T0354961

The Leap

The Leap

Jay J. Drummond

Order this book online at www.trafford.com
or email orders@trafford.com

Most Trafford titles are also available at major online book retailers.

Printed in the United States of America.

ISBN: 978-1-4269-6312-4 (sc)
ISBN: 978-1-4269-6313-1 (hc)
ISBN: 978-1-426-96314-8 (e)

Library of Congress Control Number: 2011905574

Trafford rev.04/06/2011

 www.trafford.com

North America & International
toll-free: 1 888 232 4444 (USA & Canada)
phone: 250 383 6864 ♦ fax: 812 355 4082

Acknowledgments:

I'd like to take this opportunity to thank the renowned art critic, artist and author Kim Levin for her encouragement and support in my endeavor to write my first book. The endless times she would read sections and say how good it was and in the same breath say, "Now do it again and it'll be even better." Her guiding nudges were and still are deeply appreciated. Without them this book would not have been possible.

I want to thank my older brother Larry Max Drummond and his wife Judy for their help and support in very difficult times. Their faith in me and their help when I needed it most is humbling.

I would also like to thank Martha Nilsson Edelheit for reading an early draft and her detailed constructive criticisms.

And last but not least a big thank you must go to Richard Lukin for reluctantly reading and in his inimitable sarcastic manner, giving me priceless tips for improving my writing.

I'd like to dedicate this book to my daughter Britta who I love more than life itself. May she and her wonderful husband Thomas have the opportunity to enjoy the fruits of this world before mother-nature reclaims the earth from us.
Jay J Drummond

3/11/2011

Introduction to

The Leap

A science-fiction novel by Jay J Drummond

Hi my name is Robert Manning, I'd like to explain the setting you're about to enter and a little about what took place from 2010 to 2120. The technology and abilities we have these days seemed impossible a hundred years ago, just like space travel and computers a hundred years prior to that.

From 2010 to 2035 we battled with recession and often borderline depression. Then it was over and the super-powers of the world went back into high gear and it seemed we were entering a new era of prosperity.

Energy sources were highly improved, new sources and resources were created and it looked like the whole world was going to profit from it.

Many countries had space programs and bases with settlements on the moon and Mars.

We brought pollution to a stop by 2060 and even the Chinese had been convinced and participated. The world population was decreasing and the standard of living improving. At least for those who could stay out of the reach of the ever increasing earth quakes and weather catastrophes.

There were still many problems and obstacles in our way and not all peoples got along. Most of it however could be settled without wars and terror. However there was no getting out of the way of the huge tsunamis that were now devastating islands and continents bordering the Pacific

Ocean. As the earth quakes and volcanoes increased small countries were being wiped off the map.

By the end of 2080 the North Pole was nothing more than open water, Greenland had very little ice left and half the South Pole was without snow and ice.

We had managed to prevent the Gulf Stream from collapsing by installing pumps and underwater ramps to help prevent freshwater dilution. We actually thought we could control it.

The tropical storms that cross the Atlantic Ocean each year just above the equator had begun producing more and more category 5 Hurricanes. Parts of Florida, Texas, Louisiana and the Chesapeake Bay area were reduced to little more than wet-lands.

The islands of New York City had thirty five foot sea-walls around them as the ocean had risen dramatically. After 2085 Southern Florida no longer existed. It was becoming clear that the world was changing and we would not be able to stop it.

By 2090 our scientists projected an ice-age that would cover most of North America. By 2095 it was clear that the earth had changed its orbit and we were headed into a possible global white-out which would destroy 99.9% of all life forms and we were among those who wouldn't make it.

We of course had stations on the moon and Mars but they would not be able to sustain themselves indefinitely.

The UN put out a call to all the top authorities in every part of our lives that had specialists. They gathered scientists and technical experts from all over the world. They were to design an enormous space ship that could sustain life indefinitely. The specialists were to be part of the construction team and later part of the crew.

By 2098 several space stations were assembled and minerals were being brought from earth, the moon, Mars, and the moons of Jupiter and Saturn in order to create this huge space-ship.

Construction was going on 24/7 as we were trying to out-run Mother-Nature.

The quality of life on earth was deteriorating at a breathtaking pace. Storms were killing hundreds of thousands if not millions and entire countries were simply disappearing. It was not going to get better and everyone knew it. That's a recipe for catastrophe and catastrophic was a good description for what was going on, on a global scale.

In June of 2103 I had finished my four year training as observation specialist with the CIA. I had been trained to observe large gatherings and still see the details, individual actions of people and their body language. I was the best in my class.

I was contacted by the UN and asked to be a part of the space program. They told me that the voyage must be observed and documented by a neutral party and that was what I was trained in.

I accepted and was flown to the space-ship while it was still under construction. The people building it were to become the crew. That way when it was finished it could be launched regardless of the conditions on earth.

This would not be a ship full of potbellied billionaires with their beautiful young ladies. This would be a quest to save our species with the people selected as capable of doing exactly that.

Now turn the page and discover my interpretation of your future.

C2010Jay J Drummond

"The Leap"

By: Jay J Drummond

CHAPTER I

We're not going to be able to stay here much longer. An ice-age is now inevitable. Now that the ship is complete and the biospheres are up and running, I believe the count-down can begin.

It's been a long and narrow road to get to this point. We're about to leave our solar system on an epic journey across the galaxy and with a bit of luck beyond.

With the inevitability of a great ice-age humans have managed to put most of their differences aside and have created a star-ship large enough to contain itself indefinitely.

It is to be capable of galactic and possibly even inter galactic travel.

This enormous vessel has a radius of more than three quarters of a mile and is over four miles long. It rotates creating artificial gravity on two levels and can sustain more than thirty-five thousand people.

The truly difficult part was having all the countries capable of non-hostile communication put their heads together and bring fourth thirty five thousand people who are not only highly trained but are also emotionally fit enough to (most likely) master this task.

A vote was taken and English has become the universal language. It no longer serves a purpose to have more than one.

Thousands of animals and birds have been brought aboard this vast vessel and are able to roam the grass fields and woodlands created for them. They will be utilized and harvested as needed.

Our green-houses are huge multi-layered structures and are attached to the vessel. It's amazing how little sod is needed to grow the plants we use as food.

Returning to earth is not an option.

My name is Robert Manning and I've been chosen to document this adventure, its successes, its failures and the people who make it possible. I'm not a great writer but an excellent observer.

For over seven years materials have been brought here from earth, the moon and all accessible planets and moons of our solar system. They've been forged, bent and formed to create the largest moving vessel ever imagined.

It's actually two enormous oval tubes, one inside the other. This creates two individual units, which are of course one inside the other. Each unit is hundreds of feet high. The outer hull of each is the base or floor. When rotating, gravity is created and you could believe you're still on earth.

The vital instruments and working quarters are on the inner deck. The earthlike atmosphere, wooded areas, animals and living quarters are on the outer deck. This is like a dynamic city and we will most likely spend the rest of our lives here.

There's no reason or need to explain how we got to this point. Scientists have been warning us since the beginning of the twentieth century. No one knows for sure if we created the changes or if it's just another of the many cycles that the earth has been going through since its beginning.

Fact is, we're entering an ice-age that, according to our scientists, will escalate into a global white-out, and little to nothing will survive. It's not the earth's first global ice-age and the only thing that survived the others was microscopic organisms that were able to flourish far below the earth's surface.

The stations on the moon and Mars were unlikely candidates as their environments can not be manipulated to sustain life on their own. All out-posts are to be maintained as long as possible and who knows, we may find a habitable planet and be able to return and rescue many of the survivors on earth.

Our knowledge extends to the boarders of our solar system, which till now, was a very big area. I guess we're about to experience just how small and insignificant our solar system really is.

That is, provided this thing doesn't explode once the power is turned on. Most everything on this vessel is experimental. Theoretically our air will be cleaner, the ship will be faster, the energy source more powerful than anything ever attempted on earth; I could go on and on but at some point it begins to scare the hell out of me.

The people aboard this vessel are different, "professionals" are no longer people who are taller than others and can throw a ball through a hoop or chase a little round ball back and forth over a hundred meter field. They are people who have the ability to concentrate on their work like few others and can relax without watching others do things that they are not capable of. Truly, they are the best of the best.

Votes were cast and the overwhelming majority here opted to christen this great star ship "Enterprise", after the popular fictional 20th century starship. We all hope its adventures will be similarly exciting. It is an astonishing piece of art and contains the combined dreams of all the top scientists of the world. Its outer hull is of four inch thick titanium slabs. They are 25X25 meters square and have been installed overlapping each other much like fish scales.

We exploited Earth, Mars, Jupiter's and Saturn's moons and our own moon to find enough titanium to complete it. Then it was coated to prevent ultra violet exposure. I have no idea how or who came up with or invented the coating or for that matter, what it really is. I do know that it works! We've experienced major solar flares with absolutely no penetration.

We've mastered anti-material and believe we have harnessed its power which should enable us to create force-fields to protect us and the ship from unwished collisions and heaven forbid, "attacks by aliens".

Yes, we're going to go so far and see so much that statistically it is not possible NOT to find other life forms. Who knows we may even be welcomed by them. We have no intention of taking over a populated planet. The policy is to be, if welcomed, we stay, if not we move on.

Anti material is our prime source of power and propulsion. It's so powerful that it's like having a chain of atomic bombs thrusting us forward and at the same time creating a force field to protect us from being crushed by the thrust. We're all anxious to see if it actually works.

As I said, this technology is not only new, it has never been tested. We've unleashed our scientists and abolished bureaucracy, giving them the opportunity to create things we "thought" possible but didn't do because people in powerful positions saw a disadvantage for themselves or it seemed too expensive at the time.

This unleashed fully supported strategy has produced the ability to bend time and space. Einstein told us that it could be done and our scientists have turned his calculations into reality (we hope).

They have given us the ability to create "Leaps" which will enable us to travel unimaginable distances. I will elaborate later.

We also have two smaller escort starships which will be traveling with us. They are manned and are for exploration and additional protection. Their captains will answer to the captain of the Enterprise who is a civilian.

We have just celebrated the year 2120 which is to be a new beginning for mankind. The chaos and drama unfolding on earth has become unbearable and almost all communication has been severed. We can not change what is taking place. Our goal is to maintain the species not prolong the inevitable.

The time has come. Cpt. McCain has ordered final loading and boarding. We're to leave our geo-stationary orbit in four days. Suddenly it is all becoming a reality.

You can almost feel the adrenaline in the air. All goodbyes have been said as we have been a part of this ship for many years.

Now we and we alone will determine if mankind will survive.

The "Bridge" is the heart of our vessel and all vital instrumentation can be found here. Its eight thousand square feet have been masterfully utilized.

A back-up system is in a secondary location and an emergency remote system is in one of the escort star-ships.

Security on the Enterprise is not a problem, we all know why we are here and monetary reimbursement has been abolished. Truly, we are all for one and one for all.

Manning the bridge is Cpt. Kathrin McCain, a strong Scottish woman with the heart of a saint and the temper of a wolverine. She's 5'11" tall, has an athletic body and long red hair. Her presence demands attention.

She has proven herself and her skills as captain on countless trips to Mars and the moons of Jupiter where she found and directed the harvesting of minerals needed for this project. She founded colonies on the moon, Mars and Europa, which is one of the moons of Jupiter. She was also one of the main organizational entities at the UN ensuring diversity in the choice of star-ship occupancy and keeping private enterprise influence out of the big picture.

She's not one who debates an issue and asks for opinions.

Jerry Chapman is second in command, known as #1. At 6'2" and one hundred eighty pounds he too is a renowned captain and statesman and has proven leadership abilities at the UN. He's well known for his ability to think problems and obstacles through from top to bottom.

Kim Lien is Ship's Counselor and Advisor to those in command. I say those as she has made it clear she will not be dictated to. She makes herself available to those who are in need of psychological help and/or advice and who request her opinion or are in need of her help.

She is strikingly beautiful and petite. Her long sandy colored hair is like that of a lion and she moves with the grace of a stalking cat.

Her advice, intuitions and visions are based on her knowledge and ability to see things as a third party in a clarity that others can only dream of. She is calm, cool and collected and has the ability to enable a person to be all he or she can be without stressful side effects. No doubt, to maintain ones wits will be vital.

Lars Berger is our Science Officer, with German precision and know-how this 6'4" athletic man will decipher what we find and how it can be utilized. He is truly the Albert Einstein/Steven Hawkin of our day. It was he who created our power source and he will also conduct our "Leaps".

Lin Chi, Propulsion Systems Officer, a small mild mannered martial arts master, will ensure smooth sailing. He is a renowned pilot and mathematician whose calculations have saved many a mission. He's a master in Yoga, Kung Fu, Karate, Jujitsu and a few other martial arts that I can't pronounce. He's the most graceful person I've ever seen.

Victor Akwete Kofi, Life Support: This long lanky Nigerian will ensure that this vast vessel maintains the ability to sustain life. This 7'2" Nigerian not only coordinates the vast machinery that is in place but also ensures that the trees and plants are constantly filtering over-used air and are replenishing it for us.

Bianca Lambert, an attractive woman with beautiful long platinum blonde hair and a smile that could melt an iceberg is our communications officer. She is an accomplished linguist and speaks over thirty languages. She learned some of them in a matter of hours.

Once under-way, the ship will be partially managed and propelled via artificial intelligence unless there are abnormalities in the program which would of course require looking after. That will enable Mr. Chi to concentrate on other aspects of the propulsion process. Which, as you can imagine, are very complicated.

There are no windows on the Enterprise. Outside images are projected onto screens. The images are created by sensors and cameras which enable zooming in on an object and asking the board computer what you are looking at. The screens are distributed throughout the ship making it possible for us all to "enjoy" the trip.

I've been informed that a route has been chosen and the escort star-ships have left orbit. They will verify our route once outside the solar system. It would be very unpleasant to collide with a star or rogue planet, or for that matter, anything.

Each of these "escort" ships is over a thousand feet long and armed to the teeth with technology and weapons. The propulsion systems are the same as the Enterprise and they too can educe "Leaps". They have the ability to participate in a "Leap" created by the Enterprise or if necessary create one of their own.

Once we're outside the solar system and a good distance from debris that could be dragged by the vacuum created as we gain speed, we can accelerate to almost the speed of light. Our scientists tell us, "That's the easy part". Scanning the route and avoiding collisions will be a real challenge. It will not be without stress and mixed opinions, we're glad Counselor Lien will be there to help maintain equilibrium. She radiates a calmness with her gracefulness and beautiful big brown eyes that seem to penetrate body and soul.

Actually, she and I have become very close and enjoy the comfort and warmth of a newly born friendship or partnership. I could not imagine this journey without her.

On January 10, 2120 at 24:00 hours the order to leave orbit has been given. Cpt. McCain has given the speech of her life and has unmistakably outlined our past, present and goals, "Our future".

This almost six foot tall athletic red head who's mere presence demands attention has created strict guidelines and at the same time left room for each of us to enjoy a freedom never known on earth. She's made it clear, "This is not a democracy." Positions and titles have been given, back-ups are established and requirements for the next generation are in place.

There will, no doubt, be differences in opinions but they will be settled in a quiet and civil manor. Failure to master this goal would lead to banishment and banishment is terminal.

She turned to Mr. Chapman and said; "# 1 take us out of here." "You know what? I've always wanted to say that." That created a smile on everyone's face and helped reduce the tension.

He nodded to Lars Berger and the engines roared to life. That was a magical moment.

Mr Berger, our science officer, has also made it possible for us to view each of the outer planets as we pass them possibly for the last time. They are truly beautiful and still hold many secrets.

A stillness has overcome the entire ship and for the first time since I arrived four years ago, there are no scurrying feet, no loud commands, no hammering or welding, no opening and closing of hatches,... we're saying good-by ...and we know it!

As we pass the outer asteroid belt, a glass of champagne for each and every passenger has been poured. Counselor Lien politely reminds us how easily our judgment can be influenced and requests moderation. Personally I feel like drinking two or three bottles. I'm sure we all do. There is so much fear, hope and anticipation in the air that I find it hard to breathe. We're nearing the point of no return.

Cpt. McCain has requested Mr Chi, Propulsions Officer, to initiate the main thrusters. This is a first! Everything leading to this point has been theory.

This propulsion system can accelerate us to almost the speed of light in less than four hours or explode with the force of a mid-size star at the end of its life.

The thrusters have been constructed in such a manor that they can be reversed and used as brakes, much the same way a jet engine works. They estimate that at full speed we should be able to stop in "only" five hours. "How reassuring."

As the thrusters begin their work, a slight force is felt pushing us ever so lightly toward the back of the ship. We're moving ever faster and nothing has exploded. The sigh of relief is so great I almost threw up. Smiles were exchanged throughout the bridge as the stress subsided. Slowly we all regained our composure. I realized I was actually sweating. The feeling was a lot like standing on the ledge of a sky-scraper and experiencing a gust of wind threatening to blow you off. I wonder how long it's going to take to get used to it.

Our lighting on the Enterprise has been so programmed to resemble day and night thus enabling our body functions to continue in a semi normal manor.

Our first month underway on board the Enterprise has been full of excitement and mixed emotions. Imagine, in 2031 on our first trip to Mars, it took four months to get there.

We just flew through two thirds of the entire solar system in twenty nine days at barely more than impulse speed.

Most of us have conquered our fears and doubts and are trying to become one with our new environment. All systems are and have been functioning as they should and communication with our escorts is intact.

They have even managed to dock with the Enterprise and exchange congratulations.

Our goal, although not yet made public, is a solar system just over nine hundred light years from us near the star constellation we call Orion. There is a yellow sun with at least six orbiting planets. Many believe the area to be the origin of life itself. At least it seems to be the most promising of the many options.

It is inevitable that we try our secondary propulsion system, which, so I am told, is not a propulsion system at all. It is so far beyond my comprehension that I can only explain the theory and what happens if successful.

With an enormous power surge shock waves will be created in time and space. The waves will grow in front of us. When two of them touch near the top we will accelerate and pass through the point of contact. (The Leap) The waves will flatten and we will have traveled several light years in a matter of seconds.

Not that it really matters but I would like to think we'll know where we are once there. I would be lying if I said I'm not terrified, but then, I think we all are.

Once this theoretical system has been successfully tested we will be the most flexible and fastest entity ever known and ever imagined by humans.

"Truly on a Star Trek"

Cpt. McCain has decided to send one of the escort star ships through "The Leap" first. It too has the power to do so on its own. Size is irrelevant, so if one makes it there and back, so can we all. She, Cpt. McCain, is not well known for her patience and long preparation procedures. The leap is to take place in forty-five minutes. This is not something that can be discussed, it is an undisputable order. unaware of the event and perfectly content with the moment. Had something gone wrong we would have vanished happy. It was truly a magical moment.

Having said that, I'm happy we didn't.

The escort starship chosen accelerated and disappeared into the void. It put several million miles between us and its sister ship then initiated the surge. It executed "The Leap" and was gone. Within ten minutes it was back. Upon being questioned by Cpt. McCain and Lars Berger, all our hopes and dreams were confirmed.

"The Leap" had become a reality and we have found a way to be faster than the speed of light without trying to outrun rays of light.

Instead of celebrating her success Cpt. McCain immediately gave the order for each vessel to pass through the wave created by the Enterprise, three vessels in one "Leap". This should ensure we all land near one another.

Lars Berger was given the order to initiate the surge and before anyone had the time to be "afraid" we were through.

While all this took place, I believe I was the most fortunate person in the fleet as I was holding Counselor Lien in my arms. As our bodies melted together we passed through time and space unknowing and oblivious to the moment. There was no sonic boom, no flash of light and no thrust forward. We were totally at peace with the universe.

That said, I'm glad we didn't.

Chapter II

Once on the other side we were less than half a light year from our goal. Our computers were picking up the first images of the solar system which was to be our goal. Not unlike our own, the planets have mostly hostile or no atmosphere. One or two are questionable.

Should we find a habitable planet, groups have been chosen and/or there are volunteers who will stay and populate it. The pre-requisite is that we do not interfere or destroy intact living systems.

If the inhabitable planets we find are populated with intelligent life we will only leave people there if requested by its people, or whatever they may be.

If attacked we will use all our strength to demonstrate our invulnerability and power, without the extermination of another life form. "At least that's our goal".

We certainly have the power to totally destroy a planet the size of earth. We wouldn't even have to shoot at them. A simple "fly-by" at full power would suck the entire atmosphere off a planet. Cpt. McCain and counselor Lien have made clear we humans have done enough killing for power and greed. No one or place has anything that we must have and/or need for survival. I would like to think we could exchange ideas without forcing an alien lifestyle on them. We're all full of anticipation, hopes and primeval fears.

One of the escort starships has been sent to explore the solar system. As it entered the system's outer asteroid belt we begin receiving detailed information about the stars' six orbiting planets.

None of the planets are or ever will be inhabitable by humans. There are, however minerals and water we could use on two of them and Cpt. McCain has sent shuttles to explore the options and possibilities of acquiring them and possibly discovering new minerals or life forms.

This is all very exciting and for the first time requires team-work from a large percent of the population. This is our first large-scale test as a functioning unit without help from a neighboring planet or the Earth.

While all this is going on, plans are being made for our next goal. It's amazing to observe these officials on the Bridge as they matter-of-factly make their plans, creating and determining the future of man-kind.

It seems that Cpt. McCain has decided to circle the Milky Way's spirals at the approximate depth of the earth or a bit less. This will require gigantic "Leaps" as we will encounter bands of stars and bands of pure space.

It's believed that Dark Matter is more concentrated in areas void of stars and Lars Berger will have his hands full measuring something that has never been measured to project the success of doing something that has never been done. I wish him luck.

After only nine days of exploration and mining of local minerals it seems we have overstayed our welcome. A solar eruption has caused minor damage to two of the shuttles which were on the surface of one of these desolate planets. People weren't harmed as only a chosen few were allowed to participate and they were all inside the shuttles as the eruption took place.

Several hundred tons of mineral ore have been secured. The water was too far beneath the surface to make it worth-while going after it.

The planet they had landed on is a little larger than the earth. It has two moons but has no detectable life forms. The minerals are like or very similar to those on earth or so I'm told.

The order has been given to leave this solar system at impulse speed. As was to be expected, it will be days or weeks before the calculations for the big "Leaps" are available.

We have more than enough to do with everyday life and its challenges. Maintaining air filters, humidity, temperature, food preparation, recycling systems, purified water and air to breath keeps everyone on their toes. We would all like to think its routine but it's not.

There are three intact systems for everything on the Enterprise; one working, one back-up and one in maintenance. To date we're only simulating major maintenance as all systems continue to work as designed. Alone that fact is amazing.

Cpt. McCain has requested that #1 (Jerry Chapman) conduct a walk-through of the two escorting star ships. He has a very good feeling for detail. I'm sure he'll be inspecting every nut and bolt.

I've been granted permission to accompany him and his team. The plan is to have them dock with us one-at-a-time and so long the propulsion systems don't have to be tested they will remain docked throughout the walk-through. They will dock in such a manor that the rotation of the Enterprise will grant them gravity. The rest of the time the crew wears magnetic shoes which helps create an up and down, everything not fastened down floats. Only the enterprise maintains artificial gravity on eighty percent of the ship.

The crew members can even make small jumps and float from one station to the other when needed. That takes a lot of practice. I'm hoping we'll stay docked so we avoid the nausea of weightlessness.

The ships are large and conveniently constructed. Other than the living quarters and propulsion systems they are open and practical. Weapons systems are integrated into the bridge and everything is easily accessible. There are no windows but there is a giant screen at the front of the bay which gives the effect of looking forward through glass and of course in full 3-D.

Although these ships have no more fire-power than the Enterprise they do have more, much more! As the Enterprise fires one proton torpedo at a time these star ships have the ability to fire four at a time at four separate targets and at the same time they are capable of firing two separate lazars which can melt most metals at a distance of over a half a million miles.

They move with astonishing agility and can out maneuver any previous flying machine ever made by humans.

I'm glad they're on our side.

The crews consist of a captain, first mate, nine other officers and two hundred able men and women. Their individual skills are among the highest ever achieved by a potential strike force and although deeply feared and respected they are as normal as you and me.

It's very interesting to see such a fearsome fighting machine function without someone screaming orders and people running aimlessly in all directions. They remain calm their orders are given into their head-sets without causing panic. Their actions have purpose and the results are devastating to their enemies.

Although it would have seemed logical to have a clone army I am happy it was not necessary.

These people are rotated through the Enterprise on a monthly basis and one would never know that they were a fighting team unless you witness it here on these mighty battle ships.

We started our rounds in the living quarters, they were spacious and comfortable. It was interesting to see the safety belts they wore to prevent them from floating around in their sleep. Then we checked the machine rooms. All compartments and rooms were of course individually sealed with independent life support systems. The most interesting part was the bridge. Most computers operated with three dimensional holograms. The chairs had loose fitting clamps which applied pressure to the legs just above the knee in order to hold their user in place. The captains' chair had an array of instruments attached to the arm rest so the captain could take over a station should it fail. The large directional viewing screen was like a window and it was amazing to see objects zooming by us.

After eleven hours the walk through was over and if it had been an inspection they would have both passed with flying colors.

I asked Jerry Chapman, "Doesn't it make you nervous that everything runs so smoothly?" He said "There are a hundred things that go wrong daily. The maintenance crews are constantly in action. We should all be grateful for their competence. I'm amazed that we haven't had major problems." I began to realize how much I have been taking for granted. Every drink of water and every breath of air have to be created or recycled and it seems that thirty five thousand people have become a well functioning dependable unit and all that in only eight months.

We returned to the bridge in silence and admiration of those making all this possible. Jerry with his notes and me with my thoughts.

As we enter the bridge we witness the most heated discussion since we left our solar system. It seems that Lin Chi, propulsions and Lars Berger science officer do not agree on the methodology created to make Leaps of over twenty light years. Mr. Chi said, "I have no doubt once created the "Leap" itself, is relatively easy. Just how do you propose I create such a surge?" Mr. Berger, "I would like for you to concentrate the surge into a circle not more than two miles wide. That should increase the surge's power by eighty five percent. The waves created will propel us well over the required twenty light years."

Mr. Chi, "That means all three ships will have to pass through in less than two seconds. Do you think that that's possible?" Lars Berger, "Do you see a problem with that captain?" Cpt. McCain not being one to participate in a heated discussion ended it by saying, "I would like to hear alternatives, if there are none within seventy two hours, we'll execute the plan in place."

Mr. Chi was about to comment as his eyes met those of the captain. He slowly exhaled and said "I'll insure we have the power when needed". He glanced at Lars and returned to his station.

We managed to help neutralize the situation by changing the subject and discussing the escort ships walk-through with the captain and Lars Berger.

Kim Lien quietly sat down beside Mr. Chi and did what she does best. She managed to calm him helping him to relax and concentrate on the goals and tasks at hand. It's a lot like taking a tranquilizer without side effects.

Although Lars was extremely interested in the battle ships and the walk-through he politely excused himself from the conversation and began his research for possible alternatives.

After a short while he paused and walked over to Chi. He placed his hand on Chi's shoulder and said, "When you have the time, I'd be grateful if you'd help me with these alternative calculations. I'd like to live through this just like you."

Lin Chi managed a small smile and said, "I'll be there as soon as I can, and thanks."

It is by no means easy to observe all this without commenting. So far no one has asked for my opinion on anything and it is certainly not my intention to superimpose upon the most renowned experts humanity has to offer. The captain periodically reviews what I have written and is, so far, without comment. That's as good as it gets.

It seems we'll be traveling at impulse for at least the next three days. I've decided to ask Kim to take a walk in the wooded area and possibly go swimming in one of the ponds. This would be our first unscheduled break in ten months. Not that we don't have free time but there's not a lot of it. She said, "That's like a wonderful idea, will you ask her or should I?" I said, "I'll ask, after all it was my idea." Kim said, "I've never seen the artificial sky created over the meadows and wooded areas." That made two of us. We seldom have the time for such recreation and have grown accustom to keeping close to our work incase we're needed and/or in my case, in case something exciting happens. This would be as close as one could get to a short vacation.

I walked over to Cpt. McCain and asked, "Cpt. I would like to request a twenty-four hour leave of absence." She looked at me for what seemed to be a long time and then said, "And I suppose you'd like to take my ships counselor with you?" Some-what taken by her insight I said, "With your permission, yes." There was another short pause as she glanced at Kim. She said, "You have one day provided I don't need you. I'll see you both at 07:00 day after tomorrow at breakfast. You are excused." I thanked her and returned to Kim. I looked at her and said, "She said yes." Kim said, "I know, she was actually happy that someone finally asked for some free time. Breaks are long over-due but she was uncertain how to initiate them." I asked, "How do you know things like that?" She smiled and said, "I am who I am."

As we left the bridge Kim looked at me with a soft smile and eyes that could melt a glacier.

She said, "Lets go to my quarters and cuddle, I miss you." I tried to answer her but no words came out, it wasn't necessary. We walked in silence and anticipation.

We spent the next several hours in perfect harmony, feasting on one another's needs and desires. Her lips were hot, wet and intoxicating. Her small, soft and perfectly formed body and glowing eyes seemed to hypnotize me as we drifted through time and space.

As the daylight hours were about to begin in the meadows, I kissed her softly waking her. I asked, "Would you like to go look at the sun-rise? Maybe we'll even see a few animals." She smiled softly and bit my lower lip, "Yes, let's shower. I'll wash your back if you wash mine." We kissed again and once again our bodies melted together.

After a refreshing shower I said, "I'll pack our bathing suits and a few things for us to eat while you finish getting ready." A perfect day was about to begin.

After a spectacular sunrise which was actually created by a high altitude water mist on the slowly brightening lights. We had a wonderful walk and a refreshing swim in a crystal clear pond. Then we decided to have a picnic and the day melted away.

After returning to Kim's quarters we began hypothesizing on and about the future. It is all so different now.

On earth people would not see a future although it was right in front of them. Here, we can not possibly see a future but we are all willing to create one.

It seems that humanity needed to find a reason and purpose for its existence and it also seems we were successful. At least it seems we are moving in the right direction.

It's amazing how little time we spend thinking about earth and its destiny. Naturally we have its entire history and location documented but our thoughts tend to reach forward not backward.

Should Lars and his team find a means for time travel we could possibly spring forward so far that the white-out would have passed but I'm not sure any of us would want to. Or maybe back and try to warn them. But that would serve no purpose. The white-out was inevitable.

This freedom we've achieved is amazing and exciting. The population is strictly regulated which helps keep everything in balance. We no longer thrive on personal achievements, almost all our individual achievements benefit the entire population and gives one a since of purpose. For the first time in documented history we are actually free.

A wonderful day has come to an end. I asked Kim, "Would you like to go back to the bridge in the morning to see how far along they are with the leap?" She smiled and said, "Yes I would and I know you want to." Then she kissed me and the night faded away.

The next morning as we walked to the bridge I noticed a star we were passing on one of the many screens.

One of its planets was actually visible. "I wonder why we're not visiting that system. Kim said, "Why don't you ask? I'd like to know as well."

Once back on the bridge we reported in to the captain who was already seated in the ready-room for breakfast. I mentioned the solar system we're passing and enquired about it.

Cpt. McCain said, "It's an extremely large star and a number of the planets around it make Jupiter look like a marble. The gravity is so great in that area that we could loose control of the Enterprise. Large stars are notoriously instable and tend to have very short lives. When it implodes it could very well create a black hole. We don't want to be anywhere near it when that happens." I asked, "How close are we?" "We're just under 0.5 light years but it's closer than I care to be.

Then I enquired about the progress with the leap. It seems that Lars, his team and Lin Chi have been unable to come up with a possible alternative.

The work is now being invested in the concentration of the pulse into a two mile circle in order to create enough power for such a great leap. All are certain that the window will be very short but we should be able to cross the first band of void space in a single bound, theoretically.

Two hours ago Cpt. McCain sent one of the star ships into the void. All scanners, detectors and measuring instrumentation have been concentrating on it and the dark matter surrounding it since it left.

During breakfast Lars Berger, Lin Chi and others joined us. Out of curiosity I asked no one in particular, "What is dark matter?" Lars answered, " We still don't know what dark matter is but we do have a confirmation that it is there. The star ship has actually had sensor readings indicating an infinitely small amount of friction as they pass through it. For the first time, we have touched dark matter.

Lars addressed the captain and said, "We're at our wit's end with math and theory. I'd like to request that the star ship in the void fire a small pulse. After measuring the results I believe we'll be able to calculate how much power we'll actually need to cross it."

Cpt. McCain spoke briefly with Lin Chi then agreed to his proposal.

After breakfast she contacted the star ship's captain and ordered them to initiate a small pulse in a direction that could cause no problems.

It was amazing to watch the results on the screen. It seems that the concentration of dark matter gives the pulse much more to push against. That means that much greater leaps can be made through it with considerably less power than anticipated.

The only thing left to calculate is how far the leap is to be and the power needed to create it. There was a big sigh of relief from everyone.

It looks like our next big step is going to happen soon.

Cpt. McCain decided to get some rest and ordered #1 to use the long-range sensors to investigate a group of stars on the other side of the void. He's to look for intact solar systems, preferably with planets near the size of earth. That would ensure an acceptable gravity and increase the likelihood of recognizable life forms, both plant and animal. It is to be our next goal.

As Mr Chapman scanned through them he asked me, "Do you see one you like? We'll need to look at all of them and you can decide where we start if you'd like." I said, "How about the one on the left that seems to be more brilliant then the others?" "OK , lets' start there."

When he increased power we could make out at least three planets, one of which might be the right size. It was noted and we moved on to the next and the next. There were over thirty to check. Then it would be a process of elimination to find the right one.

I noticed a disturbance on the other side of the room and went over to see what was going on. Victor Akwete Kofi, Life Support has discovered a water contamination. This is the first time that we've had a contamination of anything on the Enterprise. He reported it to #1 and began a process of elimination to find the source. Y now it had drawn the attention of everyone on the bridge.

After several hours he discovered that some of the ore brought on board during our last stop was contaminated. Having found the source he quickly solved the problem by isolating the source.

Then he went to Lars Berger and said, "The contamination I found was a life form in the ore brought on board. Would you like to have a container of it put into a quarantined lab to study it?"

Lars almost fell out of his chair. He quickly noted where the ore was from, when it was found and where it is to be located while in quarantine. Mr. Chapman gave his consent to the plan and Lars initiated it.

This first potential disaster was found, contained and fixed in less than nine hours. On top of that Mr Kofi had discovered the first ever registered life-form outside our solar system and even if it was but a microscopic organism, it is alive and alien. One of man-kinds biggest questions was answered.

Does life exist outside our solar system?

Upon returning to the bridge Cpt. McCain was brought up to date with the events that had happened. She was pleased that everything had gone so smoothly and without panic.

She said: "I am very pleased with your response to a potential hazard. Mr Akwete Kofi, you have guaranteed yourself a place in our history books." There was a round of applause for Victor Akwete Kofi and he smiled. Then she said "Now, show me our newly discovered aliens."

It was but a single celled life form but very different in comparison to anything found on earth. It was a large single cell, almost a millimeter long and it seemed to be feeding on lithium.

Cpt. McCain, "Mr Berger, this would be an excellent subject for a doctorate for one of your students. Don't you agree?" Lars nodded and reluctantly said, "Yes, I wish I had the time to do it myself." He reluctantly appointed Jose

Calderon, one of his favored student physicists and relieved him of most of his other duties. Things went back to normal on the bridge

Cpt. McCain asked Mr Chapman, "Did you locate a solar system worth exploring?" He said, "Yes, it's twenty five light years from our present position, has seven planets and three of them are approximately the size of earth."

She then asked Lars Berger if the calculations were complete. He said: "We should be ready within the hour." She ordered the star ship to return from the void and both to take escort positions along side the Enterprise in preparation of the "Leap".

So much had been happening lately that we almost missed our first anniversary. The captain opened all channels of communication throughout the Enterprise and the escorting star ships.

She said, "Colleagues! Comrades! Esteemed Members of the Enterprise and its escorts, I would like to take this opportunity to commemorate this day with you. January 11, 2121.

We have now been under way for one year. Each and everyone on these star ships has proven themselves time and again and although our journey has just begun I am certain of our success.

This is so much more than just a quest. We will determine if the human race is to exist or parish. We will explore this galaxy and most certainly find inhabitable planets where we can thrive.

There will be obstacles in our path and we will undoubtedly have to master them. Since our departure we have successfully implemented all the futuristic ideas which made this journey possible, for example, anti-material as fuel, outwitting time and space and moving faster than the speed of light to name but a few. We have done so as a team and all this without faltering. I would like to thank each and every one of you for your hard work and devotion in this quest to save mankind.

Now I would like to ask for a moment of silence in memory of those we left behind."

The pause was deafening, for a moment time seemed to stand still. Then she politely said, "Thank you" and signed off.

The people who were not on the bridge were not informed of every move we made and not made aware of an upcoming leap or for that matter the actual event of a leap before it was over.

This was to prevent nervousness and possible wrong or over reaction while working. Cpt. McCain did her best to confine stress to the bridge, after all, there was nothing that anyone could do to change what was about to happen.

Another mile-stone was about to be placed. We are about to make a leap of over twenty light years through void space.

After making the rounds on the bridge and speaking briefly to each of us, Kim Lien consulted with Cpt. McCain. She said, "As I had expected, no one is overly nervous and the leap will take place without so much as a second thought. The crew is showing an absolute trust in your leadership."

Cpt. McCain, "I truly hope it's justified. I'll be so relieved once we're so far along that most everything we do is something we've done before. I believe I'm nervous enough for all of us."

Kim asked, "Would you like to go to your quarters and gather your thoughts?" Cpt. McCain, "I'd like to go to my quarters and hide but it would serve no one. We've been here long enough. It's time we did this."

Cpt. McCain addressed everyone on the bridge and the officers of the two escorting star ships. "The calculations have been made and downloaded into the main computer. I will initiate a ten minute countdown on the bridges screens. I expect all of us to pass through within a fifteen second window. Each battle ship is to give me an oral confirmation of my orders." The response, as expected, was instantaneous.

She nodded to Chi and said, "You may begin." Mr. Chi started the count down and we all watched the seconds disappear.

The pulse was initiated by Lars and as calculated the waves, which we could see on the screen, were growing at an astonishing speed. The point of contact was calculated and the ships were all stationed for acceleration through the leap. Three seconds before the waves met, the ships accelerated toward the leap-point.

One would expect to have time to absorb what was happening but that's not the way it works. We were through and all three vessels were accounted for in less than nine seconds.

Chapter III

Cpt. McCain asked Lars for a confirmation on our position. He looked at her then at the screen then back to her. "I can not confirm where we are but I know where we are not."

It got very quiet on the bridge and Lars began the calculations in order to pinpoint our position. "I miscalculated the leap by 0.0012%, calculating from our last position we failed our goal by 0.472 light years."

Cpt. McCain, "None the less, we made it. Mr Chi, set a course to correct the problem and initiate at .25c, which was one forth the speed of light. Then she turned to Lars and said, "That's not like you, I demand a report on how that happened." Lars responded, "I'll make it a priority."

After several hours Mr. Chi informed Cpt. McCain that he'd have to initiate a deactivation of the acceleration. She replied, "Initiate and justify."

Chi neutralized acceleration and explained that the acceleration force field that was protecting us against being squashed during acceleration and deceleration periods was faltering. "We are at 0.14c and will have no problem maintaining this speed until the problem has been solved. As I have not detected a hard or software problem I'd like permission to leave the bridge and check the reactors." "Permission granted." He quickly left the bridge for engineering so there was little to nothing to do while waiting.

Dinner was about to be served and it was one of those rare occasions when we were to have fresh meat. I asked Mr Kofi if he knew what it was to be. He said, "I believe it is bison, what a treat." I looked at him and could not help laughing as I said, "surly not Buffalo wings" and we all had a good laugh.

After a fine meal of bison steaks with lots of trimmings Kim suggested we go for a walk. There was nothing special going on at the moment and Mr. Chi had not finished his inspection of the reactors.

We received permission to leave the bridge and walked toward the elevator. Kim said; "Would you like to take a walk in the woods?" I said; " yes, sounds great and a little naturally created oxygen sounds good."

Kim; "The captain has approved fifty five pregnancies and a lottery is being held in a few days to see who gets to be among the first. Do you intend to have children?"

I said, "Not that I don't enjoy the act of creating them but I really don't feel I would or could raise a child properly. You're the only person I'd consider as a mother for my children and I can't imagine it being a wish of yours. If I'm wrong please tell me. I'm a potentially good father and I'd be honored and happy to fulfill your need or desire for parenthood." "No," she said, "I find my life, my work and my partner fulfilling enough. "Then I guess we'll just have to keep practicing, just in case."

We walked through a wooded area with huge hardwood trees and even saw a pair of squirrels playing in the branches. Our time together was precious and watching the growth and advancement of this mini cosmos had become a favorite pastime of ours.

When we got back to the bridge Lars was just finishing with his theory of how he had miscalculated the leap. Cpt. McCain was not at all pleased and said: "Distraction!?, you're telling me that giving up the research on the alien life form distracted you from your duties?!!"

Kim squeezed my hand and asked me to back away and to sit looking in another direction. She wanted to participate in the discussion before it got out of hand. I did so and she approached Cpt. McCain and Lars. She said, "Mr Berger, you surely don't believe you can or ever could examine the entire galaxy single handedly?"

There was a pause and then Cpt. McCain said, "You are to keep us alive and to advance our knowledge by improving what and how we do things. Should you have the privilege of examining an alien life form it will be one that you can talk to. On this bridge I will accept no less than 100% effort and should, another calculation be wrong, I'm sure you will have a reasonable reason for it. Do you find that acceptable?"

Lars realized that she had just given him a very big compliment and that he had done something that could never be repeated. He said, "Thank you, may I return to my post?" "Permission granted."

Cpt. McCain said to Kim, "Mr Berger seems to be under a lot of stress." Kim: "It almost looks like he's bringing it upon himself. May I see his itinerary and that of those under him? We sometimes bite off more than we can chew." She nodded in acceptance and excused herself.

Kim went to Lars and said: "Mr Berger, you do realize that this is not just a job? There will be no end, no retirement and no one else to confirm your decisions. You are the top human physicist in the universe. The loss of your attention to any degree could certainly cause our extinction, please do not loose sight of that." She turned and walked away not wanting an answer or comment. Lars was lost in thought for a moment then turned back to his work.

Kim checked the work schedules of Lars and his crew and as she had imagined, he had taken on far too many responsibilities. It seemed to be only a matter of time before he would break down or burn out or make a mistake that could cost us all dearly.

Kim presented her findings to the captain and asked if the she'd like to proceed or should she? Cpt. McCain said that she would take it from there and asked that Kim stay and assist her.

She summoned Lars Berger to the ready-room to discuss options. As he entered and she said: "Please, take a seat. Counselor Lien has brought to my attention the burden you have placed upon yourself and your crew with your work Schedules.

I want each and every one on your team and of course you examined by our main medical computer and of course Dr. Kahn. Once processed, your itinerary will be issued by the Main a i computer. I expect breaks to be taken when scheduled and overtime must be approved by me and me alone.

If you believe we are moving too fast say it. Time and speed have no significance here. If our pace is too fast we will all suffer. Our very existence depends on our decision making and actions.

This is not a disciplinary action. I'm actually glad it occurred on the bridge and will be solved without it becoming a problem throughout the ship."

After a great deal of thought Cpt. McCain summoned #1 and said, "I want you to have the medical crew review all work schedules for everyone on the ship. If the work-load seems excessive it should be processed and revised by the main a i computer. I realize this will be a long process but I want it done as quickly as possible. I am not asking for end results today. I want it addressed and executed as efficiently as possible. Please start with those in the most sensitive positions. Any questions?" #1 asked, "Would you like to go first or shall I?" She paused, smiled and said; "I will, you may carry on."

Lars had joined Mr Chi in his search for the problem with the force field. Upon returning to the bridge they met with the captain and #1. Lars said, "It seems we are going to have to recalculate all the force fields periodically." #1 "Can this be programmed into one of the alternate a i computers?" Lars: "yes" Chi, "As there is no problem with the propulsion system I would like to return to my station. Lars, "I will appoint a programmer immediately. I'd like to propose giving us an additional 24 hours to ensure the programs are functioning as they should." Cpt. McCain, "Thank you, you may continue."

One of the battle ships has docked with the Enterprise and William Turner, its captain, entered the bridge and asked Cpt. McCain if she would like to test the strength and accuracy of the photon torpedoes. It seems we're going to be passing an array of potential targets.

"Yes, that is a good idea." She assigned #1 to the task.

Captain Turner said, "We'll be passing an asteroid field soon. The targets will be approximately the size of our moon. I will return to my ship and co-ordinate the strike from there. You will have the first shot. Once the damage has been assessed we will destroy what is left.

I've chosen three targets that we'll be passing. They'll be about ten minutes apart and somewhere between two hundred and fifty to four hundred thousand miles away. Good hunting sir." Mr Chapman smiled and said "thank you."

Sixteen minutes later a red alert was issued by Cpt. Turner. It was quickly confirmed and implemented on the Enterprise. Cpt. Turner announced that he was under attack but due to the opponent's location he could not defend himself. He forwarded coordinates and requested that the Enterprise assist him.

Upon receiving the position of the so-called enemy #1 fired a torpedo at it. The impact and explosion was so great that the small planet instantly became a ball of fire.

Two or three seconds later four torpedoes were fired at the same target by the battle ship. They were so placed that they hit the planet in a square, each a thousand miles away from the other.

Upon impact the planet turned to dust and fire. While we all stood in awe of what had just happened the alarm went off again and the same procedure was repeated. After the third small planet dissolved before our eyes Cpt. Turner dropped code red and thanked his people and the Enterprise for its assistance.

It seemed that it was nothing more than business as usual. We knew we had powerful weapons but had no idea how devastating they could be. I asked Cpt. McCain, "Do we really need that kind of power as a defense?" She looked at me and said, "If that weapon would be fired at us our force-shield would repel it. There's no telling what kind of a defense an unknown species could have, or weapons for that matter.

I would like to think we could hold our own but I do not underestimate what others could have. Let's hope we continue to use ours to eliminate obstacles in our path."

After all the excitement and discussions that followed things calmed down and it was business as usual.

It seems life is becoming more human-like and routine is taking over. There are many small discrepancies and obstacles in our way but Cpt. McCain and her officers seem to be handling them masterfully. Everything appears to be back to normal and we're again nearing a group of stars with planets that may have life on them.

Cpt. McCain has decided to do a first-come first-serve surveillance of each solar system. Lars has calculated arriving at the first of them in eleven and a half hours. I have no doubt he's right. Cpt. McCain has given the order to go fully automatic. That means we are all to go get some rest in anticipation of an exciting arrival.

For over four hundred years we feared a i and what it might decide to do to us. Finally only forty years ago, we found we could also program fear. When something out of the "norm" happens the a i automatically calls for help. That prevents it from turning on us; or so the experts say.

I glanced at Kim and she smiled back. Captain McCain said, "Counselor, please accompany me to my quarters."

It seems I'll get more rest than I had hoped for.

After a good and restful sleep I was the last to return to the bridge. We're approaching a solar system with seven planets. One of them is showing life. The bridge was busheling with all sensors and scanners at full power.

The life-form is believed to be organic and very primitive as there isn't much atmosphere around it. None the less it'll be exciting to see what these "plants" look like. Captain McCain has sent one of the star ships with two shuttles to investigate.

Jose Calderon entered the bridge. He asked Cpt. McCain if he could speak to Mr Berger. She nodded a yes and decided to accompany him.

He looked at Lars and said: "I must have overfed our aliens; they have grown to an average of fourteen millimeters." Lars asked, "At what point did they become multi-celled?" Jose, "They didn't, they just grew, and they are all still growing as single cells."

Lars, "I would think we are going to have a problem with space and food for them." He addressed Cpt. McCain: "I'd like to reduce the alien population to one thousand and dispose of the rest via a self-destructing vessel that we could fire into the void."

Cpt. McCain asked, "Isn't that a bit radical?" Lars looked at her and said, "It very well could be but most importantly, I believe it to be adequate. Imagine several billion one celled life forms possibly a meter long running out of lithium as a food source and changing their diet to titanium."

Cpt. McCain, "Yes, please take care of that at once." Lars, "Mr Calderon, I want you to segregate one thousand of these life forms and inform the disposal crew when they may begin disposing of the rest. You will move the life forms to a new location and the area utilized so far is to be cleaned to a molecular scale.

Have you found a sufficient method of liquidating the aliens?" Jose, "Yes, if they are exposed to pure oxygen, they implode." Lars: "Once the bay has been cleaned it is to be flooded with oxygen. I want a daily report on your progress." Jose: "Yes sir."

He took his leave and the captain enquired about the progress of the star ship and the shuttle teams as if nothing had happened and Lars replied: "I'll contact them at once.

Lars now realized he had never lost control of the alien project and was very happy with the way the captain managed the situation.

Lars contacted Jimmy Cheedle, one of our ace pilots who was presently flying the lead shuttle.

Lars, "How is the research and surveillance of the planet going Mr Cheedle?" Jimmy replied, "Fifty eight percent of the surface is water. There are beings moving in the water but we're having difficulty getting a look at them.

The surface seems to have a form of algae growing on it. I'd like to have permission to land." Lars looked at the captain, who had been following the conversation.

Cpt. McCain, "You may land but I would like for you to send out robotic exploration units. Keep your vessel at least five hundred meters from all sources of water. I want an update hourly."

Jimmy chose a place that seemed to have no alga on it and was eight hundred meters from a water source. Upon landing, the robots were deployed, one toward the alga the other toward water. Jimmy, "Mr Berger, May I have the robot enter the water once there?" Lars, "Yes, I would like both its cameras on and sending data directly to my station on the Enterprise.

I want you to deploy a stationary observation unit with three hundred and sixty degree surveillance then leave the surface of the planet immediately. You will then hover at twenty five thousand meters." Jimmy, "As you wish."

As one of the two moons of the planet became visible for Jimmy he realized why he was to leave the planet. The moon was so near to the planet that its gravity was dragging water. It was like the tide on earth but over forty meters high and capable of a lot of destruction. The robots would automatically adapt to the situation and were not in danger. The shuttle would not have been so fortunate.

"Good call" said Kim as she watched the water rush over the surface. "I guess you won't be looking for dust storms". Lars smiled and said "If I don't, there will surely be one."

Victor Akwete Kofi, "Captain, I could certainly use a few hundred cubic meters of fresh water. Did one of the shuttles take the filter system with them?" Cpt. McCain, "You may contact them, confirm they have all the equipment necessary and that the filter system is there, give them exact quantities and tell them where to deliver it."

Chapter IV

While all this was going on Lars Berger, as if in slow motion, turned to Cpt. McCain, his face expressionless in a voice that could not be questioned said: "Captain, we're being scanned......!!" A silence fell over the bridge, Cpt. McCain said, "Reconfirm!" Lars did so and said: "As I said, we are being scanned. The puzzling part is, I can not confirm from whom or from where, it is definitely not coming from that planet."

Cpt. McCain, "I want both battle ships to return to the Enterprise at once, I herewith declare a state of emergency. All battle stations are to be manned and all scanning units answer to Mr Berger."

Kim, "Captain, may I suggest that our actions appear more inquisitive and less threatening." Cpt. McCain, "No aggressive action is to be taken without consulting me first; battle ships please confirm my orders." The orders were confirmed and it seemed like we were all holding our breath in anticipation.

Lin Chi: "We have incoming!" Cpt. McCain, "Incoming what and from where?" Chi, "I can't tell where it came from. It is twenty five meters across and nine meters high. I don't believe that it is a weapon."

Lars, "I can confirm that it is not a weapon and that it appears that there are no life forms aboard it." It stopped about a thousand miles from us, which in space is right next door, it hovered there for over forty five seconds and then simply disappeared without a trace.

Lars, "Captain, it seems that who or whatever they are they want us to know they're there but are reluctant to show themselves." Captain to Lars, "Are you saying they could be right beside us cloaked?" Lars, "Yes, I believe that is what I am trying to say."

Kim segregated herself from us and appeared to enter a meditative trance. After several seconds she opened her eyes and addressed the captain, "I am certain we are not being observed." Lars confirmed, "We are no longer being scanned."

Cpt. McCain, "Mrs. Lien, did they feel your presence?" Kim: "I can't confirm it but I believe they did. I felt nothing hostile in their presence. It was more like inevitability in our meeting. I can say without a doubt, we will meet whoever or whatever scanned us and it will be on their terms. If hostility was their goal we would no longer exist."

Cpt. McCain canceled the alert and gave the order to continue where we left off. Lars initiated a replay of what had taken place on the planet during the last five hours.

The stationary viewer was under water for an hour and a half and no life forms passed in front of the cameras. The robot on land had three different forms of alga and the robot under water had viewed a form of jelly-fish. Lars said: "If there are predators then there is also something there that they feed on. We'll collect samples and continue the search." Captain McCain said: "Please carry on, Mr. Chapman, Mrs. Lien and Mr. Manning will accompany me to my quarters."

Lars contacted Jose Calderon, who had been studying the single celled life form from our first stop. Lars: "Mr Calderon have you completed your study of the life form?" Jose: "Yes sir I have, I would like to keep one of the large ones as an exhibit item." Lars, "Very well, the rest is to be disposed of in the same manor as we did the others and the space utilized is to be decontaminated.

How big did the biggest get?" Jose, "It is seventy one centimeters." (Just over two feet). Lars, "I trust you have more than enough for your doctorate?" Jose, "Yes I do, thank you." Lars: "We are going to have a lot to do in the very near future. I want you to make three teams of two scientists each and be ready to start receiving specimens within twelve hours. For now on you'll answer only to me, doctor Calderon. Jose smiled, nodded that he had understood and left.

In the captains quarters Kim Lien, Jerry Chapman and I were asked to be seated. Cpt. McCain said with a sigh, "We have a well planed procedure should we find an intelligent life form before they find us. Needless to say, we have overestimated our abilities and capabilities.

I need a course of action and/or a plan for our first intelligent terrestrial contact. It appears that those who have found us are not hostile. That, of course, doesn't mean that they will be back before others find us. Our battle ship captains are not well trained in diplomacy and I doubt very much that other life forms will realize they are confronting our entire species."

Jerry Chapman, "Our shields are constantly engaged in order to deflect debris in our path. I suggest we increase the power to deflect all weapons we can imagine. We must also bear in mind that their technology will be at least as good as ours. If we can prevent them from damaging the Enterprise it should at worst create a Mexican Stand-off giving us an opportunity to communicate, negotiate get the hell out of their range."

Cpt. McCain, "Thank you. I believe that to be an excellent plan. Ms. Lien, what are your thoughts? Kim, "A passive approach should enable us to make friends and if not and we are seriously attacked we could always make a Leap. Upon any and every confrontation a Leap should be calculated and programmed in case needed. Until we have grown and have a base established I believe retreat to be our best defense."

Mr. Chapman, "Good point, I believe it's time to begin construction on new vessels. We have a greater chance of survival if we as a species are in more than one place at a time. The vessels should be large enough to sustain life and travel on their own. We should be able to produce one every five to seven years.

They can be connected to the Enterprise via force-field during construction. This will allow our population to grow and decrease the likelihood of being exterminated by a foreign force or within. The infrastructure is in place."

Kim, "Mr. Chapman's suggestion is the most exciting and the most ambitious thing suggested since our departure from earth, truly a long-term goal which has the potential of helping secure the future of the human race."

Cpt. McCain, "Mr. Chapman I want you to document your proposal on the ships construction. The library has models and blueprints that can be used. Then present it to me as a workable plan without disrupting our ability to function.

I'll have Mr. Berger strengthen our shields.

You may return to your posts."

We left the ready-room in pure disbelief of what we had just discussed.

When Cpt. McCain returned to the bridge she addressed everyone present: "I'd like everyone to review the Log-Book at the end of their work period. We are going to make some changes and I would ask that you adapt as quickly as possible. Mr. Berger, Mr. Chapman is going to start construction of another star ship. Please see to it that everything needed to function independently is installed."

Lars, "Captain, I would like to request we build a smaller vessel first, one to be used for the study of extra-terrestrial life. It makes me nervous to bring these beings on board the Enterprise." Cpt. McCain, "An excellent idea, until its completion life forms are to be studied in their natural habitat and all information downloaded into the secondary system. That will enable us to visit more planets and invest more time in our expansion."

Jimmy Cheedle was ordered to recall the robots and to return to base.

Cpt. McCain, "Escort ship A is to scan the other interesting planets of this system and as the information is going directly to the secondary computer system Mr. Berger will determine if the exploration is worth while."

Lars then informed Jose Calderon that the newly formed teams will not be needed and confirmed that the decontamination was complete.

Cpt. McCain, "Mr. Chi, will you please assign work crews to begin construction of the science vessel? Once completed, I want the same crews to begin construction of the new star-ship. The list of materials needed will be presented to Mr. Berger and filled as needed. Please bear in mind that no sector is to suffer under this new project."

I, as observer, can not help but wonder how all these new goals are to be met without friction and having barely finished my thought Mr Chi reported to the captain that a crew member has refused to modify his work schedule and threatened to organize a strike.

Cpt. McCain immediately had him arrested and has called a hearing.

As I said before, she has the heart of a saint and the temper of a wolverine and this poor fellow is about to feel her wrath.

She had him escorted to the bridge and is showing the hearing via video throughout the entire fleet.

Cpt. McCain, "Mr. Jonathan Parker, as you are a well trained aerospace constructionist and are at present head of maintenance on the outer decks, you have been chosen to construct a much needed vessel for our science team. I have been told that you have not only refused the position but have threatened a strike. Is that true?

Mr Parker, "Yes Cpt. McCain, I feel I am doing as much as anyone else here if not more and that the additional work is out of order."

There was a pause and I could actually hear my heart beating.

Cpt. McCain said, "As was explained to each and everyone on this venture, this is not a democracy and my orders will not be disobeyed. Mr. Parker, you have made your choice and therewith sealed your fate, you will be released into space through air lock 4-A. Immediately!"

Kim Lien gasped and said, "Please Cpt. McCain, is there no other way?" Cpt. McCain sighed and said,

"I wish there were." Therewith Mr Parker was escorted away and the captain said, "I expect each and everyone to give 100% all the time and demand even more from their superiors. We will miss Mr Parker and his expertise. You may continue with your duties."

Later, on a routine update of events given by Mr Berger, he noted that a mere thirty five thousand people were chosen to save humanity from extinction and that no one should ever forget how many others are depending on them to do their part. "This is not a game or a test where we have the option of doing it over if we make a mistake. We have one chance and we're in the middle of it. Should we fail we will cease to exist."

He went on to explain that the vessel to be constructed will hold extra-terrestrial life. "It is a safety measure to keep all personnel out of harms way. Then we will construct another vessel similar to the Enterprise and will divide our strength and knowledge into two parts which will travel independently from one another, thus hopefully doubling our chance of survival.

The work-load will increase in the near future and everyone will be affected by it. Please try to remember why we are here."

He concluded with a symbolic thank-you to each and every member and asked that they, among themselves, thank and appreciate each person's deeds.

I was grateful for his words and believe most everyone else was too. Kim came to my quarters and we had a cup of soothing tea together wishing it had all not taken place and grateful that we were not captain and leader of this mission.

She said, "I need some fresh air. Let's go for a walk in the meadows."

We walked in silence hoping the events of the day would not affect our objectives. I asked Kim, "Are you going to speak to Cpt. McCain about this?"

She answered, "No, not if I can help it. It was a problem that had to be solved and any other choice she could have made would have shown weakness and vulnerability. Although I could have never done it, she made the right choice. I and the rest of us know she didn't want to, that's enough.

We need to put these thoughts aside and get on with the job of survival.

I believe our newly acquired "friends" were watching as all this took place and they too have formed new opinions and we can only hope they did not find weakness in the captain's actions."

"Yes", I said, "that is food for thought."

She squeezed my hand and we finished our walk in silence.

When we returned to the bridge we found everything was business as usual and the new construction project was to begin in five days. Mr Chi was enjoying the change of pace in his work, the captain and Mr Berger were deciding the size of the work crews.

Cpt. McCain looked up and said, "Ms. Lien glad you're back. I have a job for you." Kim squeezed my hand, smiled at me and walked toward the captain. "How may I be of service captain?"

Cpt. McCain said, "I want you to form three work colonies. They are to consist of two engineers, one foreman for each group within the colony and no less than one hundred eighty workers per group. You can get the details from Mr Berger and Mr Chi. I expect you to match these people to ensure work quality. I also expect these people to have ample time for R&R. Any questions?" Kim said, "Thank you for your confidence. I'll get started at once."

While all this is going on we are nearing another solar system and this time we've got goals. We need minerals and ore. One of the star ships has left formation and is deploying satellites around two of the mid-sized planets in order to determine if life exists and if there's anything we can use on the surface. Suddenly all these things we're doing have purpose and I feel we've all once again, grown a great deal, it's a good feeling.

Cpt. McCain asked me to follow her to her quarters. She asked me to be seated and said, "I'd like you to spend some time mingling with the various members of the fleet.

I would like to think that we've made our position clear to all but if it is not, our policies will need adjusting. In this process there will be no good and bad guys and I do not want names. I would like to hear about the people in animal care, health care, education, maintenance, food preparation, etc., a good mix.

There are no specific questions you should ask, I want you to listen to what they are saying and read between the lines.

You are an observer and that is what I want you to do. You will not be held responsible for your opinions of what you have seen, heard and learned.

We will speak again in two weeks."

I was happy to get such an assignment. I thanked her and took my leave.

I went over to Kim to tell her that I would be gone for a while but as usual, she already had sensed what was happening. We would see each other when time permitted.

I took my leave of the bridge not really having a goal. As I walked the corridors thinking how great an assignment I had, I found myself in one of the many cafeterias, got a cup of synthetic coffee and sat down at a table with three crewmen already sitting at it. One of them asked who I was as they had not seen me before.

I told them I am the one documenting the journey in order for us to have a record of what has taken place during our quest. I told them I felt compelled to meet as many people as I could in order to document things as accurately as possible.

Another one of the three asked if this was some kind of a means of control. No, I said, "control is not an issue, we all have the same goal and we all want to survive. I'm writing a history book, the good, the bad and the courageous people who are trying to make this journey a success."

The third man spoke and said, "I guess we sometimes forget just how grave our situation is and how important it is to all of us to have the same goal.

From what you have seen, do you think we're going to make it?"

I answered without hesitation, "Yes, I do. I have seen what this ship, its crew and the people who make everything possible are capable of. I believe we will find one or more planets where we can, if you will, start over again and man-kind will leave its mark throughout the galaxy.

My writings are accessible to all, if you would like and have the time, take a look at them. My name is Robert Manning and I am happy to have met you."

Therewith I took my leave.

As I walked further down the corridor I saw a sign on a door: "clean room." Curious about it I asked the man at the door if someone could show me around. A very friendly voice he said, "Certainly, I'll arrange for a tour and during that time you can shower and be dressed in proper attire." That took me a little by surprise but I followed him and was shown to a room where I showered and put on what seemed to be a space-suit.

A young woman met me at the door and introduced her self as Mary. She said, I hear you are interested in the clothing production.

"What, I said, clothing?" She went on to explain how instruments and gauges of microscopic size are integrated into the clothing.

At any given time one can be, via the smart clothing, treated for many life-threatening illnesses such as heart attack or stroke and many other things. "You mean to tell me that everyone is protected by this kind of clothing?" "Yes, she said, everyone. Unless the dosage is inadequate you would never know it is being administered.

If an acute case occurs the emergency room is notified via the clothing and someone is sent to help that person at once."

"I just thought we were all very healthy." "As well you should, she said, that's the whole idea. There are however just as many nasty little viruses and bacteria on this vessel as we had on earth. We've simply learned to keep them in check."

As I watched the clothing being made there was no indication that a high-tec alteration was taking place and it could certainly not be felt in the fabric.

She told me I could learn more from the physicians.

I thanked her for the tour and information and left for my next adventure.

My next stop was naturally sick bay where all medical procedures were performed and studied. There are forty eight physicians thirty one residents and fellows in training, sixty five RNs and another thirty four in training. Over one third of these people are in research and endeavor to ensure that we evolve as if we lived on a planet and that we're always up-to-date in the battle of the ever changing viruses and bacteria that are so egger to attack us.

I stopped to talk to one of the practicing physicians, I told him who I am and spoke of the tour I took through the fabric production center and asked if he'd mind telling me a little bit about his work. He introduced himself as Dr. Bibal Khan, he was pleasant and accommodating and said he'd be glad to show me around.

He showed me an array of instruments that have replaced many of the specialized physicians of the twenty first century. Most all physicians now are surgeons or internal medicine certified. They are trained on these instruments and can do most procedures non-invasively. Nano robots are now part of everyday medicine. They are robots that are so small that they can be injected into the blood system or released into the body by taking a pill. Once inside the body they do what they are built to do, for example, removing gall stones by chiseling them away so they can be flushed naturally or cleaning out partially blocked arteries. They are, according to Dr Khan, short lived and the body disposes of them as it would food passing through the digestive system.

The technology in the clothing is quite similar he said. It does the low-tec procedures and we take over when it fails.

He went on to explain that they also grow spare parts when needed. I laughed and said, "You're kidding, right?" He smiled and said, "not at all, come with me. I'd like to show you something."

We went to a computer and he pulled up my profile, then he asked if I was interested in my health. I said yes so he proceeded.

He said, "according to your last examination your heart will start failing in about four years. We could put you on medication and it would help but not solve the problem.

The tissue sample we took from you four months ago is being utilized to grow you a new heart. It is not a fast process and we'll need another eleven months before it is a functioning organ.

When that is accomplished we can maintain it until it is time for the transplant. It is an exact duplicate of the heart you have without the defect and the DNA used is your own thus eliminating surgical complications and possible rejection by your body.

Would you like to know your life expectancy?"

Not really, I said, "What is the average life expectancy for any of us?" "We are now capable of maintaining a high quality of life for approximately one hundred and seventy five years, but we're improving on that constantly."

Once we find a habitable planet we may need to modify those who are chosen to stay. This could change the life expectancy some. Our main goal is to maintain our human nature.

"How can you change them", I asked.

"It's really quite simple, we can have them grow long hair over the entire body in order to keep warm, they could be made capable of hibernation if necessary or they could be much taller or shorter.

It's all genetics and simply a question of what we need to do in order to enable us to survive comfortably in an altered environment.

That was, although fascinating, a really scary thought and I hoped it will not be necessary.

"What happens to us when we die?" Dr Khan replied, "We are cremated unless punished like Mr. Parker.

He was given a pill which had no immediate effect. Three hours after being released into space the pill was detonated. The detonation is so dramatic that all DNA is destroyed to ensure that no hostile beings get access to information that could be used against us." At that point I got a little faint and very uncomfortable.   "I assure you, he said, at minus 360 degrees his death was instantaneous and painless."

"You're highly trained in human behavior and I trust equally skilled? What do you think happened or went wrong with him?"

He looked at me for a moment and said, "Off the record, I would say the he was acutely home-sick. That's a condition that we can not treat. His mind could simply not adjust and therefore he became a danger to all of us.

A chosen few of us were present for the execution. He seemed to be happy that his suffering was about to end."

There was a brief uncomfortable pause.

I thanked him for his time and insight and returned to my quarters to digest and document the day.

Once back at my quarters I decided to have a scotch instead of my regular cup of tea and I trimmed my little bonsai bush while contemplating my very existence and realizing just how thin the string is that it's hanging from.

After finishing with my plant, my update and my scotch I slept long and deep.

The next several days passed without surprise and I was growing accustom to my newly appointed job. Learning more and more about how everyone keeps busy and admiring each of them for their courage.

On the morning of the ninth day Kim met me at the door as I was about to leave. She asked if she could come in for tea.

"Sure, I said, it's very nice to see you. Do you have the work crews put together?" "Yes, that was relatively easy, how are you doing?" "I'm learning a great deal about what it takes to keep us up and running and how well the people have adapted to their new environment. I've gained a great deal of respect for those who thought this whole thing up and then actually put it together."

"Don't over-do it Robert. You must remember you are the one on the outside looking in. There is no good, no bad, no right and no wrong. What you see you document and then you relax…. Would you like to relax together?"

"Yes, I'd love to……… She pressed her warm beautiful body against mine and time, work, goals and problems ceased to exist.

Later I was awakened by a wonderful soft voice saying

"Feed me I'm starving", I gave her a kiss and said, "how about a shower and me taking you to dinner?" She smiled and said, "A short shower, I'm hungry." We showered together. Watching the pearly soap run from her hair and race down her beautiful body seemed to make life worthwhile.

We walked to a near-by restaurant that overlooked a peaceful wooded area and ad a fruit salad. Then she returned to the bridge and I went off to meet the people who maintain the wooded areas and meadows.

As I crossed one of the fields I saw a young athletic looking man with long brown hair, a red bandana and bib overalls was examining the roots of the different grasses.

"Are you a botanist", I asked? Yes, he replied. "What are you looking for?"

"Nematodes, he said without them the system can't work." "What are nematodes", I asked. "They're microscopic beings that turn dirt into food for plants. Actually it's a little more complicated than that. I'm trying to ensure that these plants, insects and animals stay happy and healthy and it all begins with nematodes." "So, are the insects and animals happy?" He gave me a big smile and said, "Yes sir and when they're happy I'm happy."

"You sound like you like your job." "Job? This is no job, it's enjoying life and helping other living beings do the same. Just look at the grasses, wild flowers and that cow over there; I think she's actually smiling. Today is a good day".

"I'm Robert Manning; I'm a writer, what's your name?"

"I'm Eric Van Stahl" "Eric, would you show me around and tell me what I'm seeing and how you manage to have so many happy plants and animals?" "I'd be delighted to sir." "You don't have to say sir to me." "That's just the way I am sir, showing a little respect never hurt anyone."

We walked the meadows and then the wooded areas and I found for such a young person he was a wealth of knowledge. His soft voice and happy-go-lucky attitude gave everything around him a positive twist. With a big smile he said; "Now I'll show you how we make all this happen."

We walked to an elevator that was very well concealed among the trees, vines and bushes. He pushed a button on what seemed to be a limb of a tree and a door opened. We entered a room about eight by ten feet. He said with a sheepish smile; "You might want to hold onto the rail. This is an industrial elevator with only one goal, get there.

The door closed and with a sharp click we began to ascend. I thought it was going to push me right through the floor.

"We're now at nine hundred feet and above the haze and clouds and as you can see there are giant hydraulic pumps that ensure there is enough moisture in the air when it needs to rain. It's really cool cause you can't see this from the ground at all. Most people just think the stuff down there grows all by itself. We can also determine the temperature, humidity and barometric pressure from here which guarantees you a high quality of life."

"Wow this is spectacular, how many people does it take to manage all this?" It's amazing sir, we have more than we need because so many people ask to do volunteer work with us. I think they use it as vacation or therapy or maybe even both."

"I can understand why, you make it possible for us to stay in touch with nature." "That's right sir, if we can stay in touch with nature we can stay in contact and context with ourselves. I think that's a lot like maintaining sanity, don't you?" "Yes Eric, I do and it's fascinating to hear your point of view. I assure you, you've helped me in more ways than you'll ever know." He said; "Thank you sir, I'm glad you appreciate it."

I said; "That elevator is quite a ride too." "You'd be surprised how many people use it as a joy-ride or just plain entertainment." "Well, I'd like to think that you may have some special way to make it go down a little slower than it went up…. Please." He smiled and said, "Yes sir, I can do that."

During our descent I noticed that the walls were of glass and the view was spectacular. The way up had been so fast and furious that I was only aware of the guard rail I had clung to. I thanked Eric for the tour and I went on my way.

My two week excursion was over and I returned to the bridge to report to the captain. We went to her quarters and while having a cup of tea she asked, "What have you learned about the people that you didn't already know?" I thought my answer through and said,

"Nothing actually, they are all highly skilled in what they do, they seem to enjoy their work and seem to have adapted to their new environment."

She then asked if there were disturbing comments and opinions pertaining to the problems involving Mr Parker.

"Chosen few commented and none of them seemed to be upset about the incident. Mr Parker seems to have been an exception and his fate inevitable and as such, accepted by everyone I spoke to. I found that these people enjoy their work very much and seem to be realistic and optimistic about the future."

She seemed to be content and a little relieved with my answer. She asked if I needed some time off or would I like to join the crew on the bridge. I chose the bridge. We finished our tea and went back together.

I asked, "Should I go through the log-book and try to get up-to-date?" She answered, "Mr. Manning, you're up-to-date, you can't possibly write about every move we make. I trust you have documented the last two weeks, have ended that chapter and you may now continue with the present. Actually, nothing exciting happened but you're welcome to ask Mr Chi and Mr Berger so you don't feel like you're walking into a void." I thanked her and went off to greet the others.

Lin Chi brought me up-to-date on the construction of the research vessel. He said, "The actual construction began yesterday and can be observed via video from three satellite cameras. I think it's going to be easier than we thought.

At the moment it looks like a big pile of rubble being dragged by force fields. Shuttles are racing back and forth to and from the Enterprise moving building materials and equipment. The construction workers are all suited and are working under extreme conditions. And most of them are actually enjoying it.

The different minerals and ores are melted down, mixed and formed near the propulsions department. That's a lot like on-site manufacturing. The reactors emit more than enough heat to melt these metals. Large plates are poured which will create the outer hull. As you can imagine, at 360 degrees below 0 there is no problem getting the metal to cool. The job is keeping it from exploding due to the shock.

This phase will last four weeks. After that there will be an interior that can have force fields in its openings. That'll allow the void to be flooded with air. Although the workers will still be weightless, the work will become much easier. There'll no longer be a need for space suits. It's exciting to watch it grow." "That's astonishing that you did that in two weeks." I thanked him and walked over to ask Lars for an update.

He said, "Nice to have you back. How was your excursion?" "It was very educational. I'll tell you all about it later. What have I missed around here?" "The satellites that had been placed around the moons and planets, which had been deemed worth exploration, have been a very valuable resource for our research. All the life-forms we found were extremely primitive and presented no immediate threat to any of the excavation crews.

None of the planets were inhabitable, at least not in the near future.

Cpt. McCain has decided to stay here long enough to excavate enough material to complete the first vessel. That'll give our scientists ample time to document the animal and plant life. It seems that there is oxygen down there but it's bound in the sea water. It'll take thousands of years for enough plant life to form in order to create enough oxygen to sustain large air breathing life forms.

The scientists have considered planting a few ferns and grasses but Cpt. McCain hasn't decided if it's a good idea to interfere with the planet's evolution. On the one side it would probably be advantageous to us at some time or other and at the same time we could be destroying other life forms."

Lars said; "With the thought of being observed by someone or thing and possibly being held responsible for mistakes made, caution seems to be a good idea.

I've had an area on a viable planet enclosed and sealed. Plants have been set and are being maintained but are not directly exposed to the environment and can't multiply outside the complex. They seem to be thriving and actually growing reproductive roots which formed in only nine days. About now it would be good to know how long it took for that process on earth."

I spoke to Lars about Eric Van Stahl the young botanist I had met. "He seemed so well informed and so in love with his work and plant-life that I feel he could be of use to you and your experiments. I'll bet he'd be just what you need." Lars; "We'll see I'll have one of my students to bring him to the bridge." He turned to a young woman standing a few feet from us. "Would you please ask Mr. Van Stahl who is in gardening to come to the bridge?" She smiled, nodded and left the bridge.

When Eric got there introductions were made and he, Cpt. McCain, Lars, Kim and I sat down at the conference table in the ready room to discuss the prospect of initiating foreign life in an unknown environment.

Lars went over the environmental conditions of the planet and where it seems to be in its development. Then he explained the details of the green house he had constructed and that the ferns were growing reproductive roots after only nine days.

Eric said, "That's perfectly normal, you shocked the fern when you placed it there and it's the ferns way of countering possible death. What we need to find out is if the plants formed by the reproductive roots are healthy. If yes, as far as the plants are concerned, you can release them, they will of course grow to tree sized plants or bigger if they find enough food and water.

It's going to happen anyway, the composition of the air down there is almost identical to that of earth four hundred million years ago. It looks like the planet has ample water and a moon to stabilize the climate?" Lars said, "Yes, water and stability are no problem. The sun from which the planet is influenced is a relatively young middle-sized star. It's a lot like ours was on earth. The distance between them is virtually perfect for growth and the planet is minimally smaller than earth. The moon is closer to the planet than ours is to earth but it's also smaller."

Eric; "Sounds like an opportunity to me."

Cpt. McCain asked Eric, "If we release these plants, what's the worst thing you can imagine happening to that planet that wouldn't happen any way?"

"Captain, I'd have to be God to answer that. I believe we're all on borrowed time and if we can make things better for life forms, regardless for how long, then we should. Planting the ferns, provided the second generation is healthy, is a good thing and will help create other life-forms. It's simply giving evolution a boost, not changing it."

Cpt. McCain; "Mr Berger, if the plants are healthy how many would you plant?" "I would like to plant ten thousand evenly distributed in the areas most likely to sustain them. Eric could help me decide where they would best off."

Cpt. McCain, "Ms. Lien, do you feel comfortable with what is being said and what it's leading or could lead to?" She responded, "Eric seems to know what he is talking about and

Lars is not trying to change the process of evolution. I feel no hesitancy, it sounds exciting."

Cpt. McCain, "So be it, provided Mr. Van Stahl agrees that the second and third generations of the ferns grown on site are healthy, they may be distributed. Only ferns derivative of the plants grown in your green house on site may be planted.

I want this entire conversation to be in the log book as a permanent file and give that rock a name."

Eric said, "Let's call it Future." Everyone agreed on the planet's new name and it was documented, planet Future.

Cpt. McCain said, "Mr Van Stahl I would like to thank you for your help and ask that you co-ordinate the plant inspection with Mr. Berger. You realize of course you will need to travel to the planet and verify the plants are in good health?"

"It would be an honor captain."

Eric and Lars excused themselves from the table and proceeded to make their plans for the upcoming plant inspections.

Kim and I excused ourselves and left the bridge. "I'm hungry," she said. "What do you feel like eating?" "How about a duck?" "That does sound good, let's go to the Out Look were there's a nice view over the meadows." I took her by the hand and we strolled down the corridor. I asked; "What do you think of Eric?" She said; "He's an interesting person with a great attitude. Where did you find him?" "He was working in the meadows. He even took me up nine hundred feet on an elevator into the artificial sky. It was amazing and I might add one hell-of-a-ride."

The duck was excellent as usual and we topped it off with chocolate cake, chocolate ice cream with chocolate syrup and a little dab of whipped crème.

I asked, "Do you think all the erotic things they say about chocolate are true?" She smiled and said, "I certainly hope so." We laughed and went for a walk in the meadows.

As we walked we were suddenly interrupted by an extremely loud crashing sound that shook the entire space ship.

The captain announced over the intercom that we had been broadsided by a comet the size of a two story house traveling at an estimated sixty thousand miles an hour. She went on to say that we did not even get a scratch. Our force-fields held and no damage has been reported.

"That's reassuring on the one side and scares the hell out of me on the other." Kim smiled and said, "I guess we better utilize the fact that we're still alive." "You're not hungry again are you?" She lightly punched me on the chin and said, "Come with me."

The next morning on the bridge I asked Lars if any of the cameras had captured the impact and if it had disrupted the ongoing construction. He said, "Like captain McCain said, nothing within our force fields was damaged and yes, we did get it on camera. The problem is that even when we slow it down to twenty five frames per second it's still just a flash.

I created those force fields and should know what they are capable of but I would not have guaranteed us surviving something like that."

I asked, "How did that thing sneak up on us like that?"

"Easy actually, first it was obscured by the sun, then by a moon and then popped up from behind that planet we're next to. By the time our sensors noticed it we had two seconds to brace for impact.

We've placed long range sensors just outside the solar system to help avoid it happening again. We might be in some kind of asteroid belt. I'm still checking that."

The captain joined us and said, "Mr. Manning, I'd like for you to see what happened via the archives and then have Tanya Petrov, from the observation crew, show you what everything looked like before during and after the impact. Document it with illustrations and I formally request an honorable mention of the accomplishment of Lars Berger in regard to our force fields. We are all still in awe and shock of what has taken place. Thanks to Mr. Berger we're still here."

Lars thanked her for the honor and they began discussing the next solar system to be visited. I excused myself and walked over to speak with Mr. Akwete Kofi.

"Good morning, how are you doing?" "Great, he replied, I just became a father." "Wow, really? I hadn't even stopped to think about things like that for a long time." Is it a boy or a girl?" "We wanted a girl, her name is Kikuyu and she is our pride and our joy." "Again, my very best wishes to you and your wife and may Kikuyu have a long and prosperous life."

"Are you participating in the construction of the new vessel?" "No, not yet, once the outer hull is complete I'll send a crew to install the ventilation, conduit and water systems. We've probably got another thirty days before that happens.

Please excuse me I have a lunch date with my family." "Lunch, that's a good idea I think I'll go get some too."

I informed the captain I was going to lunch and asked where I could find Mrs. Petrov. She gave me directions and I was on my way.

After lunch I went to the observation deck. That's actually an odd name for a room that has no windows. There are screens everywhere on the walls and the sensitive areas are viewed in 3-D via holograms placed in the center of the room in a circle, all-in-all a very impressive layout.

I asked if I could speak to Tanya Petrov and the man I spoke to pointed to a stunningly beautiful woman who was doing her best to hide her beauty and look professional.

I walked over and introduced myself and told her why I was there. She led me to a desk with a large screen and we were seated. She explained that the camera is simply a stage one observation camera and zooming etc. was not possible. It did however take twenty five frames per second.

She turned it on and scrolled back to about forty five seconds before impact. "In the next forty five seconds you will see one thousand one hundred twenty five individual picture frames. The last two contain the entire event." Then she started the re-play.

It was like watching grass grow, the side of the Enterprise was being observed from an angle of forty five degrees. The construction on the new vessel was on the other side and further toward the back of the ship so it was completely out of view, it was simply the side of the enormous structure.

Then there was a flash and the picture vibrated violently. The pictures after the event were identical to those prior the event.

"How did you determine the size of that thing and what it really was?" "I'll show you the last three frames prior to impact. As you can see in the first frame, although a little blurred, it is a block of ice. Taking the objects in its background into consideration we could determine its size. Then in the last two frames you see its destruction. It literally disintegrated upon contact." "Very impressive, thank you. May I have access to these pictures on my computing station?" "Yes, I'll arrange it. Is there anything I can help you with?" "No thank you, that's all for now."

I guess the really strange part of it was that the force field could not be seen and the comet simply seemed to explode a few meters from impact with the Enterprise. I wonder what would happen if you held your hand out and touched the force field. Is it a solid like glass, does it feel like liquid, would it shock you?

When I returned to the bridge I asked Lars if he had a few minutes he could spare for me. He asked me to get myself a tea and be seated at the conference table, he'd be there shortly.

Half an hour later he joined me with apologies and a cold cup of coffee and said "How can I help." "I have some questions about the force field." He smiled, "Yes, most people do." "What is it and can it be touched?" "You should think of it as a very strong magnet. A magnet has an end that attracts and an end that repels. We're using the "repelling" end. In short it's a magnetic field. He smiled and said, "Just in case you understood that. I'll do my best to loose you with this one. The other part of your question is of course hypothetical. The energy used to create the shield is to say the least, enormous. No one has ever attempted to penetrate a shield at a slow speed.

Hypothetically, it could be done. Practically, I don't want to be there when it is attempted. I hope I have answered your questions adequately." Of course I didn't so I said; "Yes, of course you didn't!

I asked; "Do you think it makes the space it's in thicker?" "I guess you could see it that way. And the faster an object tries to travel through it the thicker it gets."

While Lars and I were finishing our discussion I noticed Cpt. McCain walk over to Lin Chi and I heard her say, "I've noticed a variation in your concentration. You seem to have something on your mind something that's bothering you. I'm not sure how long it's going to take for you to resolve it so I'll do it for you."

Chi looked at her with concerned eyes and started to speak. She raised her hand rejecting his reply and said, "Yes, of course you and your wife may have a child if that's what you want." Chi almost fell off his chair. He jumped up and for an instant I thought he was actually going to hug the captain.

With a tear of joy in his eye he asked if he could have a few hours off to inform and celebrate with his wife. Cpt. McCain said in her official dry voice; "Do you have anything pressing that can't wait?" "No, I'm up-to-date with everything." She said; "You're dismissed; we'll see you here on the bridge at 07:00 tomorrow.

He gave her a short bow and each of us a happy look and quickly left the bridge. Cpt. McCain smiled and seemed very pleased with herself.

She went on with her work as if it had been business as usual. Kim confronted her. "How long have you known?" "Since shortly before the good news from Mr Akwete Kofi." "My deepest respect for how you handled it." "Thank you, sometimes I even surprise myself."

We all applauded and were happy for our colleague and very pleased with our captain. She smiled and said, "OK, who's next?"

The rest of the day went by uneventfully and as I was leaving the bridge I asked Kim if she'd like to spend the evening together. "Sure, but as you know…. " "yes, I know, you're hungry, so am I and it's your turn to decide where we eat. How does such a small person manage to eat so much and stay small?" She said; "It's not how much; it's what, with whom and how you burn the excess calories taken in."

"Well pretty woman, you are certainly doing it right." We laughed and walked toward the restaurant she had chosen.

Over dinner she told me she was taking courses to improve her telepathic abilities. "Really, I didn't know there was a teacher and for that matter a person who could get anywhere near your powers." "Thank you, it's not a person it's a program. It's recorded on a microchip and installed in an earpiece that I sleep with.

When I wake up mornings I'm always a little smarter than I was when I went to bed." Do you actually hear it?" "No, not really, the on switch is programmed that it registers when my deep sleep phase begins and it then turns itself on. After an hour it turns itself off so I still get the rest I need."

I asked, trying not to sound sarcastic; "Have you noticed an improvement?" She smiled and then said with a concerned expression; " Let's say I'm getting better at it, I don't know if it is an improvement or an invasion of other people's' privacy." Until I learn to control it properly I hear a lot of other peoples thoughts that I'd really rather not hear." I had a sip of wine and said; "I wish you luck with that one." "Yes, as do I."

She looked me in the eye and said; "I can read thoughts and I see in your eyes that you are ready for desert." "You really are a mind reader. I'd actually be willing to share a piece of Key Lime pie with you." "Wow. I didn't see that one coming!"

We had desert and went for a long relaxing walk.

While entering a wooded area we saw a huge whitetail buck. His antlers were fully developed and he seemed irritated. Stop, I said, "That buck is in the process of putting a harem together and he's very aggressive during this period. We stood a while and watched him challenge two other buck and then slowly wander off with three doe. Kim asked, "Will they mate now?" "No not yet, the buck will have to wait till the doe are ready, during that time he'll try to assemble more doe and he'll be challenging and fighting with other buck for another few weeks.

They only have sex once a year but then the strongest of the buck have a lot of it and don't always live through it. I guess if you're going to work at something so hard that it endangers your life it might as well be sex. And it insures the future population has his genes."

"That actually exciting, are all animals breeding at this time" she asked. "Most of the big ones probably are; they try to have their young in spring." "That must mean they've done something to the weather that makes the animals believe its fall. I'll bet Eric had a hand in that.

I have an idea!" "What, she asked" "Lets go to the dairy farm and while they're milking the cows you could see if you can pick up on any of the cows' thoughts." She frowned and said; "Their thought process is most certainly different than ours." "An alien's will almost certainly be different too, yet we are all hopeful you'll be able to communicate or at least feel hostility if present." She smiled and said; "OK, let's go give it a try."

We walked to the dairy farm, which consists of seven milking stations. (Most of our milk and milk products are produced synthetically.) There were two cows in an enclosure and we asked the person who was tending them if we could conduct a short non-invasive experiment on one of them.

He said yes so we walked over to the enclosure. I asked; "How do you normally do what you do?" She walked over as close to one of them as she could get and looked it straight in the eye. For a few seconds they seemed frozen in time. Then she looked at me and said, "The brain is not advanced enough for real communication but it does seem to be content."

"Do you think you would have picked up on that a month ago?" "I don't think so, I had to concentrate and search its brain with other methodology. Thank you, I believe you've helped me take the next step in the evolution of my abilities. This is amazing. I've always known that these abilities are in me but having them and being able to use them are two different things."

"Does that by any chance obligate you to come to my place with me, have a cup of tea and maybe stay the night?"

"No, but that was a really good try. I'll go with you and have the tea and we'll see if you have enough charm to make me want to stay."

"That's fair."

When we got back to the bridge the next morning, Kim discussed her new findings with Cpt. McCain and asked if she could leave the bridge to consult with Dr Khan on a few neurological questions she had. Cpt. McCain gave her permission and she was off.

The bridge was quiet as most of the crew was still at breakfast. I sat and enjoyed watching the stars wiz by.

Chapter V

Cpt. McCain thought up another adventure for me. She's decided I should document some of the exploration going on and has asked captain William Turner of escort ship "one" to take me along so I could get a first-hand look at what is taking place on the planets we are exploring and utilizing. "He'll meet you at the port on deck 2 at 13:00 today. You'll take the tools you use for documentation; clothing and food will be furnished." She smiled and said with a mischievous smile, "They have everything necessary to help you be comfortable in a weightless environment.

I've followed your documentation of this quest and am impressed with your enthusiasm and ability. This is by no means a form of punishment. Cpt. Turner has been given orders to ensure your safety and well being. I believe it invaluable for future generations to know what we did and how we did it. Your strength is documenting once you've seen and questioned a process. Go and do exactly that for our future generations. I wish you a pleasant journey."

I thanked her for the complement although I'm not exactly thrilled about a weightless environment. It nauseates me.

I decided to go have some lunch while waiting for Cpt. Turner to pick me up.

At 12:50 I went to the port on deck 2. Cpt. Turner had sent Jimmy Cheedle, an ace pilot I had met while doing a walk through a few months ago. He's about 6'2" and moves like a panther. Jimmy was certified as the best pilot ever trained anywhere. He picked me up in one of the shuttles. They're built to transport up to eighteen people. They're also utilized like tractor trailer rigs and can attach to large containers and transport almost anything. It was an honor to get such attention.

Jimmy gave me a change of clothing and asked that I change while still on the Enterprise, "Once we separate there will be no gravity. The suit will help you cope with the change. Here's a pill to ward off motion sickness. You'll need one every twelve hours for three days. By then you should have adapted."

I took the pill first to make sure it was working when we took off and then changed into a suit that seemed to have many layers. It was very comfortable and the sock-like boots had soles of rubber with a high percentage of iron oxide it them. They, via a Velcro-like substance, attached themselves to the legs of the suit and became one with it.

When I came out of the dressing room Jimmy smiled and said, "Hey, you look like one of us. Are you ready to go?" "Yes, I suppose I am," we walked down the ramp and got into the first air-lock, then the second and then the shuttle. Jimmy checked a gauge he was wearing. He looked at me, smiled and said, "You seem to be filled with anticipation." "How do you figure that," I asked. "Your pulse has gone up considerably. Try to relax if you can, you're in a taxi, nothing more." "Thanks, I'll do my best."

We sat down and strapped ourselves in, then he pushed a button and we were no longer attached to the Enterprise. No longer being a part of it we were instantly repelled and found ourselves about five hundred meters from it.

Jimmy asked, "Did you ever get to see the whole Enterprise after it was finished?" "No, I can't say as I did. Do you have time to show it to me?" "I've been instructed to give you a tour of it and the area if you would like." "It sounds good to me." And therewith he pushed a lever forward and we lunged into the void. He went out into open space about thirty or forty miles and faced the shuttle toward the Enterprise The shuttle had large windows that covered the top half of the front and continued along the side for about six feet. It offered a fantastic view. I said, "Wow, I'm aware of the dimensions but I had no idea it was so huge." "Yeah, overwhelming isn't it?"

The Enterprise was pill shaped with an uneven surface. The propulsion/energy producing part is behind and separated from the main vessel. It is held together by a beam that comes out of the center of the Enterprise and entered the center of the reactor. The Enterprise was rotating, the reactor was not.

"Now we'll circle the Enterprise and you can see all of it. To your right is escort ship two and we'll see number one on the other side. Again he pushed the throttle forward and I noticed it was a joy-stick. We flew closer and then flew the length and circled it twice.

Now I'll show you the exterior of the escort/battle ship. It has the form of an arrow-head and is by no means small. At a little over a thousand meters long and two hundred feet thick, it almost looked menacing.

"If you look to your right the planet you see is the one we're all excited about. I'm to take you there tomorrow." "It looks so far away, how long does it take to get there?" He chuckled and said; "It's amazing how fast these shuttles are. We'll need less than twelve minutes actual flight time."

We made our approach from the rear of the star-ship and as we neared a door opened. As we got closer my eyes got bigger. "Are we really going to fly into that little hole?" "Yes, that way the shuttle's protected when docked and we won't need space suits. It takes less than five minutes to flood the bay with breathable air once the hatch is closed and in an emergency that thing can close in seconds." I remember seeing the hatch from the inside during the walk-through. It looked a lot bigger from that perspective.

Once we actually got there I realized we had more than enough room to get through. Jimmy expertly flew into the bay, turned the shuttle 180 degrees and set it down. The hatch closed, lighting was turned on and we prepared to exit. He said; "Once you release those straps you'll be weightless. Please try to keep at least one foot on the floor at all times. If you do start to float, don't fight it, you'll eventually make contact and will note that you can walk on the walls and ceiling just like you can on the floor. Actually, that's the crap that makes you nauseated. Don't do it if you can avoid it."

I planted my feet on the floor and released the straps holding me to the chair. With no effort on my behalf I stood up. I looked at Jimmy and he smiled, "Fun isn't it?" What a sense of humor.

I practiced walking for a few minutes in the shuttle where I could reach the ceiling and brace myself if need be.

When the hatch of the shuttle opened it was at least ten or twelve meters to the floor and there were no steps. Jimmy put one hand on an overhang above him stepped into space and gently gave himself a shove toward the floor. I did the same and was pleasantly surprised how smoothly it went. I asked if we always had to jump. "Heavens no, when you're on a planet with gravity that would be a long drop, there is a ramp out the rear of the shuttle that we can use."

I was then greeted by Cpt. Turner and he re-familiarized me with the ship. "Make yourself comfortable and then you're welcome to do a little exploring on your own here on escort ship 1. The crew has been instructed to be accommodating but you must understand that their duties come first." "Yes, of course, I appreciate your hospitality and would like very much to take a look around."

I therewith excused myself and went off exploring the ship. There were two bays with two shuttles each. There were also two huge container vessels in each bay. That was what was used when transporting ore, minerals and water from planets to the Enterprise.

Then I entered the living quarters of the crew. I said hello to those who were off duty and not sleeping and asked where I would be sleeping. One of the crew said, "right over here sir. It's more comfortable than it looks." He showed me a little container which was one meter in diameter and two and a half meters long. "Actually it's a lot more comfortable than it looks and it keeps you from floating around in your sleep and out of harms' way during battle." There were lockers where work and sleep garments were stored. The crewman explained that each garment that was placed in the locker was cleaned and disinfected while hanging there.

The shower and personal relief bay was next to the room of sleeping units and lockers. Once clean, you are automatically blow-dried and also disinfected. While in these rooms you wear magnetic slippers that were strapped on, all in all very efficient. I thanked everyone for the tour and continued my tour.

I re-entered the break-room and asked where I could get something to eat. I was told by one of the crew, "This is it, break-room cafeteria and lounge in one. There are five meals served here per day. Here's a menu that you can choose from. If you're booked to be on a shuttle or elsewhere the meals are automatically sent with you. Just don't forget to place your order."

A woman dressed in white said; "As you can imagine, our meals are special, which means a lot of the things you'll be eating will be served in tubes. The quality and taste don't suffer under the process. Actually some extra vitamins and minerals are often added making it healthy and very nourishing. I thanked them for the information and menu, made my selections and noted the meal schedules.

I entered the main bay and asked to be shown to engineering. It was the space in the middle rear of the ship with the bays for the shuttles on either side. Like on the Enterprise there was a large unit behind the space ship attached via a huge pipe. "What's that out there," I asked. A woman approached me. She was about 5'8" with short blonde hair and a pair of pliers in her hand. She introduced herself as Edita Romero, head of engineering. "That's the oven. It's where anti-material is produced. It produces so much radiation that our strongest force fields are needed to protect the ship and us from exposure. It creates the power for everything in and on this vessel." She went on to explain how the power was distributed and stored. When she finished I wasn't really sure I had fully understood anything but at the same time was very impressed.

A buzzer sounded and I asked if it was an alarm. She smiled and said, "In a way, yes, it's time to eat. We tend to stay so busy that we get lost in time. Even in an emergency situation at least one third of the crew is required to eat on time and the rest within two hours of being notified. That insures clear thinking and an alert crew." We walked toward the break room and she asked if there were any further questions about engineering that she could answer. "Yes, I said, do you work in engineering on the Enterprise as well?" "Yes I do, it would be a waste of talent not to."

We had our meal; I thanked her for her time and information and went back to the bridge. I found a spot to be seated and spent the rest of the day observing.

After a while the buzzer went off again and this time I noticed that exactly one third of each group departed for the meal. I asked Cpt. Turner if I could wait for the second phase and when it would be. He replied, "Yes, you may, the board computer has been programmed to have a large tolerance for deviations of your itinerary. The second wave will be in twenty minutes."

After the meal I was shown to a fitness room. They explained that I'm required to work out no less than forty minutes before retiring and as that will be in two hours I should watch the others and when ready ask the instructor for assistance.

I watched for half an hour and then confronted the instructor. "Hello, I'm Robert Manning. I'll be here for a few days and have been instructed to see you about a fitness program."

He was a perfectly formed person who, no doubt, didn't have a gram of fat anywhere. "Hello, he said with a smile, I am Goro Shima, fitness director." He turned the computer on and entered my name. A list appeared. Goro said, "This list can be viewed on any screen in this room. Your access code is 123RM. I will show you each instrument and how it is best utilized. You will please do this once per day."

We went through each of exercises and he certainly helped me limber up. It was more like waking all the sleeping parts and massaging them. After finishing my exercises I thanked Mr. Shima and went to the sleeping quarters. There was a locker with my name on it. I opened it took out the suit I was to sleep in, took my shower and changed.

I got into the cube I was to sleep in. It was small but padded on the inside. A screen turned on and a voice asked me to say my name.

A second after saying Robert manning I heard a very faint ssssssst.

I woke up refreshed and feeling great. With no real sense of time I got out of my box wondering how long I had rested. I showered, exchanged clothing and went to the break room to get a cup of coffee. It was just as the buzzer rang. What great timing and I was certainly hungry.

While finishing my meal and working on my second cup of coffee Jimmy Cheedle entered the room. "Good morning," he said and almost everyone replied. He got his food and sat down across from me. "Are you ready for an exciting day?" "Absolutely, where are we going?" "We thought you might like to take a look at a few objects we've been studying and then go down to planet Future and take a look at the life forms and plants that have been growing there in a green house." "Sounds good, when do we leave?" "Right now if it's OK with you." "Sure, why not?"

We finished our coffee and went to the shuttle bay. Jimmy said, "We're going to take a container with us. One of the crews has located ore that can be used for construction of the research vessel. We'll be picking up and delivering the first load." We strapped ourselves in and Jimmy started the shuttle, connected to the container and we were on our way.

We flew to a near-by asteroid belt and he pointed out some rock formations that seemed to be glowing. "That's new for us and no one has figured out what it is or if it could be utilized. They're not radioactive and that surprised everyone. We may have stumbled onto a new energy source free of pollution; or something that could easily destroy us, we just don't know." I asked, "Has anyone tried to get a sample?" "You and I think alike. But the answer would be no. Until Mr. Berger gives the go-ahead we're all to stay clear of it."

Jimmy pushed the throttle forward, made s steep bank and flew straight at the star supporting this solar system. I asked; "How close can we get before we melt?" "That's not something I want to test. I can accelerate more efficiently when utilizing the star's gravity but I intend to break off long before it starts getting hot. It's like I promised you, we'll be there in ten minutes." He moved the joy-stick ever so slightly and we lunged toward a faint spot in front of us. "We'll *do a slow fly-by of the excavation site and then drop the container off. Then I'll hover ov*er open water to give you a look at a primordial soup. After that we'll visit the green house."

As he had promised, we were there in ten minutes; now we had to enter the atmosphere.

He bounced along the surface of the planet's atmosphere slowing us down. We circled the planet three times before we were slow enough to enter. As we entered we suddenly had a white hot shield in front of us. The shuttle shook violently and slowly the white hot shield went to yellow which changed to red and finally faded. The planet came into view. It was a lot likr flying over a dessert.

The strip mining location became visible ahead of us. As we approached, the turbulence lessened and the flight became smoother. We took a look at the excavation site, dropped off the container. There were only ten people with heavy equipment on site. We spoke briefly with them via head-sets as there was not enough breathable oxygen for us to get out of the shuttle. Then we flew another fifteen minutes to get to open water. Jimmy stopped the shuttle in mid air for a closer look. I was astounded that he could do that in an atmosphere and directly above a planet that has the same gravity that earth has. Of course that was the first thing I questioned. I asked; "How are you doing that? There's no sound of roaring engines or thrusters and yet we're suspended in midair, or whatever that is out there."

He said; "I'm using a force field just like the one that protects the star ship. It's repelling us and I am using just enough energy to neutralize the effect, ergo, we're suspended." Visions of Si-Fi movies were flashing through my mind. It's still hard to believe we're where we are doing what we do.

Having digested my crash course in the use of electromagnetic fields and accepting the fact that although we are less than fifty feet from the water we are not going to fall in, I decided to check out the water contents and hoped I would see some kind of life form swim by.

We hovered for about half an hour and nothing exciting happened so I suggested we move on. Jimmy accelerated and we were soon once again over dry land.

We arrived at the green house without incident and landed about a hundred meters from it. Jimmy said,

"You're going to have to suite up for the trip outside. The temperature is OK but there is almost no oxygen in the air. To avoid claustrophobic feelings I'll give you a helmet with a 360 degree view. The suit itself is very light and non-restrictive. Your air supply will last for three hours. Thirty minutes before you run out you'll hear a very loud beep. At that time we'll return to the ship.

Please be very careful not to damage the suit. If you're exposed to the atmosphere, and live through it, you'll be put into quarantine for six weeks. Take it from one who knows, that's not fun."

After suiting up we went to the rear of the shuttle where there was a ramp so we could descend. The landing gear of the Shuttle kept it almost twenty feet off the ground. It was a special feeling to have real gravity holding me in place. It's been almost seven years since I was last on a planet. It gave me a sense of extreme co-ordination, like I could walk, run and jump with no problem at all. Jimmy said, "That super feeling about your co-ordination is your brain lying to you. If you can't jump twenty feet on the Enterprise, what makes you think you could do it here?" "I understand; do I need to watch what I step on in regard to puncturing the suit?" "No, not really, your suit's soles are of pliable plastic and can withstand a lot. The suit itself, on the other hand, is twenty two layers of extremely thin materials that help maintain a comfortable atmosphere and are not made to withstand being punctured. Just try to walk as you always do, it'll be OK. Let's go over and have a look at the ferns."

We walked to the green house, which I had pictured as a little glass cube with a watering system attached. It was the size of a football field and at least a hundred feet high. "Wow, that's a big green house." "Yes, we have no idea how big these plants will get and Mr Berger said he wanted ten thousand of them."

Upon entering the building Jimmy began measuring the oxygen content of the air. "Is it enough to breath; I asked." "No, but it's considerably more than outside the structure. What do you think of these ferns?" "They're really big and look almost like trees." "We think so too and these that are only about six inches high are the third generation. Once Eric Van Stahl gives the go-ahead they'll be planted on pre-determined locations across the planet. It should be a relatively green planet in a hundred years." "Only relatively I asked." "Yes, this planet doesn't wobble like the earth. Its equator is extremely hot and will probably remain desert. Its poles are very cold and will probably always be frozen. Everything between the two should produce life in abundance. We hope a certain amount of weather patterns will start appearing and will distribute the perception evenly across the planet but you just never know for sure."

"You know a lot for a pilot." "Its simply being around scientific experiments, I'm constantly exposed to very smart people and most of what they do I find interesting. Some of it sticks and I get smarter. I guess that's the way it works."

We went outside and took a walk so I could see the mosses and alga that are growing there. After a few minutes a buzzer went off. That was our cue to return to the shuttle. "That was an exciting two and a half hours and I thank you." "I'm glad you enjoyed it and hope you have the information you need for your documentation." "I always do. It seems like a new adventure begins every minute." "I know exactly what you mean."

We returned to the shuttle. Then we flew back to the excavation point and connected to the now full container. "Unless you have unfinished business on escort ship one I'll drop you off on the Enterprise when I deliver this load of ore."

"Sounds like a good idea, that'll give me the opportunity to see how it's processed." "Pull your straps real tight, leaving the planet with this load is going to require quite a little burst of energy and it'll most likely get a little bumpy."

Knowing Jimmy's since of humor I knew I should brace myself. He pushed the throttle forward and everything began vibrating, he looked at me, smiled and said, "We're off the ground are you ready?" I nodded and he pushed the joy-stick forward again.

With a roar and violent shaking we lunged forward. At first we were traveling almost parallel to the planet then he pointed the shuttle upward and pushed a second throttle forward.

With another burst of energy we accelerated very quickly and within thirty seconds we were out of the planet's atmosphere and gravitational influence.

Jimmy said; "So, it's smooth sailing from here on. We're not going to be traveling quite as fast on the way back so the trip will take about forty five minutes."

I asked, "What does that container weigh?" "Out here nothing but as we left the planet it was just over three hundred tons." "How much can you remove from a planet at one time?" "That's pretty well it. I've never had to use the back-up power source before to get off a planet. I must say, it packs quite a wallop." "I'll go along with that."

I tried relaxing and enjoying the view on the way back. It had all been very exciting and I'll have a lot to write about.

When we got to the Enterprise Jimmy attached the container to one of the ovens which are connected to the exterior of the reactor. The ore was removed from the container, ground to a course sand, melted down and separated.

While still in a liquid form the metals are mixed to create whatever alloy is needed at that time and poured into its final form. Only the actual pouring of the alloys takes place inside the Enterprise as gravity is a pre-requisite for pouring. Then the finished product is taken to its final destination.

Jimmy flew me to deck two; "You've certainly made this an interesting trip. I hope we can do this again some time." I thanked him again for his time and effort and we said our good-bys then he was on his way.

I went to a nearby restaurant and had a meal that did not come out of a tube. Not that it's bad, I just prefer being able to identify what I eat. Then went to my quarters to catch up on my reports and have a real shower.

I wrote for the rest of the day and then thought I'd test Kim's skills. After showering and relaxing for a few minutes I sat in a comfortable chair and concentrated on her and tried to depress everything else. Then I started calling her in my mind. I called and called but didn't feel anything in return so I gave up.

While I was making a cup of tea my door buzzer rang. It was Kim; she smiled and said, "You called?" "As a matter of fact I did, I'm in need of your presence. Do you have time for a cup of tea or possibly more?" "Yes, she said, the tea sounds good and so does the more." We drank tea and chatted and as always the hours melted away.

The next morning after breakfast we returned to the bridge together. Cpt. McCain was about to have a meeting or discussion period and asked us to join them.

She said her good mornings and ensured herself that there were no outstanding critical problems that needed immediate attention. She went on to say, "I;;ve been informed that the star system we're in has resources that require three more weeks to excavate.

I'd like Mr Berger to finish his experiments and planting on the planet we call Future and ask that Mr Chi has the construction site secured for a "leap" within three weeks.

Mr. Kofi, do you have everything you need in place?" He replied, "I will have everything within fourteen days."

She turned on a hologram which was built into the table and our next goal appeared. She asked Lars to explain the situation. "We've studied the near-by solar systems very carefully and believe that this one has the highest potential of supporting life. If we're right then our friends who payed us a short visit may live there.

This will most certainly induce a reaction." Cpt. McCain, "Ms. Lien, would you like to comment?" "Yes, thank you, although there was no apparent hostile intent on their behalf you must know that they could consider our actions hostile. I am uncertain how quickly I can read their intent. We need to do this with the utmost caution."

Lars, "We're looking for extra-terrestrial life and I believe we can prove ourselves equally interesting to them if they allow us to communicate. If we don't show an interest they may allow us to pass and that would be unfortunate to say the least." Mr Kofi, "Unfortunate would be if they blow us to pieces."

Cpt. McCain, "Upon arrival we will not have our weapons systems activated; we will however have our shields at maximum strength. They've seen that they can withstand the impact of a comet.

I believe us to be safe for at least the time it takes to induce a second leap. Just in case we're welcomed with hostility, Mr Berger, how much time do you need to induce a second leap?" He looked at Chi and asked, "Will we have enough power?"

"Yes, power is not a problem." Then I could create a second leap in less than nine seconds. I'll prepare them both at the same time."

Cpt. McCain, "We'll discuss and finalize this in two weeks. Are there any questions and does anyone have any other business that needs the bridges attention?" No one spoke and the meeting was adjourned.

Cpt. McCain and Kim meandered toward the coffee machine conversing on what I believe to be the thoughts and emotions of those present at the meeting.

I asked Mr. Kofi how his daughter Kikuyu is doing and he replied with a big smile, "Thank you for asking, she's doing very well and growing fast. How was the trip and most of all was there oxygen in the green house?"

"The trip was very interesting and enjoyable, as for the oxygen, Jimmy Cheedle said there was almost enough to be able to breath. Their confident they'll be able to create an inhabitable atmosphere within a hundred years or so." We talked small-talk for a while and then he had to return to his station.

Two weeks passed and once again we found ourselves sitting at the conference table discussing the "Leap". It seems that everyone finds it's a good idea and we're all a little worried about the aliens and what they could do to us if they didn't want us to be where we are going.

Chapter VI

As the captain was about to speak our main power source put itself in safe mode, dim red infrared lighting came on and all monitoring screens pointed at one object.

Cpt. McCain, "Well ladies and gentleman, I guess we're about to find out what they think of our idea. Mr. Chi set a course directly at that vessel and accelerate to impulse." She looked around and saw puzzled faces. "We will not send the escort ships as that could be understood as a hostile act.

Cpt. McCain to escort ships, I expect you to remain stationary and alert, acknowledge." They repeated the command and we advanced on a starship with extraterrestrial life-forms on it. The silence was overwhelming. I wanted to run and hide but there's no place to go.

We stopped just short of one hundred miles of the vessel. It was less than half the size of the Enterprise. It had a disk form that was a lot like what we had pictured in sci-fi films. The outer edge of the vessel is about five hundred feet high and seems to be rotating around the star-ship. Mr Chi believes it to be their source of energy.

We faced each other for over thirty minutes, which seemed like hours. Cpt. McCain looked at Kim and Kim surged her shoulders. "I feel no aggression coming from them."

The silence was broken by a voice saying "I am Kotar of the Ty and am from Korant. It is one of the planets you are about to visit. State your intentions."

Cpt. McCain cleared her throat and said, "I am Cpt. Kathryn McCain of the star ship enterprise. We are explorers and come from the planet Earth. It is fifteen five light years from here. We are in search of intelligent life forms and hope to exchange our knowledge."

"You may send two representatives of your peoples to our vessel. There will be no weapons on the transporter or with the representatives. We have translators for them. Our atmospheric requirements are similar to yours and we have a form of what you call gravity on board our vessel. Please send them at once."

The captain looked at Kim and Kim looked at me and my heart almost stopped. Cpt. McCain, "It's apparent that they are not going to eat you. Ms. Lien will search their thoughts and you will observe. There is much that can be said and there is even more that must not be said. You will not expose any of our weaknesses or the number of our population, be it here or elsewhere, understood?"

We nodded and she sent for Jimmy Cheedle in a disarmed shuttle. "If you opt to document them and their ship in picture, ask them first and Ms. Lien, I expect you to invite representatives of theirs to return with you. I'm curious to see what they look like."

Cpt. McCain then replied to the Ty, "We will send our ship's counselor and our historian. We thank you for this opportunity." "So be it, we await their arrival."

When Jimmy arrived he was summoned to the bridge. He reported to Cpt. McCain and she said, "Mr Cheedle, I want no heroics and nothing fancy. When you deliver Ms. Lien and Mr Manning you will politely take your leave and wait to pick them up from what you consider a safe distance. Take food and water with you. I can not say how long this visit will last. When they return they may have guests with them, treat them as such." He nodded, glanced at us and said, "Ready?"

My fear had changed to pure terror and I was trembling, Kim took my hand and said, "Consider them foreigners from an exotic country. They invited us and I can only hope we are so wise when it's our turn." We walked to the shuttle in silence. Upon arrival Jimmy explained to Kim how she was to secure herself in the seat and about the upcoming weightlessness. I think that bothered her more than meeting the aliens.

Jimmy, "This is going to be a very short trip. When we get there you'll simply disregard me and leave the shuttle. I'll wait for clearance and then detach and station the shuttle a few miles from their vessel. I'll not return to the Enterprise without you." I had never seen him so serious. We acknowledged his commitment and were on our way. As we neared the Ty vessel a large door opened on the side of the ship. At the same time we saw Jimmy release the joy-stick. I think a tractor beam or remote control must have taken over and the shuttle glided in and landed inside the alien space-ship.

Kim and I walked down the shuttle ramp into the bay.

There they were. They were humanoid with very well formed bodies that were about seven feet tall. Their facial structure is more pronounced than ours. The bone above the eyes and the cheek bones are pronounced than ours. They looked extremely powerful.

After we had cleared the shuttle ramp four of them approached us. One held out his hands, elbows close to his side and his palms up. It was as he were saying (look I'm unarmed). We did the same and smiled. The one who came to greet us spoke. He spoke slowly as if searching for the right words, "We welcome you to our transport; I am Timlayar, consular on board this vessel."

Kim introduced herself and then me and we were asked to follow them. The ship is very different from ours as it is not made of metal. It seems to be made of some kind of carbon fiber or plastic. The corridors are like tubes running through the structure giving it structural strength. The floor part of the tube is about twelve feet wide and has a slightly rough structure for grip or traction.

The induced gravity is considerably less than what we are use to and it makes it a little hard to walk slowly. I guess that's why they are so large and seem to have wide feet.

We were taken to a conference room to introduced to the captain. Timlayar said "I have the honor of introducing the counselor of the great ship Enterprise Kim Lien and the ship's historian Robert Manning." Cpt. Kotar's eye met ours. He smiled and greeted us in the same manor Timlayar had greeted us. We returned the greeting. Then he said; "I would like you to meet my science officer Maylar. Once again we did the palms up greeting. Then we were asked to be seated. Water was offered as refreshment in quart sized glasses. We all picked up our glass, poor Kim needed both hands, and while trying to make eye-contact with everyone at the same time we all drank.

Kim said, "It is our custom to present a gift to people we meet for the first time. I would like to present you with this hologram of our home planet, its size, people and other life-forms that share the planet with us." She placed it on the table and turned it on. They looked, checked some of the data and thanked her. Cpt. Kotar, "We inhabit two planets in our solar system Korant and Suboro. We have a civilized history of more than five hundred thousand of your years. We welcome you as a people to accompany us to Korant if you would like."

With that Kim and I knew they either had access to our computers or have visited the Earth. How else could they know how long one of our years is?

Cpt. Kotar addressed Kim; "I will allow you to enter the thoughts of our counselor Timlayar for a brief look at who and what we are. Then you will return to your ship." "Thank you and I would like to invite one or two of your crew to return with us to meet our captain."

Cpt. Kotar, "I thank you, first you will join thoughts with Timlayar, everything you can see in him he can also see in you. Then we will take the next step."

We both knew that Timlayar would almost defiantly be able to get more information than Kim could but it was a fair and even offer that couldn't be refused.

They sat across the table from each other, Timlayar reached out with both hands and Kim's hands disappeared inside his. They closed their eyes and it was silent for about thirty seconds. Kim's eyes opened, she smiled and said thank you.

We got up, made eye contact with Cpt. Kotar, Maylar and Timlayar. Then we returned to the bay where Jimmy was waiting.

Cpt. Kotar, "Speak to your captain and have her contact me when she is ready." "I will and thank you."

The trip back was brief and gave us no time to talk. We went straight to the bridge and Kim spoke briefly with Cpt. McCain then the captain asked us all to join them at the conference table.

Kim explained what we had seen and what had been said. When she came to the part where she and the Ty's counselor telepathically exchanged thoughts she paused and said, "They are much further advanced than we are. They have however acquired their knowledge and way of life through trial and error as we have. They live on two planets which are very near to one another. They are both the size of Mars so they have less gravity than we do. The warmer of the two planets, Suboro, is utilized for agricultural purposes and Korant is for the dominate race.

It seems they have three species of humanoids and each does what they can do best. We would be tempted to say that two of the three species have been enslaved. That is however not the way the Ty interpret it. They have a system that has worked for several hundred thousand years and as there are no revolts and they seem to be content there is no reason to judge them.

I am certain that the Ty counselor was capable of restricting what I could see and yet I couldn't feel that he was holding anything from me. I believe we should invite them to come over to the Enterprise and then visit their planets."

Cpt. McCain, "Mr. Manning what was your impression?" "They were certainly not hostile, at least in our definition of hostility. They do however have purpose in their actions so I believe that they see an advantage for themselves through us and that we should at least endeavor to act and re-act the same in self-defense." Mr Chi, "Do you feel that we have reason to fear them?" "No, but I do know that once in their solar system we will be at their mercy and that means our entire species. That worries me a little." Cpt. McCain, "Indeed caution must remain a priority. We will however do as Ms. Lien has advised and visit them.

Mr Berger I want to know exactly how close we can get to their solar system and still create a leap without harming them. A leap to safety will always be programmed and ready to initiate. We will utilize the escort ships to get close enough to use the shuttles to fly down to the planets. There must always be a ready and able crew in place here on the bridge of the Enterprise in case we're threatened."

Lars nodded and said, "I believe we have the perfect opportunity to train the crew of the new star ship to be built. Cpt. McCain, "Mr Chapman, I want suggestions for your replacement as you will be the captain of the new ship." Jerry Chapman (#1) was taken by surprise and for a moment was speechless. He said, "Thank you captain and I will find you a worthy candidate."

Being number one is like a vice-presidency, you have the knowledge and the expertise but no one wants your opinion. Jerry was truly a happy man and very deserving of the promotion.

Cpt. McCain, "When the two Ty come here to the Enterprise. I want Mr Berger to be in an escort ship when they arrive, after all they are telepathic. Mr Chapman, Mr Manning Ms. Lien and I will greet them and we will meet in conference room number four. Any questions?"

Kim mentioned that water should be served from one container and poured into large glasses for everyone. "That's what they greeted us with and I believe it to be custom." Cpt. McCain, "So be it, this meeting is adjourned. If any of you have any additional ideas or thoughts please let me know." She stood, addressed Kim and said, "Come with me, I think we should take a walk.

Cpt. McCain said, "#1 you have the bridge, please send another invitation to the Ty. They are welcome to send two representatives at their leisure. Also send them our means of telling time and send them a functional clock via computer. That way they can tell us what time they are coming." Then she and Kim left the bridge.

Lars had lots of questions for me about the Ty as he was not allowed to confront them yet. I explained that they really aren't very different than us and promised to have a number of cameras on during the meeting. An alarm sounded at his station and we both ran over to see what was wrong.

A shuttle has had a malfunction and a blast of energy from the fuel system has catapulted it toward a planet. Lars said, "If it enters the atmosphere at that speed it'll disintegrate." All we could do was watch it on the screen.

A beam shot out from the ship of the Ty directly at the shuttle. As it hit it the shuttle came to a complete stop and then slowly pulled out of the gravitational influence of the planet, then the beam disappeared.

Jerry Chapman and Lin Chi were watching as it happened. The whole thing took place in less than ninety seconds. Jerry immediately paged the Ty and thanked them. He went to voice communication and said, "I, as second in command of this ship, would like to thank you personally for saving our crewmen and our shuttle. I look forward to meeting you."

He also sent the invitation, an explanation of our time and a clock.

Lars said, "So, it is possible to create a tractor beam. It can not only affect a smaller vessel, it actually neutralizes and takes control of it. I must say, that was impressive."

Mr. Chapman told an orderly to find the Captain and let her know what had taken place. "You will do this privately, if she wants others to know it happened she'll tell them." "Yes sir,"

Lars, "I'll be done with the planting tomorrow and I believe we have ample ore to finish the research vessel. Theoretically, we could leave this solar system whenever we want. The Ty seem to be watching every move we make, thank goodness I might add. I wonder what the captain will think about it."

Mr Chi had the shuttle brought to the Enterprise for repairs and told its pilot to report to the bridge.

Kim and the captain had gone to an early lunch and I suppose the captain now knew everything about the shuttle and visit that we know.

When she returned she was again updated, and she addressed Lars. "Mr Berger, this changes my perspective considerably. You will of course be present should the Ty send representatives. Ms. Lien will school you in protecting vital thoughts. It's an amazingly simple thought process which we hope will help protect information we determine classified. Then you will report to me and we'll discuss what we deem classified."

Kim sat down with Bianca Lambert, communications officer who had now become an important factor. "We need to know their language for a better understanding. I'll also want your opinion of their ability to fully understand our word and thought process. This is vital as a miscommunication could be devastating." "This is exciting after all of our other languages were discarded I almost considered my education a loss."

"You'll have more than enough to do. It looks like we're going to encounter many more intelligent life-forms than we had anticipated." "Do you really think so?" "I'm certain and you'll again be speaking many languages."

Therewith Kim had let the cat out of the bag. During her mental lock with Timlayar she realized that they communicate with a number of life-forms from other solar systems.

The Ty have announced that they will visit us tomorrow morning at eight o'clock. We were reminded to be at the main dock shortly before eight.

I glanced at Kim and said, "Do you want to go get something to eat?" "Yes, I'm starving I'd like to visit the restaurant overlooking the meadows, they have such wonderful salads." "Sounds good to me, are you done here?"

She said, "Not quite but I'll be with you in five minutes." I walked toward the bridge exit. On the wall next to the door was a screen and the camera was focused on the Ty's star-ship. It is certainly an impressive object. Kim came up from behind me and said, "Don't tell me you want one of those for your birthday." "OK I won't but you know I do." We laughed and were off to the restaurant.

Over dinner Kim said, "I'd like to teach you how you can protect your thoughts." "Do you think I'm at risk?" "I believe anyone coming in contact with a life form that has the ability to telepathically scan your brain is to a certain extent at risk.

We don't know if they can plant ideas in people and therewith control them and we don't know if they would do it to us if they could. For the time being everyone coming in contact with the Ty will be closely watched for variations in his or her behavior. W're not going to risk enslavement." "Wow I had no idea you had discovered so much about them."

"That's part of the problem. I can sense what they are capable of but not necessarily if they actually use the powers they have the way I interpret them.

We should give them the benefit of the doubt without putting ourselves in danger." "Is that why I need this mental blocker?"

"Yes, but I am by no means sure it will work." "I have faith in your abilities. Let's go for a walk and try to relax a little.

We left the restaurant and walked for over an hour. Kim spotted a big oak tree and said, "Would you like to sit and rest under that tree for a while?"

After we were seated she asked me to relax. "I'm going to kind of hypnotize you but don't worry, I won't turn you into a rabbit." We smiled at each other and then she said, "Mentally you're as well protected as you can be." "You installed a protection system in me and I don't even know it's there?" "Yes, something like that. If your subconscious mind feels it's being influenced by an outside force it will automatically block it. You'll notice it if it happens. You'll need to contact me at once.

If you notice any changes in your ability to remember or you notice a loss of creativity let me know." I gave her a long slow kiss and asked how long it had been since she made love under a big tree. She smiled and said, "OK it looks like the creativity is still working. Let's go to my place before this gets out of hand."

Chapter VII

We got up early the next morning, had a good breakfast at the Look-out and went to a waiting room just outside the bay where the Ty were to arrive. The others were already there and waiting. At exactly eight o'clock their shuttle arrived.

Cpt. Kotar entered the landing bay with Science officer Maylar at his side. I had explained the greeting gesture in advance. We greeted one another and made our way to the conference room.

Once we were seated, Kim sat very close to the captain. Cpt. Kotar said, "Ms. Lien, we know your abilities and understand your protective actions and I assure you and your captain we will not misuse our abilities and we wish you no harm."

We believe we can in some ways be of service to you as well as you to us. I would like to invite you to visit our planets and there we can exchange things both parties consider risk free.

Cpt. McCain, "I thank you for this opportunity and hope we can become friends." "As a starter please explain how you learned our language and then how to pronounce the words. Your lips don't seem to be in sink with what I hear." "I believe our science officer Maylar can do that better than I."

Maylar, "We tapped your computer system, down loaded what we considered of interest to us, then listened to conversations until we could create sounds like you. We tapped your computers on our first visit. We have bionic translators implanted. We speak in our own language and you hear what we say in yours.

We sent a probe out and it gathered the information needed. When we encounter other life forms they are not always as friendly as you are." "I understand, I suppose if we had the technology to do that we would act and react similarly."

The water was served and we toasted to a prosperous future. Kim seemed relaxed and content with how the conversations were progressing. I was a little amazed at their honesty. There was another ten minutes of small talk and Cpt. Kotar announced it was time for them to return to their ship.

Cpt. Kotar, "We will be returning to Korant later today. As we have different propulsion systems I would suggest you follow when you are ready. Korant is the forth planet from the star that sustains us."

Cpt. McCain, "Thank you and we will be there in a day or two." "Once you enter our solar system there will be escort vessels to show you the way in. They are of course vessels that we use as protection and they are heavily armed but then so are you."

We walked them back to the main dock and they took their leave.

As we were walking back to the bridge Lars said, "I guess we can officially call this "First Contact" and against all odds it looks like they're friendly." Cpt. McCain, "Ms. Lien do you feel the meeting went well?" "Yes I do, there were no hesitations in any questions asked or answers given and honesty is almost always a good thing."

Once back on the bridge Cpt. McCain notified the escort ships that they were to name their vessel as we will be referring to them more frequently in the near future. Cpt. Turner needed no time at all and asked if the name Adventure would be OK and Cpt. Atilla Zarka said he would like to call his Freedom.

Cpt. McCain, "Well, that was quick and painless. I trust these names were already in circulation?" "Yes they were" said Cpt. Turner.

Cpt. McCain "Have the names engraved onto the exterior of the ships for all to see. All vessels and materials are to be secured and prepared for a Leap. Mr. Chi as soon as possible you will take us out of this solar system and maintain a course toward Korant at impulse. I will be in my quarters, number 1 you have the bridge."

Lars was busy preparing for the Leap and calculating the emergency Leap should it be needed.

Bianca Lambert, communications, had found a way to eavesdrop on the Ty and has been recording their conversations. She was determined to learn enough to follow what they were saying before we get there.

Kim approached me and said, "You look lost, are you OK?" "Yes, I guess so it's all pretty overwhelming. All of these things happening at once and a path being laid before us instead of us creating it and,... " Let's go for a walk, we've got time, don't we?"

We walked through the wooded area and she said, "This is all inevitable, try to accept it for what it is. Think about it, there's no good, no bad, no right, no wrong, this has all been going on longer than we've existed. We are finally becoming a part of it."

"Well that's exhilarating and certainly not the way I was looking at it. I guess I was just afraid." Kim said; "We all are, that's part of it, we'll have to earn our place in the galaxy but I believe we're so fortunate that we're actually going to have help doing it." I said, "Thank you, I needed that." Kim gave me a soft kiss and said, "I know."

"Let's go get some food and have a picnic." "I'd love to but you can imagine how much must be accomplished before we get to Korant. Let's just have a nice lunch together and return to the bridge." I'd have much rather pulled her into a room and made love to her but she was right. We walked to one of our favored restaurants, had lunch and returned to the bridge.

Captains Turner and Zarka were discussing the roll of the escort vessels in the visit to Korant and Suboro with Cpt. McCain and Jerry Chapman. They would be traveling almost constantly between Korant and the Enterprise. Lin Chi was taking care of unfinished business regarding the research vessel. It'll have to be physically attached to the Enterprise and the building materials will have to be stored in the shuttle bays.

I asked Lars if he knew what was going on and when we were leaving, he said, "We're to take the Leap at 1800. That should put us just outside their solar system by 0700 tomorrow morning. Maylar sent us information on their time system and it seems that we're almost identical, at least when we arrive.

From what I understand the star ships are having seating arrangements installed for their shuttle service so they can transport up to fifty additional people each trip. Then the shuttles will take them to the surface." "Who's going first?" "Cpt. McCain has decided that Jerry Chapman will lead a party of six, Jose Calderon science, Bianca Lambert Communications, Kim Lien, Eric van Stahl the animal and plant expert, and you." "Me?" "I know several who would gladly trade with you." I said, "I guess it is quite an honor."

Lars said; "I follow your writings very closely and look forward to your version of First Contact." "Yes, its' mind boggling when you consider how far we've come in less than six years and now we're actually visiting inhabited planets."

We were all asked to join the captains meeting. She announced to all that Lars Berger had calculated the leap and

94

the co-ordinates would not be disclosed. The escort ships were to pass through with us and maintain close contact to the Enterprise. Then we will travel to the solar system in formation. Cpt. McCain, "The Enterprise will as discussed be stationed just outside the solar system and both escort ships will be utilized for transportation to and from the planets. I want the areas around the planets scanned constantly. If we were to be unpleasantly surprised it would almost certainly come from a remote satellite. If fired upon there will be no return fire. Hold your shields at maximum and retreat." Cpt. Zarka, "What is our course of action if the shields are penetrated?"

Cpt. McCain, "That's why we'll have two ships there. If one is damaged the other is to power up and be at the ready. If I can not get the situation under control I'll be the first to return fire. At that time you may release your ships wrath.

Should the fire-power be overwhelming we will make a leap. Cpts. Zarka and Turner will be on their own. They are to retreat if possible. A meeting point has been established and you can get that information from Mr. Berger after the meeting.

This is for everyone on the bridge, you all need to relax for a few hours and prepare for high stress situations. Prepare yourselves mentally for the worst and make certain that we do not instigate an intergalactic war. You are the best that the human race has to offer and I expect you to ensure that we continue to thrive."

Then the meeting was adjourned. When I got up my legs almost gave way. My entire body felt numb. This was like reading a scary book and suddenly finding yourself in the middle of it all.

I needed some company and to unwind. I walked over to Eric Van Stahl and asked if he had a couple of friendly riding horses that Kim and I might use. He nodded, "Yes sir Spook and Danny, I'll go with you and help saddle them up." "Just a minute, I haven't asked Kim yet." I went to Kim and asked if she'd like to go horseback riding. She got a big smile on her face and gave me a kiss. "I didn't see that one coming." The three of us took our leave of the bridge and went to the riding stables.

We rode for almost two hours and I had not seen Kim so happy in a long time. I must confess that smile on her face made me feel better too. When on horseback all sense of being on a space-ship was gone. It helped me find my "Happy Thought" and it looked like it was working for Kim too. Once back at the stables we brushed the horses down and led them to their pasture. It was time well spent.

After we had washed up and were ready to leave the stables Kim looked at me and said, "In ten minutes we're going to make the Leap. I can feel the tension on the bridge from here." "Do you need to be there?" "No, I can't help at this point, I'm as fearful as they are. Lets go get something to drink." We thanked Eric and walked to the restaurant.

As we walked she said, "So, we're there. The Leap had taken place and we are now close enough that they can see us coming." "Do you feel anything hostile?" "No nothing at all, which I suppose, is a good thing."

We had a cup of tea speaking very little and when finished Kim asked, With a sheepish smile Kim said; "Do you still have some of that old scotch you're always bragging about?" "Yes I do and I would say this occasion defiantly merits a glass." She said "Let's go have a drink and relax."

We went to my quarters to talk but couldn't find the words to discuss the upcoming events. So we had a glass of scotch and faded into our own little world.

We woke up around 0500, took a shower and went out for breakfast. When we left the restaurant the meadows were being watered via artificial rain. There was a beautiful rainbow and we decided that it was a good omen.

Kim looked at me, smiled and said, "I feel good how about you?" "I feel OK, kinda and I am looking forward to this adventure or new era."

We arrived at the bridge just after 0600. We're now nearing the solar system and could see it on the main screen which was like a huge front window. It seems that all had been said and everyone had their eyes fixed on the screen.

Now we could make out vessels that were traveling from one planet to the next. Maybe they only lived on two of the planets but it seemed that they utilized all of them.

The Enterprise stopped just outside the outer asteroid belt and sent a greeting to the Ty. It was promptly returned and they announced they would send a welcoming committee.

Capt. McCain addressed Major Vogel, head of security.

"I want a small presence in the docking areas at all times. It will be noted who comes, who goes, who brings something aboard and what that something is and who takes something with them and again, what that something is." "Are the officers to be armed?" "Yes but don't over-do it; I believe laser pistols to be adequate. They are to be set so they don't melt a hole in the exterior wall if fired. It goes without saying that the Enterprise must be jeopardized to justify using them. There are to be no threats or commands made with drawn weapons. If a weapon is drawn it is to be fired.

Please remember that this is a mission of peace and you will be cordial and friendly. We do not have the upper hand here and could easily be enslaved or worse."

Kim walked over to Capt. McCain and said, "Please don't allow the security guards to be armed. If we are attacked it will be from outside and our surveillance systems are more than adequate. They should be there to show the guests to their destinations regulate substance control and report abnormalities. I fear we would be risking far more than necessary as alone the size of the Ty can be intimidating."

Capt. McCain looked at her for a long moment, turned to Major. Vogel and said, "Major Vogel, We will follow Counselor Lien's advice. The security teams are not to be armed. Any questions?" "No, I understand fully." "Then implement it at once." "Yes mam"

Fifteen minutes later a squad of six security officers in dress uniforms appeared at each of the docking areas.

At 9:15am the shuttle arrived. The Ty were escorted to the main conference room and it was explained that this meeting would be on-screen throughout the Enterprise and its escort ships. They were very proper and at ease, as if they had done this many times before.

We were given a short version of their evolution, customs, rules and general way-of-life. Over-all it was very informative and practical. This would help avoid surprises and unwished fears of the unknown. They also explained that they had taken the liberty to study my documentary and were therefore relatively well informed on our situation. That did not go over well with the Captain. She replied to Counselor Timlayar, "In the future if you want information I would like for you to ask for it and we will do our best to accommodate." He said he would pass the request on to Cpt. Kotar as all visitors are cleared by him before contact with the planets is allowed.

Timlayar went on to say, "The air on Korant is almost identical to the composition on the Enterprise. When visiting, you are to take food with you to avoid contaminating each other with possible unwished germs, bacteria and viruses."

He went on to explain that there are three levels of peoples on Korant and Suboro and that they would prefer if we would restrict our visit to the Ty, at least until we understand how things work.

Cpt. McCain, "When will we be visiting your planet?" "We are trying to select an appropriate time for you but we have a twenty two hour day and your morning is near our resting period." "That will not be a problem, I will select a visiting party and they will adapt to your time schedule." "Then they may arrive at 23:00 your time tomorrow. They will stay for five days and then return to your ship for orientation as you are out of reach for direct communication.

Should you wish to continue your construction project you are welcome to mineral deposits from our two outer planets. Our vessels will not come within one hundred thousand of your miles of your ship. We have placed you in what you would call Quarantine."

The meeting was there-with officially over and they took their leave.

We returned to the bridge where Cpt. McCain addressed the six person visiting party. "You heard them; you will be cut off completely for five days. Is there anyone who does not wish to be on this assignment?" None of us spoke and the captain asked Kim if she could feel any excessive anxiety. She replied with a no.

"Well then I'd say we're as ready for this adventure as we're going to get. While away Kim Lien will be in command Mr Chapman will lead the group, her decisions are to be considered my orders. "Questions?" Again, no one spoke. "You are all relieved of all duties until 22:00 tomorrow. Try to rest if you can."

We excused ourselves and left the bridge. Kim and I decided to have lunch at our favorite restaurant and walked in that direction.

Kim asked, "Are you alright with the fact that I'm in command?" I smiled and said, "The only difference is that it's now official. You're the well balanced one among us and the only one who could possibly still have some kind of contact with the captain. I sure as hell don't want the job." "Do you think the others feel that way?" "Who gives a shit? You're in command and that's that, they wouldn't dare challenge you or your authority. All I ask is that you do your best to keep us alive and show no fear of making a decision. I'm sure they feel the same way. Besides, you've got Jerry Chapman to consult with."

She took a deep breath and said, "I've never had so much responsibility placed on me before." "That's not true; you need to realize just how important you are. You are the glue that holds this entire society together, if anything, you're getting a vacation. Instead of being the stabilizer for thirty five thousand, all you have to do is take care of the five of us."

She smiled and said, "Nice try, let's go in and eat I'm starving." We went in and were seated on the terrace with a beautiful view of the meadows and woodlands. The waiter brought tea for both of us and asked if we were ready to be served. Kim, "We haven't selected anything yet." Waiter, "We've taken the liberty of doing that for you." Kim looked at him smiled and said thank you. Then he looked at me and I nodded in appreciation.

Our appetizer was smoked fish with a mango salsa which was fantastic, then Kim was served boneless duck and I was served a "real" bison filet. Our trimmings were small new potatoes fresh corn and snow peas; it was phenomenal. As desert we had chocolate cake with chocolate syrup and chocolate ice cream. It was the best meal we had had in years.

After we had finished we thanked the waiter and went to the kitchen and thanked the cook. Kim, "Now it's time for a walk in the wooded area." "Yes, I agree." We took our leave and went for a long walk.

We saw Eric Van Stahl tending to some animals as if it were a day like any other. Kim said, "Let's go ask Eric if we can ride horses again." "Sure, that sounds like fun." "Should we ask him if he would like to join us?" "I think that's a very good idea." We walked over, said hello and asked him, he said yes to the horses and politely declined to join us. Eric, "Not that I don't enjoy your company I simply need this time alone to gather my thoughts. We walked to the stables and saddled the horses. He said, "I'm going to be watering the quadrants 3, 5 and 7 within the next hour. It's going to be very wet over there." We thanked him for the warning and rode into the meadows.

After an extensive ride through woods and pastures we walked the horses and talked. We took a break under our now favorite oak tree and then returned to the stables, brushed the horses down and brought them to their pasture.

Kim said, "Let's go get cleaned up, have dinner then take some food back to our quarters. I would like to stay up late and sleep in so we're semi-adjusted for the time change tomorrow." "OK that sounds like a plan and I am hungry again."

We awoke the next morning at 11:00. Kim wanted to return to the bridge for a meeting with the landing crew so I contacted them and set the time for 15:00. "Let's have lunch and go get some new clothing, it's time for a change." She smiled and said, "That sounds like something I would say and it's an excellent idea."

The options were limited due to the technology in each garment but it could be varied. After lunch we went to the clothing distribution center where we were measured by a laser scanner. Then the clothing variations were demonstrated via hologram.

We both picked out two complete outfits and they were promptly brought from the locker room.

"Let's stop and see Dr Khan for a minute on the way to the bridge." Kim asked, "Are you ill?" "I hope not." We walked around the corner to his office. As we walked in he met us in the lobby and I asked him, "Dr Khan you said my heart has to be replaced, am I fit enough to be on the landing crew that leaves this evening. He said, "Come with me." I asked Kim to go along and we entered an examining room. He put me behind a glass wall which virtually made me transparent, he then enlarged the quadrant that included my heart and its immediate surroundings. "You'll be fine" he said, "There's no apparent damage that could cause trouble within the next six months." "Thank you, I was I a little worried." "No need to thank me, I didn't do anything, you're apparently eating well and getting exercise and as you know, that's what it takes." He smiled and you must excuse me I'm late for a meeting. We left and I was a little more at ease.

Kim, "What do you mean when you say you need a new heart?" "A few weeks ago I visited his office as part of the orientation the captain assigned me with. During that visit he told me my heart would need replacing in the not too distant future and that they had already taken DNA and started a production sequence." "Production sequence?" "Yes, they're growing me a new heart." "That's interesting, is everyone checked so comprehensively?" "Yes, that's why we wear this clothing, it's full of microscopic sensors and we're constantly being scanned. The clothing's so sophisticated that it can even administer small amounts of medicines, minerals, sugar and salts."

"Very impressive, I'm going to have to get up-to-date on your writings." "Oh yes, please do!" We laughed and made our way to the bridge.

As we arrived we noticed a number of new faces. Kim said, "Oh look Hetshepsut is here. She is my second and I was hopping she would be integrated soon." "Is she your replacement?" "No, of course not but her skills are growing and she will probably be the counselor of the new vessel once completed. She has a fascinating name, Hetshepsut means foremost of noble women and her last name is Bonafrit which means beautiful soul. I said; "That's a lot to live up to" Kim; "Yes, and she does it well."

Even my replacement was here. His name is Brett Ambrose and he's originally from Sidney Australia. He's a very gifted writer and becoming a good observer. I guess there's nothing being left to chance.

The captain saw us, smiled and said, "You're not being replaced. I am however, giving each of you the opportunity to withdraw from this mission; at that time I will send your backup. There's a chance we have misread the Ty's intentions and returning could become difficult or even impossible. Although this is first contact we do not know their nature." "Eric Van Stahl said, "You can send Mary Ann back to her duties, I wouldn't miss this for anything." Kim Looked at Hetshepsut and nodded, she smiled and addressed the captain, "Eric has spoken for all of them." Cpt. McCain said, "I'm honored to have you all at my side."

We were contacted by Cpt. Kotar at 21:30 and informed that they were sending a shuttle at 23:00. He sent instructions for one of our shuttles to follow so it could be documented where the landing crew is. The shuttle may scan the surface but not land. A means of communication between the crew and the Enterprise will also be made possible.

The captain ordered Jimmy Cheedle to the bridge for a briefing. She ordered Jimmy to scan as much as possible and take pictures. She then turned to us and said, "Ladies and gentlemen you are all reminded that you represent humanity and your actions and re-actions will be considered typical of our race. I wish you a pleasant trip and a successful mission. You may now gather your things and report to bay number two on deck four. Your place in history is assured."

We walked toward the door and everyone on the bridge stood and applauded. It was a very moving moment and it finally soaked in on us just how big a step we were taking. My knees almost gave way from under me and I felt dizzy. Kim took my hand and said, "That's simply a chemical reaction to the moment, adrenaline, enjoy it."

We all went our separate ways to gather the materials we were taking with us. At 22:30 we met at dock number two.

Some very thoughtful person was passing out tea and coffee. Kim was asking Jerry Chapman' "What exactly was meant when you say I'm in command of the mission and you're the leader?" Jerry; "It's really quite simple. I'll lead as best I can. If you see fault or danger in what I do you're to make me aware of it. If I can't justify it to your satisfaction I must change it. Your authority will not be challenged as the captain and I have faith in your ability and senses. It's all going to be touch and go but from the way it's beginning I feel confident we'll see and learn a great deal and the mission is bound for success." She said; "You realize of course that once we are on Korant there is a high probability of being separated." "Yes, of course I do but we'll have to do our best to never be fully alone. I think that's the best we can do."

The shuttle arrived. It is about the same size as ours but no sharp edges. In fact I'd call it futuristic looking. Counselor Timlayar appeared at the entrance and welcomed us aboard. We were seated and strapped in. Then with no sound at all the shuttle backed out of the dock and lunged forward.

While under way Timlayar explained that a crew member would be attaching a thin layer the soles to our shoes. "We have duplicated the gravity you have created on the Enterprise in reference to your weight. It will compensate for the difference in the gravity on Korant and should make the visit more comfortable." We looked at Kim and she said, "I'll be first if it's alright." Timlayar smiled and nodded to the crewman to begin. We were all fitted with a surprisingly thin layer of additional shoe sole which increased our weight just enough that their gravity felt like ours. It's amazing how much detail is being put into this visit.

We were now nearing the planet Korant. It's about fifty/fifty water and land. The land masses appear to be spread out across the planet creating evenly distributed islands the size of Europe.

Timlayar, "On Korant we have a high counsel of fifty five Ty and 24 of other origin representatives. They document our past, ensure our present and create our future. They are elected for life and answer only to one another. Captain Kotar is one of the esteemed members. Unlike your species we have a life span of approximately six hundred of your years. Having this extra time to develop has made our advancements possible.

While on Korant you will please restrict yourselves to communication with the Ty. There are other species of humanoids indigenous to Korant and we respect them and utilize their expertise while allowing them to develop at their own pace. They are not what you would call slaves and they are a part of our system. There will also be a number of what you would call visitors or people from other systems.

We would like to have a controlled atmosphere when you meet them. It is a safety factor for both you and them. It seems that all species of advanced life forms come from a somewhat hostile origin and some are better at controlling their hostility than others.

There are nine of us that that have communicators with your language programed, and when communicating with members of the high counsel they will have additional synthetic translators to avoid one of us making an error and creating a misunderstanding. Cpt. Kotar is one of the two counsel members that speak your language. He is also in charge of all exploration and determines what species we communicate with and when that species is ready for first contact. We have observed your development for just over three thousand of your years and are quite surprised that you survived your hostile instincts and at the same time congratulate you for your progress and we enjoy the privilege of introducing you to the known and accepted galactic societies.

Please prepare for entry into our atmosphere. We will be on the ground within fifteen minutes." He lowered his eyes, and then his head, extended his arms toward the floor with his palms toward us, and then took a step backwards turned around and returned to his seat. I had no doubt that he too was a member of the high counsel.

Once in the atmosphere we could see their cities. They were hundreds of square miles with huge buildings they all seemed to be connected to one another, all in all a very futuristic scene. There were landing platforms for the various types of flying vessels at different levels and ground transportation as well. The air seemed to be free of any kind of pollution.

Surrounding the cities were forests and occasional grasslands. I saw no sign of agricultural activity. It was as if the peoples of the planet used the parts of the planet that they needed and allowed nature to provide them with clean air by allowing the cities to be surrounded by gigantic rain forests.

Eric asked, "Are the forests maintained by people?" Timlayar replied, "No, the forests maintain us. It took us thousands of years to realize that if we just left them alone they would develop much better than any influence we could ever implement. It is the origin of our life and they are not to be altered." "But surely you use wood products." "Yes we do but they come from the planet Suboro. We are very fortunate to have an entire planet that we can utilize for agricultural and harvesting of natural resources."

The pilot zeroed in on the top platform of one of the larger buildings and began his descent. It felt surprisingly familiar and there was no fear factor. Upon touch-down the hatch of the vessel was opened by people who were defiantly not Ty. They looked a lot like us. Their feet were wider and they did not make eye contact or speak.

We entered the building which seemed to be made of the same material as their spaceship. I asked, "What is the material everything seems to be made of?" "Timlayar replied, "It's carbon created with what you call nanotechnology. It is not unknown to your species. You have simply not mastered its mass production. It's harder than any metal and much more flexible."

We entered a large room and Timlayar said, "This is your living space. There is a separate resting room for each of you. You may place the things you brought with you here and we will proceed to meet the high counsel if you would be so kind." We set our things down and the ladies, as they always do, had a quick look in their mirrors. Then we continued on our way to the high counsel.

The building is absolutely enormous and the halls echoed with our presence. We entered an elevator which was also a cylindrical. Although I didn't feel it move, Timlayar explained that we were now on the top floor. He spoke to a fellow Ty at the door and the Ty entered the room ahead of us. I believe he went to announce our arrival. When he returned the double doors which were at least twenty feet high were completely opened and we entered the impressive and gigantic room.

It was like entering a grand theatre, the high counsel which was two thirds Ty and one third a mix of other species, was at the front and the audience faced them. There were many different species of humanoids seated to our left and right as we walked toward the high counsel. About thirty feet away from the counsel was a large circle. We stopped there. Timlayar looked at us, smiled and took his seat in the counsel. The counsel rose and preformed their formal greeting. Arms extended downward and slightly forward with palms facing us. We returned the greeting.

There was a large screen behind the counsel and we were on it. That made it possible for those seated behind us to see us.

Kim was asked to take a step forward and then there were several minutes of silence. She stepped back and bowed her head.

Kotar spoke, "As spokesman for this counsel I welcome you to Korant, it is a pleasure to meet each of you and we look forward to your visit here. Counselor Lien will answer your questions and your visit here may now formaly begin.

Timlayar will escort you back to your quarters where you may contact your captain on the Enterprise. We have taken the liberty of making an itinerary for each of you. Please review these, if there are questions Timlayar will answer them. We will meet again at the end of your stay. "

We made eye contact with Kim then with Kotar and awkwardly took our leave. We returned to our quarters in silence. Timlayar said he and some other colleagues would return in three hours and we could begin our exploration.

Chapter VIII

Once alone Kim let herself fall into a plush arm-chair. The rest of us stood there speechless trying to digest what had just taken place. She said, "Of all the places to begin our exploration we have come to the strong-hold of the entire galaxy.

These people are among the oldest sophisticated life forms in existence and have formed a grand intergalactic federation. This was necessary as there are outlaws and unfriendly nations throughout the galaxy. They are as a rule considerably less advanced and usually easily controlled. We were actually considered one of the unfriendlies and the counsel had at one time considered our extermination to avoid us spreading our hostility throughout the galaxy. They have made it clear that they do not fully trust us but are willing to allow us the opportunity to prove ourselves worthy to join their federation." I said in complete disbelief; "You mean to tell us they told you all that in the thirty seconds of silence during our introduction to the high counsel?" She said; "Yes, but that's not all. I know our dos and don'ts and pretty much how life is on this planet."

Jerry said; "Let's contact the Enterprise and bring Cpt. McCain up-to-date. Then we can have a question and answer period with Kim before they return.

The captain seemed quite pleased with how things are going and wished us luck.

Later Jerry said to Kim, "What if we just visit and go on our way with no desire of joining their federation." "That is not an option. We are either worthy or extinct. The amazing part is that they're not asking anything of us. They'll observe us observing them and feel that they will have a decision after this visit. They've already deemed us worthy or we wouldn't be here. We are, if you will, being put on exhibit for all to see and become familiar with."

Eric "Sounds to me like we're the animals in the cage being studied and judged." "Kim, "That's very close to what is going on, it's simply at a more sophisticated level.

Has everyone reviewed their itineraries? They'll be here to get us in a few minutes." We all acknowledged we had reviewed and understood. Jerry Chapman and Jose Calderon were teamed, Kim and Bianca Lambert were teamed, Eric was to fly to Suboro and I was invited to observe a session of the congress of the federation.

Our escorts arrived. A Ty by the name of Mimonar was assigned to me. Although she's a foot taller than me she is a strikingly beautiful creature. We greeted and proceeded toward the congressional facility. Mimonar was the first high ranking female Ty I had seen. She was not quite as fluent as Timlayar which meant she spoke a little slower. As we walked she said, "Are you comfortable here?" I looked at her for a moment and said, "As comfortable as you would be on earth. It's all very new and overwhelming. A few weeks ago we could not confirm that there is really other intelligent life in this galaxy and now I know that I belong to an underdeveloped species that with a bit of luck has earned the right to exist among far more developed peoples." "You should be very proud. You are a very young species with no experience to fall back on and yet here you are.

Many of those who have been invited were filled with fears and primeval instincts and were simply not ready to join us." "What became of them?" "They were returned to their planet with no recollection of being here. We test peoples in one thousand year intervals. That would be about eight hundred fifty of your years."

What is the purpose of this federation?" "There is wisdom and safety in numbers, although we are the oldest advanced life forms in this galaxy many of you have technologies that we have not thought of. We have found that if we share our wisdom with our fellow members of the federation and they with us, we all profit.

Once we are seated you will place your right arm in the slot on your arm-rest. You will receive an injection that I believe will be uncomfortable for you. It will enable the translation of most of the spoken languages and all telepathic conversations. You will hear and understand everything. You may not comment or ask questions. This session is as you would call it business as usual. We will be here four and a half of your hours after-which the translator function will be turned off. We can explain how to reinstate it if and when necessary."

We entered a balcony booth and took our seats. I put my arm in the slot and a very large needle entered a main artery. "Uncomfortable was a real understatement." I didn't want half the galaxy to hear the puny earthling scream so I gritted my teeth and hoped it would pass. Then I fainted.

As I awoke Mimonar was sitting beside me offering me a drink of water. She smiled and said, "Over forty percent of those who receive that injection are very verbal. You are a credit to your species." I smiled and said thank you. She explained that my brain would need a couple of minutes to get used to the translator and then everything would seem normal.

It was amazing to watch the different life forms and peoples on the huge screen behind the counsel and chairmen as they presented their wishes, problems and goals. And for me, they all seemed to be speaking English.

As the session was coming to an end Kotar addressed all present; he reintroduced us earthlings and asked that all be as observant as possible as they would vote on our future in three days.

He went on to say, "Each of you at some time or other were given this privilege and not all adapted easily. These humans have advanced consistently since we last visited their planet and merit our attention. They have developed several technologies that are unknown to us. I believe we can all benefit by their induction into this federation and have no doubt that they too will benefit."

He looked up at me and said, "Mr Manning, would you like to say a few words?" I stood, paused for a moment and said, "I will pass this information on to my captain, I'm sure she will be pleased and honored. A reply will have to come from her." "Well said, Mr Manning, this session will reconvene tomorrow at 08:00 hours.

Mimonar said, "You handled that nicely, I too believe your species is ready, please forgive me I must touch you. The next thing I knew we were walking down a long corridor. "What did you do?" "I disengaged your translation implant. It will be reinstated as needed and once you are members of the federation you will be given control of it. This is one of the many things we can do for you. We are very interested in your agriculture and energy source." "I'm sure Cpt. McCain will allow Lars Berger, our science officer and Eric Van Stahl who is already here to share what we know. I am only the one who documents our journey." "You are too modest. We have discovered that through your documentary endeavors you have become the most well informed member of your species." "That's amazing, I never thought of it that way. Where are we going?" "As our structures and building materials seem to interest you I would like to show you how we put a building together and ensure its efficiency. This will of course not enable you to duplicate what you see but should give you ideas of your own." "Thank you, although it is not my profession it does interest me."

We went to the basement of the building where there were passageways to other structures cut into the walls and I could see that the structure was actually many layers of carbon fiber. There were spaces between some of them for insulation and others for utilities. It was virtually indistructable as it didn't consist of many different objects that were connected, it was all fused together. The entire building was like one piece of carbon fiber. Instead of glass in the windows there were force fields. The power source, water, ventilation, heating and cooling systems were all integrated into the walls thus invisible. They even have subways like those in our larger cities on earth. I asked; "Is everything on the planet made like this?" She said, "No, only the objects that are costly in time and effort. The life expectancy is over ten thousand years and with maintenance at a minimum we have time to invest in other things. The construction however is costly and time consuming."

"Thank you very much for the tour it was very informative. Can I repay you with information about us?" "That would be very nice of you. I have a question for you. Do you still have mating rituals which lead to reproduction or is it simply used as entertainment?"

"Wow, I must say, that one caught me off guard. Our mating habits have remained a source of reproduction and of course is predominantly a means of entertainment. How is it with the Ty?"

"It is a form of stress control and entertainment shared with many but not openly."

We returned to the living quarters getting as close to as possible but not discussing interspetial sex.

While our first day was drawing to an end on the Enterprise Cpt. McCain was being tested by a rogue group of space pirates. The Enterprise has been fired upon several times and Cpt. McCain had asked for assistance from the Ty or permission to defend the Enterprise.

The Ty sent three small vessels and asked that their maneuvers be documented so the Enterprise would know how to handle these pirates if they should encounter them again.

They approached in a very tight formation and once fired upon separated and showered the pirates with impulse lasers. Two vessels were destroyed immediately and two more within an additional five seconds.

The last vessel was captured in a tractor beam. The Ty tried to communicate with them but got no response. Then a faint light was flashed at it and it was reduced to dust at a molecular level.

The three ships rejoined in their formation and returned to wherever they had come from.

Cpt. McCain contacted Kotar and enquired who the pirates were. Kotar said, "It's not who but what they are. They are not humanoid and they have no respect for other species or life forms. They are of reptilian decent and have maintained their aggressive nature for over one hundred millennia. We have been unable to harm them on a large scale as they are dispersed throughout the galaxy and appear only in small groups.

As you have seen, their technology is quite advanced and gets better with every vessel they overtake."

Cpt. McCain, "Again we find ourselves in your debt and thank you for your assistance and information." "We are hopeful you will one day have the opportunity to repay our assistance by helping us and our allies." "It would be an honor."

The conversation was ended and Cpt. McCain addressed those on the bridge. "Mr Kofi, Mr Chi, may I have a damage report? Mr Berger, what kind of weapon did the

Ty fire on the fifth vessel?" Lars, "I have no idea what it was but it was as close to total disintegration as you can get. I would venture to say it could very well dissolve a force-field rendering us vulnerable at best. We definitely do not want them firing that thing at us." "I want you to study it and come up with a defense."

She then turned her attention to Mr Kofi. He said; "They were able to penetrate our shields twice and managed to damage an air-lock." "It's to be repaired within three hours. Mr Chi, do you have anything to report?" "Our main power source is at 99.6% and the secondary is ready if needed. They were at no time endangered by the aggressors."

She said; "I do hope the ground crew had a better day."

We were now all back in our quarters and discussing the events of the day. Jerry Chapman and Jose Calderon had visited what we would call a university and were both overwhelmed and could hardly grasp what they had seen and learned.

Kim Lien and Bianca Lambert had conversed with humanoids from 25 solar systems. It seems we all received the translation implants and Kim and Bianca were pondering how something like that could work.

Eric Van Stahl, who had flown to Suboro, was quietly thinking about the events of the day over an herb tea. When I enquired how his day had gone he replied, I'm was amazed at the simplicity, precision and ability to utilize space for agriculture without disrupting the natural balance of an environment actually is. It would have taken us years to think of some of that stuff.

I suggested we all take a two hour break in our personal quarters in order to gather our thoughts and meet for dinner. All agreed and we went to our rooms.

I rested for an hour and a half and took a refreshing shower then returned to the main room where Jerry Chapman and Kim were setting the table for dinner. As I approached Kim said, "We've been ordered to report to Captain McCain at 21:00 hrs. That leaves us plenty of time for dinner and to chat a bit. Would you like to help prepare for dinner?" "Sure, where is the food stored I'll get it if you'd like."

We finished setting the table as the others slowly appeared. We had our meal and were about to leave the table as Eric said, "I was allowed to return with a fruit which the Ty consider a desert item. They have tested it and said it could not harm us. Would anyone like to try it? We all eagerly said yes and he went to his room to get it.

It looked like a large zucchini with a smooth three toned green outer skin. When he cut it the inside was brilliant red with perfectly round white seeds. Eric said, "The seeds are supposedly also very tasty.

Each of us received a slice and we all tried it at the same time. It was sweet, tart, juicy and exhilarating and the seeds seemed to magnify the flavor.

As it always does when exceptionally good food is being eaten, it got very quiet as we severed every bite. Then Eric said, "So, what do you think?" And we all answered at the same time. Wonderful, may we have more? We all laughed and eagerly polished off what the Ty call Ky Tauk, Eric said, "loosely translated it means sweet surprise."

At 21:00 we reported in to the captain and did our best to convey what was and is going on and we all expressed our eagerness to continue the visit.

At 22:45 all had been said and Cpt. McCain signed off without mentioning the aggressors who had attacked them. Shortly thereafter the Ty contacted us via a messenger and gave us our itineraries for the next three days. It was primarily entertainment combined with free time for personal observations. We eagerly exchanged experiences, stories, hopes and wishes of things to come. The second, third and fourth days passed without an unpleasant incident.

With great anticipation the fifth and final day arrived. We were escorted once again to the grand chambers of the high counsel. To our surprise Cpt. McCain and Lars Berger were also there. They had received their translation implants and ours were then re-activated.

Once again we walked to the ominous circle facing the high counsel. This time the counsel rose and we were greeted formally. We returned the greeting and they were once again seated.

Kotar rose and announced that they would like to offer us the privilege of joining their federation. He reviewed our past and praised our present. It seems that the vote for our admittance had been unanimous.

We were to leave a small delegation here on Korant to represent our species and ownership of our present solar system and any other we should take charge of.

The laws and by-laws of the federation were by no means stringent and did not forbid differences of opinions. They did however specify that the high counsel would have the last word in settling disputes.

After Kotar had finished his twenty minute speech Cpt. McCain was asked to speak. She did so in a surprisingly humble manor thanking The Ty and all the other peoples for their hospitality and their vote of confidence. She accepted the invitation and pledged our allegiance to the federation.

She knew that they knew our situation and that they probably had better information on our solar system than we had. She explained, "The time has come for us to create a new beginning for our kind and we thank you for the opportunity to do so in your presence and with your help."

Everyone stood, I'm estimating over ten thousand heads of state and all of them aliens who have now become our comrades, and we were welcomed with a "Hoorah!" which I imagine sounded different for every species. Then we were led to an enormous room where a banquet was about to take place in our honor. It was quite overwhelming. Kim came to my side and said, "I think we're going to make it, we're actually going to survive." I squeezed her hand and said, "I believe you're right."

We celebrated and mingled for several hours and then Kim and I went to the roof for a breather. While standing there we realized we were so high that a force-field had been activated to lock in an acceptable atmosphere. "Won't it be nice to be able to utilize all this technology?" She answered, "It's only good because it's new, soon it will become a regular part of our lives and we will be a full member of a federation that rules over an entire galaxy. I'd venture to say that some of the peoples here could even be from other galaxies." "Do you really think so?" "Well, it's certainly a possibility."

One of the porters approached us and asked if we would return to the banquet as the force-fields were being shut down and the atmosphere would become hostile. We thanked her and returned to the festivities in time for one more fruit drink before it ended.

Jose Calderon met up with us and said we were to meet the captain at the fountain in twenty minutes. We will all be returning to the Enterprise together.

It would probably take days if not weeks for us to digest what had taken place in the last several days.

We finished our drinks and made our way to the huge water fountain in the middle of the banquet hall where the rest of the crew, along with Cpt. Kotar and Mimonar, were gathered.

Cpt. Kotar was explaining how we would be escorted back to the shuttle and then to the Enterprise. We will have a week to designate the representatives who were to stay and represent our presence in the galaxy. At that time we were free to continue our voyage or stay for a while to exchange technologies and thoughts.

The Leap

Without comment Cpt. McCain thanked him for everything and then she thanked him for this opportunity, as did we all. Then we said our goodbyes. Mimonar escorted us back to the shuttle where Jimmy Cheedle was waiting for us. We thanked her said goodbye and entered the shuttle. The captain nodded to Jimmy and we were air-born.

Cpt. McCain said, "In order to comprehend what just took place I'm going to need some time with you councilor Lien. I believe we just passed through several thousand years of evolution and I don't feel a damned bit smarter."

She went on to say; "In the early twenty first century the famous astrophysics professor Steven Hawkins warned us of the possible perils of meeting extraterrestrials and although I'm pleased that he was at least partially wrong I find it hard to believe there will not be stepping stones and obstacles in our way. That said, "Damn" That was exciting!" We all laughed and agreed. As we left the Ty solar system the Ty escort returned and we went on to the Enterprise.

Once we were on board we went to a conference room adjacent to the bridge for a debriefing. Cpt. McCain decided to allow it to be recorded in case she wanted to make it public knowledge. When the debriefing was over we were given thirty six hours to relax, gather our thoughts and get accustomed to the time zone on the Enterprise.

As we left the room I asked Kim if she'd like to share the time. She said, "Give me three hours to clean up and meditate, I have to gather my thoughts and find my equilibrium. I'm of no value to you in my present state." I smiled and said, "I'll catch up on my documentation and you come by when you can." She gave me a small kiss on the cheek and left for her room.

Once back in my room I cleaned up and began writing. Before I knew it, she was at the door. When I opened it she said, "Feed me I'm starving." "OK let's go have some sea food." "Yes, that sounds good and maybe a walk in the wooded area?" Although Korant and its peoples were fascinating, it was good to be home.

We had dinner and our walk then returned to my room and made love as if there were no tomorrow. As we lay there fully spent she said, "Are you trying to get me pregnant?"

"Although I won't say yes, I can't say no. If it happens I'll be happy and if it never happens I'll be content and happy to have you. You'll be able to have children for the next thirty five years, I'm in no hurry. Why do you ask?"

She said, "I've been endowed with additional feelings and/or the ability to feel additional feelings in others. That doesn't mean I read them correctly." "It must be our wish not just mine. It's time to start getting ready for duty, let's shower together." I said, "Yes, lets." We had an exhilarating shower and made our way to our favorite breakfast spot.

Most of the crew was also there so we all sat together. Jose asked, "Have any of you decided to volunteer to remain on Korant?" We all said no and then Kim said, "You're going to request to stay aren't you?" "Yes, he said, I think it would be a great honor and I believe I could attain a lot of information that would help us improve our data transfer and over-all standard of living." I said, "We'll certainly back you in any way we can and I'm sure Lars will be thrilled to have his number one man with his finger on the pulse of the galaxy."

Kim said, "You do realize that your mission would be primarily diplomatic and there would be times that you would need to defend and/or fight for our rights and goals." "Yes, of course I understand but on top of that I would be exposed to many new technologies. I'm a scientist and feel like a child who has found a way to open the cookie jar. I'm certain I would be an asset to our cause."

Jerry, "Well, lets go see what the captain thinks of your idea." I grabbed a coffee to go and we were off.

As we entered the bridge we were met with a round of applause from those who had been filling in for us. We thanked them graciously and were then filled in on the events that had taken place in our absence. The attack by the rogue aliens was the most exciting so we were shown the replay of the event.

Lars said, "The destruction of the last vessel was the most impressive part and I've been doing my best to figure out how they did it. Although only a theory, it could be that they cloaked it.

When Kotar visited us for the first time their vessel was cloaked and we could not find it or a trace of where it had been, so we know they have the technology to cloak. I can not reconstruct or even imagine a power that would have simply reduced that vessel to a molecular level without a tremendous bang. Can anyone think of a reason why they would cloak an enemy vessel?"

Cpt. McCain, "I'll confront Kotar with exactly the same question. I honestly believe he will have a satisfactory answer.

We'll make it known on board all our vessels that a party of twenty five will be stationed on Korant and ask for volunteers. Kim Lien, number 1 and I will choose the representatives from among them." Jose Calderon spoke and told her of his wish to be among the twenty five. She said, "You may consider yourself pre-approved unless Mr. Berger has a reason for me to say no. Lars said, I think it's a great idea if you really want to." Cpt. McCain said, " I'm hopeful that there are other equally qualified and highly skilled candidates.

We'll be staying here for another two to three weeks so that we're, in reference to procedures, I mean of course their dos' and don'ts, as up-to-date as possible. For the moment ladies and gentlemen it is business as usual. We'll be holding a grand opening of the new research vessel in two days, please make that public knowledge. Number 1 I want you to ask captains Turner and Zarka to bring their seconds and best two shuttle captains from each star-ship to a 12:30 luncheon. Ms. Lien, you will not leave my side during normal working hours and I'm afraid you won't be having a lot of free time in the next few days.

Let it be known that no one from the bridge may volunteer for permanent ground duty on Korant. That includes you Mr. Manning.

Mr. Chi, I want you to create a landing crew of ten, five female and five male, you will be addressing protocol and ethics on Korant. While there I am certain you'll be confronted in reference to our energy source. Do not give more information than you receive." Lin confirmed he had understood and asked, "When will we be going to Korant?" "Tomorrow at 19:00 hours, that's about the time their day gets started. You'll spend about seven hours a day on Korant for approximately five days. I want daily reports.

Does anyone have anything else to contribute?" We were all silent and she adjourned the meeting.

Cpt. McCain asked Bianca Lambert to contact the Ty and request a meeting for her with Kotar at his earliest convince. "He can come here or I will go to him, the place is irrelevant."

After a short while Bianca reported back to her that Kotar would see her on board his star-ship at 21:30 our time today. Cpt. McCain, "Mr Berger, counselor Lien, you'll accompany me to the meeting."

The rest of the day was as she had said; business as usual.

Upon returning to the bridge after a good night's sleep I asked Cpt. McCain for an updated on the meeting with Kotar. She said, "As I had suspected there was more to it than met the eye. It seems they've been fighting the Palchek for thousands of years. The word Palchek means "scaled worrier" as they are apparently of reptilian decent. Occasionally a few are taken prisoner for questioning. They're a very brutal species and brute force is used to interrogate them. The Ty didn't want to upset us so they cloaked the vessel and took it with them.

Kotar admitted that he was concerned about making the wrong impression on us and underestimated our ability to research an event and our willingness to accept the ways of others." I asked, "So what happened to the Palchek?" Cpt. McCain said "They were of course exterminated after the questioning." "Are we still at risk of an attack? "Yes we are. It has been our good fortune that every time they intended to attack the earth the federation was able to stop them. The Ty are now willing to give us the technology to locate and trace the Palchek. Kotar said we have ample weapons to fight them but should not underestimate their resourcefulness. They are responsible for the extinction of thousands of civilizations throughout the galaxy. It seems their reason for living is to eliminate all competition for space and real-estate and at the same time secure an ample food source.

Kotar is certain that they have a base or home planet from which they're dispersed in small groups to do their work. It is however a heavily guarded secret and as their brains don't work like ours they cannot be scanned like ours can. On top of that the Ty are not able to keep them alive for a prolonged period in order to press the information out of them." I said, "That's fascinating, are we going to pursue them?" "No, we are going to go on as if they didn't exist and if confronted we will defend ourselves."

Cpt. McCain added, "You should also know that we've been given a huge facility where we'll be creating or rather growing a large number of hybrid humans from our sperm banks. They'll have accelerated growth and will be full grown, trained and equal to us in every way in less than two years. I've decided not to use clones for ethical reasons." I asked, "What's the difference" She said, "The difference is that it is human sperm meeting human eggs just like in the womb. The only thing different is that the male and female count is determined. After fertilization they're altered for quick growth." "How many are you having made?" "We're going to start with one hundred thousand. They'll be needed to ensure our presence in the areas we make our own." "Will we be able to observe their growth?" "Yes, we'll return to Korant periodically and observing the progress will be possible."

She excused herself as Lars Berger had been waiting with questions for her. They went to his station and I decided to get my third cup of coffee. While sipping on it I noticed a red flashing light at Lin Chi's station. He looked up at me and saw the question in my eyes. "No problem, it's a Ty shuttle bringing measuring instruments. They're hoping to get a look at our reactors." "Oh really, and what do we get in exchange?" "We've sent a team to Kotar's vessel to look at theirs and to at least ask about their cloaking device." I wished him luck as he sped off to meet the inspection team.

After getting permission to leave the bridge I went to the meadows to sit and gather my thoughts. After a couple of hours hunger took over and I decided to have a salad at a near-by café.

While I was eating I was confronted by one of our physicians, he said, "My name is Abu Nye, may I join you?" "Sure, please sit down. What can I do for you?"

"I would like to be one of those chosen for duty on Korant. I have yet to fill out the application but I would like to go there to study the anatomy of extraterrestrial life. Do you find that a worthy reason?"

I answered, "Personally I find it a very worthy cause. In your application I suggest you explain why you want to be on the team, what you hope to accomplish with your research and how you believe it will help the human race.

The captain will decide if it's appropriate or not. She can't say yes if you don't ask." A sigh of relief was followed by smile on his face. He thanked me twice sitting and once standing and rushed out the door. I'm sure he'll be cleared. He seemed very bright and sincere.

I finished my salad and made my way back to the bridge. Upon arrival I noticed a Ty female and our communications officer Bianca Lambert consulting with the captain. As it is my privilege and job to observe and record conversations I allowed myself to become a part of the meeting. Bianca was asking for the opportunity to trade positions with the Ty Simlayar who is communications officer on-board Kotar's starship Simu.

Simlayar said. "Kotar did not request it as it was not his idea. Bianca and I thought of it and we feel we can not only learn a lot, we can widen our knowledge of our new-found friends and help to secure a good relationship." Cpt. McCain said, "I will have to think about this and of course speak to Kotar and ask his thoughts."

Bianca thanked her and Simlayar bowed her head and said, "We await your decision with great anticipation."

As they returned to Bianca's station the captain turned to Kim and said, "I'm counting on you to keep me out of trouble." Kim nodded and said, "If they wanted to harm us we would already be harmed. I see two young enthusiastic women who have become friends and are trying to utilize their combined knowledge to benefit all." "I hope you're right I'll speak to Kotar tomorrow."

It was obvious that there were going to be a lot of changes but I have yet to see any that could be potentially harmful. When we leave this star system it will be with purpose and we will no longer be alone.

The celebration of the completion of our research vessel is today and will begin in an hour. Cpt. McCain had invited a group of over fifty dignitaries from Korant, over a third of them were not Ty. It was a bit of an over-kill so it was obvious that Cpt. McCain had something up her sleeve.

We all went to the new vessel which had a transparent ceiling and was now attached to the Enterprise, The festivities were about to begin when our star-ships Adventure and Freedom sped by firing lazar bursts that were being intercepted by lazars fired from four of the shuttles. It created an enormous fire-works display that lasted almost five minutes. She was pleased that it was being enjoyed and it was an obvious demonstration of our pilots' capabilities.

She made her speech and again greeted the opportunity to be a member of the federation and welcomed visits from all members. That too went over very well with all of them and the atmosphere became much more relaxed.

The structure of the quarantine station was extremely high-tec and we were very proud of it. It's big enough for nine scientists to conduct separate experiments without the danger of cross contamination. It can house fifteen life forms larger than elephants and countless small ones. Lars seems to be very pleased.

Kim came to my side and said, "I've been given time off till 06:00 tomorrow morning and I need to let off some steam. Do you feel up to neutralizing me?" "Here or shall I take you home?" "Suit yourself."

I'd never experienced her that unleashed and didn't know what to make of it. We left the festivities and walked toward my place. She held my hand and said, "I've found a way to release excess energy which is stored in the body and I'm anxious to try it out. She looked at me, smiled and said "You're in for a treat."

When we got to my place she said I could simply sit and watch if I'd like but she needed to relax her entire body and it would take about thirty minutes. I said, "Take your time, I'm not going anywhere."

I sat down on the sofa and she sat on the floor facing a mirror. I guess she was doing a form of yoga and self-hypnosis at the same time as she sat cross-legged and starred at her own image for a long while. Then effortlessly she placed her hands on the floor in front of her and did a hand-stand. From that position she exercised her legs doing splits that were absolute horizontal. She then slowly placed her weight on her right hand, tipped to the right and landed on her feet. She said, "Let's go take a shower."

While showering we slowly washed each other savoring every touch on every inch of each other's body. After drying off she gave me a kiss that made me want to melt. We wandered aimlessly toward the bedroom and fell into the mattress. She held her petite beautiful body against mine moving her breasts slowly back and forth to be kissed and caressed while her hands seemed to be everywhere. We made love for four hours in ways I didn't even know existed. When it was over she smiled and said, "If you can do that again you're not human." We laughed and fell into each other's arms.

We got up early the next day and went to our favorite café for breakfast. Kim seemed more at ease than usual and it was contagious. We had a great breakfast and some extra juice and were about to leave when Victor Kofi came in with his daughter Kikuyu. He came over to say hello and show us how she had grown. She was a beautiful child. We chatted for a few minutes and left for the bridge.

Upon arrival Cpt. McCain took Kim and flew to Korant for a meeting. Lars Berger was installing updated shields and Lin Chi was busy training new personnel to maintain the power stations on the escort star ships. It seemed like everything was as it should be.

I asked Lars when we were going to start building the new star ship that Jerry would be flying. He said, "We're trying to locate a solar system that can supply us with the right materials. The problem is we don't know what we're going to build it out of. Cpt. McCain is trying to borrow a few engineers from the Ty to show us how to master mass seamless-carbon production. If they say no we'll need titanium. Either way it should be started within a few months." "Then we're leaving on schedule?" "I wouldn't see why not."

"I asked Lars, Are you going to spend any time on Korant?" "Yes, as a matter of fact I'm spending a few days with their top scientists next week and I'm pretty excited."

An overhead blue flashing light came on and Jimmy Cheedle's voice came over the intercom system, "Need assistance shuttle out of control!" Lars said, "Watch this" and he pushed a couple of buttons and with a joy-stick launched a tractor beam at the shuttle. The shuttle stopped almost immediately and Jimmy laughed and said, "Give me back my shuttle!" Lars looked up and said, "Did you see that, it works! We have our own tractor beam." I asked, "Why the emergency?" Lars said, "It would be relatively easy to stop a vessel that was under control, if nothing else we could simply destroy it but a hopelessly lost vessel which is out of control and doomed is no easy target." "Was he really hopelessly lost and doomed?"

"As a matter of fact he was. We've been rehearsing this for three days. Jimmy put himself in a relatively dangerous position to help prove it could be done." "That's crazy." "Yes it is but he's one of the best and he always has an ace up his sleeve."

I asked, "Did the technology come from the Ty?" Actually it didn't, we had it all along and didn't know it. One of the science officers of the Ty pointed it out to me and suggested I implement it." "How far will it reach out?" "It is effective for almost four hundred miles. It takes a few calculations each time and I need to get quicker at it but I'm certain it'll prove itself invaluable.

We can now control every approaching vessel that gets within four hundred miles of the Enterprise." "How close were the Palchek when they attacked?" "They were seven to nine hundred miles away and never once got within range.

We could have eliminated them on our own but didn't want to start an interstellar war." "Well I guess that's a completely different topic. I'm amazed at what we're doing and yet feel very comfortable being a part of it."

Jimmy came in and wanted to talk to Lars about the experience of being in a tractor beam so I stepped aside and asked them to carry on as if I weren't there.

I listened for a short while but it soon got extremely technical so I decided to go to lunch.

Bret Ambruse, my second, was walking in the same direction so I asked if he'd like to join me. He said yes and we went to one of the many diners and exchanged thoughts and ideas.

I asked, "When do you intend to start writing for Jerry Chapman?" "I don't know for sure, he's yet to approach me about it." "Do you want the job?" "Of course, to document an odyssey like you have done would be every writer's ultimate goal." "Then tell him you want to start so you can get it from the very beginning. You'll need to put a lot of thought in how you begin and never forget, you are nothing more than an observer and should not be opinionated. People don't want to read about what you think, they want to read about what took place and that in as much detail as time allows you to create.

I have no doubt that your adventures with Cpt. Chapman and his crew will be every bit as exciting as what you've experienced on the Enterprise. Fact is, Jerry Chapman will not approach you. You're the person who decides what and when."

We finished our lunch and I asked him to return to the bridge with me. I said, "There's no time like the present, ask him if you may have the privilege of beginning the documentation and I'll bet he says yes." "OK, I'll risk it, after all that's what I'm here for."

Jerry was busy coordinating visiting parties to Korant and Suboro but when he saw that Bret wanted to speak to him he made time as quickly as he could. Bret presented his plan to begin the documentation and Jerry agreed at once. He said, "You can spend a few days with me and you'll start to see our course of direction and from there on in it's your call."

Brett thanked him, gave me a glance and a smile and sat down near Jerry to begin his observations. I'm anxious to read his first few pages.

Cpt. McCain, Kim and Simonar returned from Korant and we all gathered to find out if she had been successful. She said, "We're going to be using titanium for our next few vessels. The process is much more complicated than I had anticipated and we simply do not have the man-power for such a time consuming undertaking."

Kim then introduced Simonar as one of the leading historians on Korant and a specialist on underdeveloped species on remote planets. Kim said, "It seems that we have been watched over for much longer than we could imagine. Robert, you might want to record all this." I asked Simonar if it was alright and she said, "Yes, it is your history."

Simonar stepped forward and formerly greeted us and we eagerly returned the greeting. She said, "Your species has certain voids in your history that we feel only fair that you now learn.

Four thousand five hundred years BC counting time as you do, we visited earth for the first time. It was in the countries you call Egypt on the continent of Africa and Peru in South America.

The Ty were convinced that humans were ready to advance and needed a little guidance. We gave them a certain amount of technology that we considered harmless to your species. To mention a few, there was the harvesting of minerals and the means to create stronger metals and advanced mathematics." She blushed and said," Oh, excuse me, I, of course, meant to say, your ancestors. This helped bring the peoples together and create civilization as you know it. Such wonders as iron, steel, navigation and buildings such as the great pyramids were made possible with this technology.

Due to uncontrollable primeval instincts almost all of it disappeared in your wars and tribal disputes.

We soon realized that you as a people were still very aggressive, solving large scale problems by eliminating adversaries rather than working together with them and there was no end in sight.

We thought that the tools we had given you would enable you to prosper and share but we were wrong.

Once people had progress, they also had power and sadly they used it to oppress others. That of course made the others retaliate. The aggressors were conquered and that in turn threw you backwards in your development.

We watched it happen time and again and decided to leave you to your fate for a prolonged period.

We returned in time to observe the Romans conquer the known world and create a sophistication that we did not know you were capable of.

Then of course it all happened again and we watched you plunge into the dark ages. You were in real danger of extinction in Europe and northern Africa. By this time there were also high cultures in South America and in China so we opted not to intervene. We hopped that they would advance in a more favorable way. That was of course brought to an end by Spanish explorers in South and Central America and the Chinese were overrun by the Mongolians. It was truly difficult to watch as entire nations and cultures were destroyed.

In the early part of the 20th century we were pursuing the Palchek aggressively. We were chasing a small band of ships through the galaxy and discovered that two of them had decided to attack the Earth. As they were about to enter your atmosphere over the area you call Siberia we destroyed the vessel.

The explosion caused considerable damage to the surface but very few people suffered from it. Later we watched you enter what you called world wars one and two. We were considering eliminating your species and allowing nature to start over. One Ty voted against it. At that time one vote was enough to stop such a decision. That Ty was Kotar's grandfather.

Then through no fault of your own the earth's advantageous alignment to the sun shifted and a great ice-age began and here you are. We are happy you have mastered your hostilities and we welcome you with open arms. The federation has approved your existence and you should know that less than seventy five percent of the known advanced life forms in this galaxy have that assurance."

Cpt. McCain, "We felt that everyone should have the right to know that we were never really alone."

I asked, "How long have you been studying our fate?" "I have spent two hundred and thirty of your years gathering and documenting information about earth and nine other planets. The Ty have watched you since your beginning." Lars, "How many documented planets with advanced life on them are out there?" "We have documented over four hundred in this galaxy and there is still much to be explored." With your help we hope to welcome many other peoples into the federation." "How many of the two hundred are members of the federation?" "We now have one hundred fifty four members and you are number one hundred fifty five. The others are not yet ready for many different reasons."

Cpt. McCain then invited us to all have dinner together before Simonar returned to Korant. Kim and I went ahead to reserve a table and have the cooks prepare the dinner.

Kim, "Were you surprised?" "You know, there were always questions that remained unanswered and I think everyone knew that we would be able to answer them some day. I'm glad we found out on these terms.

Are you going to have any free time soon?" "I don't know but I'll see what I can do." "That would be nice."

The waiter, who was also one of the shuttle drivers from the star ship Freedom, asked us to follow him. He led us to a large banquet table with a view of the wooded area and a lake. "Thank you," I said, "couldn't be better. When the captain and her guests arrive please show them the way." He nodded and left us to be seated. He returned with a hologram of the fireworks they had created and placed it in the center of the table.

I said, "I know you, you're one of the shuttle pilots. Were you a part of that demonstration?" "Yes sir, I was, did you enjoy it?" "Yes, I'm sure we all did, are all the pilots capable of maneuvers like that?" "No, not all but as you saw, several of us." "It was very impressive, who thought it up?" "Professor Doctor Berger asked us if it could be done and we took it as a challenge. There's very little we can not do if we set our minds to it." "I have no doubt." I said, "Did you volunteer for this position?" "Yes I did, a lot of interesting people come through here and I often get a chance to talk to them." "So you're a pilot and a waiter?" "Most of all sir, I'm a part of the most exciting thing the human race ever endeavored to do and as you see, once again have the opportunity and privilege to speak with celebrities."

Kim said, "Would you please bring us some peppermint tea?" "I would be honored to, I'll be right back.

"That's a pretty enthusiastic young man." "Yes," she said, "we all seem to be. It's as if we had been wandering through the universe for thousands of years and have finally found our way home.

I wonder if the Ty are the custodians or perhaps the source of life on other planets. Whatever they are it is almost certain that they are more than simply another one of the many life forms this universe has to offer."

The others began arriving and gathered around the table. We talked, discussed the hologram, the fireworks, our past and settled in for our luncheon.

Later as we were leaving the café a Ty messenger approached the captain and handed her a note. It seems that a member of one of the groups visiting Korant had an accident. He stepped into a well marked secured area and his leg was cut off just below the knee by a security laser.

The messenger said, "I have been instructed to inform you that your crew member will be all right. His leg will be reattached and he will have full use of it within a week. Our security officer would like to know why he did it and what he hoped to gain by disregarding our rules." "Those are very good questions and I assure you they will be answered." She sent for our head of security Colonel Andrew Vogel.

A short time later after returning to the bridge and saying our goodbyes to Simonar Col. Vogel arrived.

Cpt. McCain handed him the message and then filled in the rest of the information. "I want you to fly to Korant and make a full report on what took place, how it took place and why. Then question the other members of the crew and any witnesses you can come up with. I would like for you to take Dr. Khan with you and have him examine the patient, physically and mentally. If he can find out how they rejoined the leg it would be beneficial to us. Colonel, I want that report in record time, understood?" "As you wish captain."

Cpt. McCain, "Ms. Lien, was that an accident?"

"I received no negativity or intent of deceit from the messenger and it surely could have been an honest mistake from someone who was so overwhelmed by his surroundings that his common since failed him." "I hope you're right.

Chapter IX

Cpt. McCain,

"Attention on deck, we will begin a countdown at 24:00hrs, in ten days we will be leaving for our next destination; make it known.

Mr Berger, I want a route planned so we can visit the Lumy and their planet of Copat as our first destination. Their spokesman, Quay-Matt spoke of large resources of minerals such as titanium in the area."

It was about to get exciting again and this time we would know where we are going and have a good idea of what we will find.

I glanced at the charts that Lars was bringing up on the screens and it looked like Copat was just over forty light-years from here. It was amazing that the distance no longer impressed me. It was simply a matter of making the calculations and pushing a button. I suppose we'll see the other side of the Milky Way before the year is over and maybe even be able to visit another galaxy in the future.

While I was day-dreaming Atilla Zarka, captain of the star-ship Freedom came to ask Cpt. McCain if the new escort star-ships were to be the exact replicas of the Freedom and Adventure or if he might submit a few suggested changes that he considered improvements.

Cpt. McCain was pleased to be receiving improvement suggestions and asked him to submit them as soon as possible. He brought forth a memory stick with detailed sketches of the present star-ships and then the improvements. It of course had nothing to do with aerodynamics as they were useless in weightlessness.

The new ships were a bit smaller with a little more power and a lot more fire-power. They included neutron torpedoes to complement the already present photon torpedoes and a twenty percent increase of power to the laser batteries.

"Very impressive" said Cpt. McCain, "we will construct two of them and each super star-ship will have one new and one old so the power is distributed equally among us."

Cpt. Zarka thanked her for her time and insight and took his leave.

It was now early evening and Col. Vogel returned with a report on the incident on Korant. He, Cpt. McCain, Kim and I went to a conference room for a debriefing.

Col. Vogel said, "I am please to say that it was but an over-site by crew member Carlos Reyes. He knew that they were on their way to a restricted area but due to a conversation he was having did not notice that he had arrived.

Instead of seeing a flashing light and three guards he simply stepped over the barrier. This in turn triggered a laser that severed his leg. It happens more often than they would care to talk about but as there are no lasting effects once the leg is reconnected, the Ty have decided it is a just punishment for not paying attention."

Cpt. McCain, "What have you decided to do with Mr. Reyes?" "Nothing, his experience was not without considerable pain and I believe he has been punished enough." She said, "So be it, thank you for your time and effort. Was Dr. Khan able to learn how they reconnect limbs?" "He remained behind as an observer." "Very well."

That was a happy end to a potentially awkward situation. There was a sigh of relief and we returned to the bridge.

Cpt. McCain gave Kim the evening off and we left the bridge together. I asked, "Are you tired?" "No, not really, why do you ask?" Would you like to go find our friend Eric Van Stahl and ask him if we could go for a horse-back ride?" "Just when I think you have a one track mind I find out you have two tracts. I would love to." We laughed and made our way to the area where we usually see Eric.

I called him via communicator. He was with a Ty and a Lumy observing a few horses running across the meadows and asked us to join them. We went over to say hello, greeted the Ty and Lumy as we had learned and said hi to Eric.

We asked if we could once again have a couple horses for two or three hours. He said, "I would be happy to saddle a couple for you. That will give my new friends an opportunity to observe what we have been talking about. I think I have to convince them we're not torturing the animals.

Please, everyone come with me. As we walked we too explained that the act of riding helped us bond with nature and the horses didn't seem to mind carrying us around.

They looked a little skeptical but willing to observe and possibly accept our strange behavior.

Once at the stables Eric brought us a couple of horses and we began to saddle them. The Lumy took a long look at the saddle and asked, "That's not the skin of an animal is it?" The discussion was headed for trouble so Kim asked if either of them would like to try riding. They politely declined and backed away. We thanked Eric, said our goodbyes and rode off.

I said to Kim, "I'll bet they think we're really strange and are still looking for contact to our fellow mammals." She said, "I'm sure by observing them closely they will also have strange habits. Just wait till all the groups return from Korant with their tales of what they've seen." "I must admit, I really am anxious to hear about it."

We rode for a half an hour and then decided to take a break under a huge maple tree. I produced two glasses and a small bottle of sparkling wine and we sat and watched the birds come and go. Another perfect evening in what seemed to be an ever improving way of life.

"Alrighty lady, I challenge you to a race and the winner gets to choose where we eat." "That's fair and I'm certain you'll like my choice." We mounted the horses and galloped off and then suddenly stopped. "Where's the goal?" "See that building over there?" "Yes." "I'll be waiting for you behind it." "We'll see about that!" ..and she spurred her horse to a canter.

We raced across the field and around the building with her half a length in front of me. As we came to a stop we encountered Lin Chi kissing a beautiful young woman.

They were startled by our sudden appearance but Lin recognized us at once and said. "Do you have a minute I would like to introduce you to the most beautiful woman in the galaxy?" Fearing we had barged in on something we shouldn't have we reluctantly said yes.

We dismounted and Lin said, "I would like you to meet my beautiful wife Maya the soon to be mother of our child. I think he was one of the happiest people I've ever seen.

With a sigh of relief, we greeted and congratulated them both. We spoke for a few minutes and then Kim said, "Robert and I have a dinner appointment that I just won and we'll be going now. Enjoy your evening, it was a pleasure meeting you Maya, you should have Lin show you where he works so we can all meet you. I said goodbye and we rode off.

I said, "I was afraid that was going to be embarrassing." "It was for them. Their culture doesn't allow them to show affection in public." I said, "Their culture is back on earth. We are here and the present is our new culture. How can we make everyone understand that?" Kim said, "We can't, we're just humans and are bound by our teachings, traditions and beliefs. Let them be themselves as they allow us to be different, it's only fair."

I said "Lets take the horses back and you can show me where we're to have our dinner." "OK, if you get there first you get to choose the desert." "That's fair" and I took off galloping across the meadow.

I believe she allowed me to win as she weighs less and rides better than me. None the less, I did win and would of course insist on choosing the desert.

We had a great meal at a place I had never been and we ended the day at her place with great expectations of the morrow.

The next morning we had breakfast with Lars and Lin and began the day by witnessing a super nova that was only ten light years away. Lars even induced small waves in time and space to help break the impact and radiation, and it worked. It seemed as if we were invincible.

The Ty were most grateful for the gesture as their methodology would have been at some cost to the environment. Or so we were told. At any rate the day was off to a good and exciting start.

Sometimes I can not believe what I am writing and accepting as normal.

The federation has contacted us and asked Cpt. McCain, Lars, Lin, Kim and me to attend a meeting of the high counsel of the federation. We of course said yes and left immediately for Korant.

Upon arrival Kotar took the floor and proclaimed that we had done more than even the Ty had to protect everyone from the super nova and although it must remain an exception he proclaimed that we must be allowed to have a seat on the high counsel. No people had ever earned this privilege in less than almost two hundred of our years.

There were no protests and it was done. We were now members of the high counsel of the most powerful organization in the galaxy. Wow!

We needed to appoint someone as ambassador. Cpt. McCain said, "We will appoint Hetshepsut Bonafrit as our representative on the high counsel. We will send for her at once."

Cpt. McCain knew that Kim and she had a strong telepathic connection and could communicate over great distances and diplomacy ran in her family.

Mimonar, "May I go to the Enterprise and ask her to join us?" Cpt. McCain, "That will not be necessary I'll ask Ms. Lien to contact her. She can be here within the hour." Therewith she looked at Kim and Kim nodded. Cpt. McCain, "She's on her way."

Kotar, "It is amazing how at ease you are using all the new technologies you have acquired." Cpt. McCain said, "They are but tools that shorten a path."

Kotar went on to explain that the counsel would like to present us with a down-load of all the known star systems in this galaxy and an explanation of who lives where and their standing with the federation.

This federation is the oldest interstellar organization in the Milky Way and Andromeda. It has ruled over the two systems for over seven hundred thousand years.

Kotar, "With these maps you will be able to visit many peoples and hundreds of systems. However, with it comes the obligation to help where needed and to allow the other peoples of the galaxies to grow and prosper at their own speed.

We have done our very best to prosper and develop at an ever slower speed in the hope to not outgrow our body and mind.

We hope you will attempt the same as the only alternative is to enter another dimension. It is of course a possibility and others have chosen to do it. We have lost track or should I say can no longer communicate with them. This system has another four billion years of life in it and we would like to be a part of it for as long as we can and we hope you'll join us."

Cpt. McCain, "We have never had so much insight and of course knew nothing of these options. We will have to discuss this among ourselves and choose the route we find most promising.

When speaking only for myself I would say I understand your point of view and would choose the same path."

In the meantime Hetshepsut arrived and Cpt. McCain explained that she would like her to assume the position of ambassador of the human race on the high counsel of Korant.

Cpt. McCain, "This is of course not an obligation that I will force upon you. If you do not want the responsibility you may decline."

There was a short pause and it got very quiet in the great hall. Then she replied, "It is with great pride that I accept this honor and I pledge to use this position to help all the peoples of the federation and secure our rights within the guidelines of the high counsel."

Kim mentally blocked all others and telepathically said to Hetshepsut, "Please take it slow and keep a low profile. We all have much to learn." She looked at Kim, smiled and nodded.

We thanked the high counsel for the honor and took our leave. On the way back to the Enterprise Kim asked the captain, "Do you feel fully comfortable with your choice?" "Of course not, I would much rather be there myself but we are going to be spread pretty thin for the next ten years and we will have to learn to depend on others.

You will of course monitor her well-being and mental state. I am certain of her abilities to function as a diplomat."

Lars said, "Twelve years ago I calculated that it would be theoretically possible for us to exist outside our bodies in less than a thousand years. Now that I have the confirmation that it is a real option I find myself questioning the advantage or even the purpose of such a transformation.

The others who have opted to take that step no doubt occupy the same time and space as we do but I would bet that they see and feel us as little as we see and feel their presence." We all looked at him and he said, "Sorry, just thinking out loud."

Capt. McCain said, "We've been out here in deep space for over four years now. It has not been easy for anyone, we have however adapted well and I would like to move on, meet a few new neighbors and get started duplicating our transportation systems. We need to find a few alternative planets for our people to inhabit and uncover the secrets of our universe. The rest I'll leave up to appointed dignitaries." We all applauded and I asked if I may quote what she had said. It was after all the summary of how we all felt.

She smiled and said, "Do you really believe that the entire crew feels that way?" "Yes, I do and I have contacts and friends on all decks.

Those who want land under their feet have volunteered for duty on Korant and the rest of us await your commands." She paused, smiled and said, "That's nice to know."

As Jimmy docked the shuttle Cpt. McCain said, "Mr Cheedle please accompany us to the bridge. Upon arrival she called a meeting of all officers on the bridge.

As we were all seated at the conference table she rose and said, "I herewith assign pilot Jimmy Cheedle the title of Captain First Class. He will be training our new pilots until a "B" class Star Ship has been completed. At that time he will be given command of one of the ships.

He will be assigned to the Enterprise until he is to replace Cpt. Atilla Zarka who will be working with Captain Chapman."

Jimmy rose from his seat, I thought he was going to faint, he said, "Thank you captain, I am honored and...."

Cpt. McCain said, "You will have your hands full for a while. I want an additional twelve pilots trained within the next three years and of course Cpt. Zarka will allow you to train on the Freedom. Don't get too attached to it and remain flexible as you will be piloting one of the new starships Cpt. Zarka can tell you all about it."

We all stood and congratulated Jimmy. He was very deserving of the promotion. Cpt. McCain said, "Cpt. Cheedle, you may have the rest of the day off. Please see to it that by tomorrow your attire is appropriate. He nodded respectfully, we all shook his hand and he took his leave.

As he left the Enterprise the other star ships and all the shuttles were in formation and gave him a welcoming salute. That was the first big promotion that Cpt. McCain had given since our journey began.

Cpt. McCain, "Mr Manning, you had asked if you could quote what I said on the shuttle as we were returning from Korant; the answer is of course yes. I would like it made public knowledge and also known that we welcome comments.

Mr Kofi, do we have everything we need to continue our journey?" "No, we still need several of the air filters changed and we are loosing pressure on deck 22 sector nine." "How long before you are ready?" "I still need three days." "No problem we have six.

Mr Chi, are you ready for departure?" "Yes, all but five power cells are at maximum charge and I expect them to be ready within forty eight hours." "Mr. Berger, are we ready for departure?" "Yes captain, we are."

Cpt. McCain said, "Counselor Lien, I want you to choose a successor for Mrs. Bonafrit and a counselor candidate for the new star ship who will serve under Captain Chapman. He will of course have to approve. They are to be chosen from your best pupils and must,... I'm sure you know what I want."

She answered, "Yes Cpt. McCain, I do and I will have them within twenty four hours."

"Mr Chi, please check with captains Turner and Zarka to insure there are no overlooked problems aboard their vessels. I am going to lunch, #1 you have the bridge."

We all had more than enough to do and the day was soon drawing to an end. I had returned to my quarters for documentation orientation when Dr. Khan knocked on my door.

"Hello Dr Khan what brings you to this part of the ship?" He smiled and said, "When we met we had a discussion about your heart. The time has come, you are a day or two away from a massive heart attack and we need to replace it before that happens."

To say the least I was shocked, I had forgotten all about it. I asked, "Are you going to put me out of commission for a prolonged period?" "No, not at all.

The procedure will take five hours and we will reseal the wound by melting the tissue back together. You'll hardly be able to see where you were opened. The actual recovery will take about three days.

I've taken the liberty of informing the captain and would like for you to come with me now if you would be so kind."

I guess I should be happy, it did last much longer than they had originally predicted. "OK, do I need to take anything with me?" "No we have everything you'll need for the next three days."

We walked to the clinic in silence. Upon arrival they gave me a gown and asked me to change and prepare for some tests. The nurse gave me a shot and said it would make things a little fuzzy but therefore painless.

By the time I realized I was changed I was also pretty well done with the tests and another nurse was helping me to bed. "You will sleep now and we'll take you into the O R at five tomorrow morning. You'll be able to have tea tomorrow afternoon.

I slowly drifted off dreaming about this huge banana split.

At about 14:00 the next day I awoke in the I C U with Kim holding my hand. "Hi there, she said, how do you feel?" "I don't know I'm not sure I'm capable of feeling anything.

They have some pretty amazing drugs here. How did the operation go?" "Dr Khan said everything went as planned and you have a brand new heart and will be just fine in two or three days."

"I remember a nurse promising me a cup of tea after I wake up, is she around, I'm thirsty?" "I'll call for her and we can ask." Just as she was going to press the button, the nurse came in with a tea pot, two cups and a few cookies.

She said, "Hello Mr Manning, I'm MaryAnn, we spoke briefly yesterday and I promised you a cup of tea. Do you have any pain?" "No, none at all." "Good, Mrs. Lien the other cup is for you, can I do anything to make your visit more comfortable?" "Thank you no, the tea will be fine."

We had some tea and Kim ate the cookies. I said, "It's amazing that one can go into a clinic with the knowledge that his heart is going to be traded out and yet all I thought about was food."

Kim said, "Yes, our brain is a wonderful machine and it knows when to be serious and when to just relax and think of pleasant things because the upcoming event is simply inevitable. You're going to need some rehabilitation when you get out of here and I've asked my Yoga instructor to assist you. I hope that was OK."

"Yes, of course it is I'm grateful for the help. As long as she doesn't want me to bend like you do. I'm afraid I'd break if I tried." She smiled, "No promises."

Dr Khan came in with two residents, they took a look at the chart, checked the computers I was attached to and stepped back so Dr Khan could examine me.

He stepped forward and placed his hand on my chest. "Is that uncomfortable he asked?" "Uncomfortable would be an exaggeration, I feel it more than I would normally but there is no pain."

"Isn't that amazing, a few hours ago I had clamps in your chest holding you open so I could operate and now you are back together with little to no discomfort.

You are an excellent patient and if you would like me to take out any additional organs please let me know."

We all laughed, I thanked him for his work and the excellent care I was receiving, he smiled and said, "Take it slow for a few days and ensure your diet is followed for at least two weeks."

"Diet, I asked, "A nurse will give you a pamphlet with a few guidelines and a suggested diet. I'll see you one more time tomorrow and you may then return to your quarters. Day after tomorrow you may resume your normal duties." "Thank You." He nodded and he and his residents left.

Kim said, "I brought you your documentation unit so you won't be bored. I need to get to the bridge. I'm very happy there were no complications. Let me know if I can help you when you get back to your quarters."

She gathered her things and took her leave.

I finished the day getting caught up with my work. The next morning I returned to my room and tuned in on the conversations that had taken place on the bridge. They are always recorded for cross reference.

Our count-down was now just under forty-eight hours. The ground crews were established and the ships were ready.

Cpt. McCain has arranged a banquet aboard the Enterprise for tomorrow evening. She has invited the high counsel and several other dignitaries. Everyone on board the Enterprise who is off duty and wishes to join the festivities is welcome.

I was feeling reasonably fit and decided to return to the bridge. As I was leaving my quarters Victor Kofi met me at my door. He said, "May I have a moment of your time Robert?" "Of course, what can I do for you?" "You know Cpt. Cheedle personally don't you?" "Yes, I do, is something wrong?" "No, nothing's wrong, I know he's interviewing young potential pilots and I have a good friend who would like to get her hands on an application and doesn't know how. Can you help?"

I said, "Sure, that's no problem, I'll have one for you by noon and you can give it to her on your lunch break." "Thank you, she'll be thrilled. So, how was the operation?" "Not unpleasant at all, I wasn't aware that Dr Khan could do such dramatic procedures in such a short time and that his patients could recuperate so quickly."

Victor said, "Yes, we are fortunate to have him."

As we got to the bridge Simlayar welcomed me back and gave me get-well greetings from twenty three nations. I have to admit it was very flattering.

Cpt. McCain said, "Mr Manning, are you certain you're up to being here?" "Yes, I'm OK and looking forward to the banquet. Are there going to be any surprises?" She said, "It wouldn't be a surprise if I told you, would it?

It will be worth while to be there and I hope some of the counsel members and dignitaries that we've yet to communicate with have the time to speak with some of us.

It will be beneficial to have many friends in the future. I was hoping that you would be well enough to attend." "I will be there and will mingle as best possible." "Thank you, it will be appreciated."

Kim came over and said, "Aren't you supposed to be in your quarters relaxing?" "Yes, as a matter of fact I am but you knew I wouldn't be, right?" "I wouldn't be a very good mind reader if I didn't.

I spoke to Dr Khan yesterday evening and he said he knew you wouldn't be able to relax but the operation was a full success and you were fused back together, the only recovery necessary is from the anesthesia and that shouldn't last longer than twenty-four hours."

I said, "Hey, you ended up with more information than me." She smiled and said, "Of course I did."

I asked Kim, "How will I know who is most beneficial to speak to tomorrow?" "I'll be helping you as best I can. You'll receive little suggestive impulses, try to follow them."

"You know, you could explain that a little closer this evening after dinner if you have time." "It will definitely be a bit later. I'm flying to Korant with Lars and the captain for a dinner meeting with five of the high counsel members." "OK, I'll see you a little later. I'm on a mission, I promised Victor Kofi some paperwork and need to see if I can come up with it." She gave me a kiss on the cheek and off I went.

I paged Jimmy Cheedle and asked if I could meet with him. He was on the eighth floor only a five minute walk from here so I went there for the meeting.

I told him of Victor's wish and he gave me a form to pass on. "I can only take this lady if she's really good, he knows that, right?" I said, "There are no obligations and you do not owe anyone a favor, you never will."

Jimmy said, "Thank you, I still have to grow into the position I've been given." I said, "No one "gave" you anything. "You are one hell-of-a pilot and have great leadership qualities. I'm glad you had time to enjoy speeding around the galaxy and doing things that no one had ever done before.

Now you have moved into a small elite group that has our very existence in their hands. I feel quite safe knowing you're protecting me." "Thank you sir." "It's a pleasure, and thank you for the application."

I went back to the bridge and gave Victor the application. He said, "I didn't really think you'd be able to do that. There are about a hundred people who would like to apply for the one of the twelve slots and only forty applications are being distributed. I can not thank you enough." "Stop, all I did was get the application. She has not yet qualified for training. However, if she does qualify I certainly hope to have a ride in a shuttle of hers after her graduation." That you will my friend, that you will."

Lars and Simlayar asked if I'd like to join them for lunch and as Kim had already left for Korant so I said yes. We decided to have a pizza as Simlayar knew she liked all the vegetarian ingredients but she couldn't imagine them combined on what she called flat bread.

After ordering we talked a little about each other. Lars asked, "How long have you been stationed on the Simu?" "I had the honor of being communications officer on the Simu for over thirty of your years." "I hope you will be happy here on the Enterprise." I'm sure I will be, there are four other Ty and two Lumy now on board so none of us will feel isolated."

The food arrived and she had an expression of excitement on her face as the waiter placed the steaming hot pizza in front of her.

I said, "I hope you like it. If you do not, you may order something else." She said, "No problem, I'm sure I'll like it. She looked us both in the eye and said, "May this food replenish our strength." We said yes, we're sure it will and began eating.

After finishing our pizzas we went for a short walk in the wooded area before returning to the bridge. I thanked them for the company and decided to go to engineering to see what was going on elsewhere on the Enterprise.

While walking I noticed several vessels on the outside monitor. It looked like they were ready to attack something.

Then all hell broke loose and several advancing star-ships were being pounded. I thought a war had broken out. One of the security guards walking by saw my concern and said, "Looks real doesn't it?

The lasers being fired are little more than red and blue flashing lights. It's a large defensive maneuver."

I said, "Thank you for the explanation, I feared the worse." "It will be over in a few minutes, good-day sir."

As I got to engineering I saw a new face, it was a Lumy by the name of Tauchin. I introduced myself and we exchanged a few words. He is a master engineer and has been assigned to the Enterprise for awhile. We spoke for a while then I continued my rounds.

I went to the room where the reactor could be observed via computer. It always amazes me to see something that can produce such an enormous amount of power.

Conor Brodie, the head of engineering and I have become friends and he often allows me to observe the process of extracting energy from its magnetic encasement. What he actually does with it in order to create the right amount of energy to supply each and every component on the Enterprise with the right amount of energy at the right time is far beyond me but he does make an effort to educate me.

He said, "You see those huge pipes going around the inside of the casing, they are accelerators. They contain many elements that have been reduced to their most basic form. Then they are shot at each other. The elements in each chamber almost reach the speed of light. When they collide it creates all the energy we'll ever need." I still don't get it but it is a tremendous lightshow.

Instead of utilizing the power for a steam engine like the nuclear power units on earth did and having everything hard wired to a system, it produces the power magnetically. There's no waste as the radiation is recycled and electricity traveling through wires is a thing of the past.

Our energy flows through the ship itself and is tapped by the different components as needed and when needed. The energy isn't turned to electricity until it enters the component it is to power. There's no loss and no such thing as too much or not enough. I don't really understand it but I do know it works.

It was getting late and I decided to go have a bite to eat and Conor said there was a real good diner only a short walk away. I asked him to join me and we left engineering.

Over dinner I asked, "Are we all set to continue?" "We're more ready than we have ever been. We have become a power to be reckoned with."

I asked, "How do you mean that?" "We are as fast if not faster than the other vessels out there, our shields are strong and our firepower demands respect.

We're receiving support from the best people the federation has to offer and have two thirds of a galaxy to maneuver in. That's what I call exciting."

"I guess you're right but I still find it hard to simply trust in everything and everyone and lunge ahead into the unknown." He laughed and said, "You have an alternative?"

We finished our meal, said good-by and I returned to the bridge. Our departure was now only three hours away. Everyone going was on board and at their station. We will be leaving the solar system in less than two hours.

Cpt. McCain gave Mr Chi and then Cpt. Turner and Zarka the order to initiate power and leave the solar system in formation.

Cpt. McCain, "Mr Berger, what are your instructions?" "Lars said, "The Adventure and Freedom will make the Leap with us. They are to maintain a fifteen hundred meter safety zone from the Enterprise. I have entered the co-ordinance into all three board computers. We are ready."

Cpt. McCain, "Are we ready? "Report" ... "The Adventure is ready," "The Freedom is ready," "Mr Chi, "Ready." "Mr Berger, initiate."

For the first time I actually felt the event. It was as if time stopped for a fraction of a second and there was absolutely nothing, a void with an epic dimension and then we were there.

Lars, "That becomes more exciting every time we do it." "Exciting?" "Yes of course, we just traveled thirty eight light-years and during that split second between the two locations we were neither here nor there, we were one with the universe and that's exciting."

Cpt. McCain, "Well, that's enough excitement for one day. Mr Chi, please maintain impulse speed until Mr. Berger has verified our position then plan the route to Copat and accelerate to 0.15, I want an ETA of 09:00.

#1, you have the bridge. We all took our leave and returned to our quarters.

The next morning at 06:30 my door buzzer rang. When I answered it, Kim was there with breakfast. "Are you hungry Mr Manning, she asked?" "Is that a loaded question?" "It most certainly is!" "Then the answer is of course, yes!"

We had breakfast and made time for one another. Kim kissed me and said, "I want desert." We made love on the sofa, floor and whatever space we found between the two.

After a refreshing shower we proceeded to the bridge. It was now 08:45 hrs and we could see our goal on the long range scanner.

It was a solar system with eleven planets and two asteroid belts. The forth planet from the star "sun" was Copat. It was a blue planet not unlike the earth. Lars estimated that fifty five percent was covered with water. That gave them much more land than we had on earth.

Three of the other planets are as large as Jupiter with many moons circling each of them. That's probably where we'll be getting our titanium minerals. We've been told that one of the moons is almost pure titanium.

It is a highly combustible ore in powder form. The work on that moon will probably be very dangerous.

The Lumy are interested in the FFC Cambridge process of creating the metal. It seems their attempts at utilizing titanium have been unsuccessful. We hope for this to be a win, win situation for both us and the Lumy. I hope it's a big moon.

Quay-Matt, ambassador of the Lumy asked Lars, "If the moon is truly of pure titanium how do you intend to reduce and harvest it without heat?"

Lars said, "That's relatively easy, we have a small canon-like thruster that can educe the same shock waves that we use for our leaps.

The waves are naturally much smaller and can be controlled so we do not use excessive force in reducing the mineral to a practical size." He asked Lars, "Will we have access to this machine of yours?" "I don't know. That will be a negotiation you'll have to conduct with Cpt. McCain.

The canon is mounted in a shuttle and can be fired while suspended above the moon or planet we utilize. It is a very effective tool and in the wrong hands could be used as a weapon." "Thank you so much for this information."

We're entering the solar system and Cpt. McCain has chosen a stationary setting for the Enterprise. She said, "Simlayar, inform Cpts Zarka and Turner that I want two shuttles from each ship to dock at 4-B within the hour.

Quay-matt, I would like to meet your rulers on Copat. Please make contact so we can arrange for a meeting."

He went to Simlayar and gave her a code. He said, Cpt. McCain you may speak at will. You are now connected to their high counsel."

She said, "Greetings, I am Cpt. Kathrin McCain of the star-ship Enterprise representing the human race of the planet earth. We have been informed by your ambassador Quay-Matt that we would be welcomed and we would like very much to negotiate with you."

A voice came back in response, "We too greet you and your people. My name is Chancellor Leo-May. We have been expecting you and welcome you at your leisure."

Cpt. McCain said, "I will assemble a landing party of my counselor, my science officer, communications officer and our historian. We will be on Copat with Quay-matt in one hour."

"Our coordinates will be forwarded. We look forward to meeting you."

Cpt. McCain, "#1, Mr. Berger will prepare a modest leap, use it if you must." Jerry nodded in acknowledgement. "Simlayar, tell Cpt. Zarka to expect us in a few minutes and give him the coordinates forwarded by the Lumy. We will take one shuttle.

I want the other three shuttles to remain on the Enterprise."

We gathered ourselves and our thoughts and followed Cpt. McCain to the shuttle. Naturally Jimmy Cheedle was piloting the shuttle. Cpt. McCain, "Cpt. Cheedle, you have nothing better to do?"

"No mam, you're about the biggest VIP we have and I'd like to make sure you and your crew arrive safely." "Thank you for your concern." "It's my pleasure."

As we entered the Starship Freedom and it departed for Copat. Within three minutes Mr Zarka was in orbit. Jimmy asked, "Is everyone ready?" There was no answer, the bay door opened and we flew out and toward Copat.

Cpt. McCain, "When we arrive I would like you to accompany us Cpt. Cheedle. We will be discussing the mining of Titanium on a moon that consists of over 90% titanium crystal.

I know you have worked with the impulse cannon and you know what it can do and what is possible without endangering others or blowing up their moon.

I am not interested in sharing the technology at the moment." "Yes mam" "And quit calling me mam or I'll demote you to janitor." We all laughed and Jimmy cleared his throat and said, "Eye Cpt. McCain. I would like everyone to tighten their seat-belts and prepare for entry it'll be a little bumpy for about a minute." No sooner said than done and we were blasting through Copats' atmosphere.

Jimmy, "I've entered the coordinates and gone to auto-pilot we'll be there in about ten minutes. Cpt. McCain, we've got a half a dozen weapons aimed at us." "What is the meaning of this Quay-Matt?"

As Cpt. Cheedle said, "They are aimed at us but not armed. They're automatic and follow any and every flying object in our atmosphere. I believe your word for that is security. I assure you it is not meant to be taken as a hostile act." Cpt. McCain, "Cpt. Cheedle, do they pose a threat?" "No threat captain, little more than a nuisance."

As we were about to land Quay-Matt said, "Our oxygen content is higher than what you are accustomed to and you may feel a little light headed for an hour or so, it will not last.

We would also like to ask counselor Lien to wear a head-dress or what you would call a helmet. It will prevent her from scanning the minds of those who do not wish to be scanned. No one on Copat has her abilities, I'm certain you already have that information."

Cpt. McCain, "You have my word, she will not scan any of your people and she will certainly not wear a helmet." There was a pause and everyone waited for Quay-Matt's answer.

The situation was getting uncomfortable since the greeting party was at the landing pad and we were on approach. Quay-Matt said, "It is highly irregular but we will allow it with the word of the good captain of the human race."

Cpt. McCain said, "The only thing Ms Lien will be on the alert for is hostility. If there is hostile intent she will know and although unarmed, we will react."

That said, Jimmy set the shuttle on the landing pad and shut it down. Quay-Matt explained that he would have to exit first and receive permission to allow Kim to exit the shuttle without a helmet. He returned, opened the door wide and welcomed us to Copat.

We exited the shuttle and were greeted with the greeting we were accustom to on Korant. We returned the greeting and a man stepped forward and introduced himself as Leo-May, Chancellor of Copat.

We introduced ourselves individually and were then led to a conference room where other Lumy were waiting for us.

The meeting lasted two hours and ended on a very optimistic note.

We were to take one of their scientists with us and he would be present for the first experimental mining attempts. Then we were invited to send groups to visit, look around and enjoy the food and air. All in all it was a successful trip.

The Lumy are a very attractive, human-like people with slender features and long fingers. Their height varies between 5 and 6 feet. They seem to be very forward and out-going. It's a lot like a person who tries to get too friendly and too close much too soon.

I asked Kim what she thought of it and she said, "We need to be on our toes as we could easily be put in a compromising position." "What do you mean?" Kim said, "They could compromise the integrity of members of the landing crews and that would at best upset the commanders on both sides. They are an astoundingly attractive people and we do not know their culture. I will recommend caution to Cpt. McCain."

After returning to the Enterprise, Cpt. Zarka of the Freedom was assigned the task of exploring the possibilities of titanium excavation. Cpt. Cheedle would pilot the impulse shuttle.

Cpt. McCain, "Cpt. Cheedle there is to be no risk taken. You will have the Lumy science officer Mr. Borko on board. He will observe the results of the impulse cannon, nothing more." "Understood." "Aye captain"

She then called twelve people from various locations together to create a landing crew. They were from medical, agriculture, building and cultural fields. Kim spoke to her about her concerns and she decided to have her instruct them on how they were to avoid unnecessary and possibly compromising situations.

I went over to Lars Berger's station to follow the progress of the excavation crew. Lars said, "They'll be deploying the shuttle in about ninety minutes, do you want to get some lunch?" We excused ourselves from the bridge and left. While walking down the corridor we noticed an asteroid shower hammering away at our shields on the over-head screen.

Lars stepped over to a communicator on the wall and called the bridge. "Lin, please let the Freedom know that an asteroid shower is headed for them and that they may need to delay the shuttle launch." "Thank you, they have been warned.

Lin asked, "Would you please bring me a large salad when you return?" "Sure, anything special on it?" "The works, I'm hungry." "We'll be back within the hour." We watched for a couple more minutes as it was impressive to see these huge bolders and chunks of ice explode upon contact with the force shields.

At lunch I asked Lars, "Are they going to be successful at retrieving that titanium?" "Yes, that's not the problem, the planet that the titanium moon circles will inevitably be influenced by removing most or the entire moon. I haven't finished the calculations but I would say the planet could pick up a wobble as its other two moons circle its southern hemisphere."

I asked, "Do they know about it?" "I mentioned it to Cpt. McCain but she didn't seem concerned as the idea to excavate came from the Lumy."

We had our lunch and took Lin Chi his salad. The asteroid showed missed the area where the Freedom had stopped and Jimmy has just left in the shuttle on his way to the moon of titanium quartz.

When he was within two hundred miles of his target he had all the measuring instrumentation turned on and fired a week burst of concentrated energy at one of the moon's higher points. Upon contact the small mountain trembled and crumbled.

The blast had also induced tremors throughout the moon and it seemed to be destabilizing. Jimmy immediately called the Enterprise and asked them to get there as quickly as possible. It is possible that only the tractor beam could hold it together. If it turned to a pile of instable rubble it would be at best difficult to harvest it or even a potential threat to the Lumy planet.

Cpt. McCain gave Mr. Chi the order to get there quickly and stabilize the small moon if needed. The Freedom moved to make room for the Enterprise. Mr. Chi was not accustomed to maneuvering the Enterprise within a solar system with planets and moons so close.

Within eight minutes the Enterprise was on site, Cpt. McCain asked Jimmy for an evaluation and he said, "I'm afraid you're going to have to grab it. It doesn't seem to be stabilizing." She gave the order and Lars initiated the tractor.

Instead of it stabilizing it began to separate and move up the beam toward the Enterprise. "OK Mr. Berger, what is our plan of action?" "We have over thirty trillion tons of titanium coming at us, I would like Cpt. Cheedle to position himself between us and the rubble and then fire another burst at it." "What is that supposed to do" she asked? "I am hopeful it will stop it from advancing. If we're lucky it should have enough gravity to reassemble itself."

Cpt. McCain, "Cpt. Cheedle, Mr. Berger will give you a signal when he deactivates the tractor, you will position yourself between us and the rubble, once Mr Berger reinstates the tractor beam you will once again fire a pulse at it. It is at your discretion as to how powerful the pulse should be. If you are uncertain Mr Berger will help with the decision. You have four minutes to complete the maneuver."

That said, Jimmy headed for the Enterprise, as he neared the beam Lars deactivated it, gave the signal, Jimmy entered the area between the rubble and the Enterprise. Lars reinstated the beam and Jimmy fired.

The whole thing took exactly forty nine seconds.

We all held our breath in anticipation of what was going to happen. As the wave hit the rubble it lost considerable speed and the rubble behind it slowly but surely collided with it and the moon did reassemble.

However once it had reassembled itself, which took thirty minutes, the moon was only one hundred fifty miles away from the ship. The Enterprise gently repositioned itself about five hundred miles away from the newly assembled moon and Cpt. McCain called everyone to the bridge for a meeting.

About an hour later everyone was on the bridge. Cpt. McCain asked us to be seated and then said, "That was a very unpleasant surprise and I feel you all handled it masterfully.

Now, how are we going to harvest it?" Lars said, "The answer has already presented itself. We will have a landing party land on the moon. Then we will fire an extremely small and concentrated tractor beam at their location. It should loosen the crystals enough that the beam can grasp them and transport them to our front door."

Jerry asked, "How do we stabilize our people so that they are not drawn into the beam?" Lars, "They will naturally be using heavy equipment and must keep over eighty percent of the machine out of the beam at all times. I believe that to be doable."

Cpt. Turner of the Adventure said, "Louis Barret, heavy equipment specialist and engineer would be ideal for that kind of work. He can crack an egg and deposit it into a glass with a bulldozer."

Cpt. McCain, "Call for him at once, I want him present for this. In the meantime lets' take a break and get some food delivered." I contacted a nearby restaurant and ordered food and drink while the others made small talk about the unbelievable maneuver Lars and Jimmy had pulled off.

Forty five minutes later the food arrived and shortly thereafter Louis Barret did too. He was welcomed to the bridge, which was quite an honor for anyone. Then over lunch Lars filled him in on the plan.

Cpt. McCain said, "Mr. Barret, do you feel up to the challenge?" "Yes, I do, I have a well trained crew and that's what we're here for.

I would like to have the machinery coated with a soft non-electrostatic substance to ensure I don't blow the moon and myself up." Lars said, "We'll get on that right away."

The Lumy science officer Jodan Borko asked, "How can we participate in the harvest?" Lars answered, "You can have transporters dock next to the tractor beam and take what you need from the rubble that is in transit." He nodded with acceptance.

Chapter X

Cpt. McCain, "We'll need nearly a year to harvest the crystallized titanium ore and produce enough titanium to build the three vessels. During that time there will be exploratory ventures into deep space with the Adventure and Freedom. We four captains will take turns utilizing the Freedom and Adventure and I will allow each captain to determine his own goals. They will naturally be cleared through me and if at all possible contact will be maintained.

In a little over a year we will return to Korant to pick up the clones and trade out any ground crew wishing to come back on board. Then #1 will assume control of the new major star ship. Cpts. Zarka and Cheedle will remain with me and Cpt. Turner and one other will be assigned to Cpt. Chapman's command.

I hope by then we have located a solar system with a suitable planet for us to utilize as a home base. It's going to be a challenge and I'm very happy you are all at my side." I asked, "How can all that be done in just one year?"

Cpt. McCain, "The Lumy have promised us a work force of ten thousand people and as many transporters as we need for one year as payment for the excavation of their titanium moon. That's more than enough labor to assist our specialists. Are there any other questions?"

There were none and the meeting was adjourned. We were all free to go back to our duties. Victor Kofi came over to me and asked, "Would you and Ms. Lien like to come to a baby shower we're holding for the Chi family?"

Kim, "Is it time for her to deliver?" "She has three more days and we would like to have a little party for them and wish them well." Kim smiled at me and I said, "We would be delighted to come, when and where?"

He said, "It will be this evening at 19:00 at the Oasis Restaurant on deck three. Gifts are not required but a smile and lots of good wishes are."

Kim excused herself and went back to speak with Cpt. McCain and I went over to speak to Mr. Barret. He looked more like a scientist than a heavy equipment engineer.

I asked him, "May I interview you?" "Sure, why not." Let's go have a cup of coffee together." We excused ourselves from the bridge and went to a nearby café.

"What does your job consist of? "I make sure the equipment is maintained and improved upon to utilize its potential as best possible."

"You can operate all the equipment?" "Yes, I can but I don't. We have very qualified operators. It's just when it gets touchy that I'm called in and that keeps me from rusting."

"Is excavation your strong point?" "No, of course not, it's construction. That's a never ending process and the on site preparation alone for a structure often takes weeks. It's all very challenging and ever changing."

"So you will not only go get the quartz, you'll also be responsible for building the ships?" "Me and about twenty five hundred others, that's what we do." "Amazing, would you please let me know when they have the bulldozer coated? I'd love to see it before it's put to use." Sure, I'd be happy to."

We had our coffee and talked for another half an hour and he said his good-bys as he had many things to attend to.

It was 17:30 when I returned to the bridge and Kim and the captain were just finishing the day.

She saw me, excused herself and walked over to me. "Are you going back to your quarters before we go to the party?" "Yes, I'd like to shower and change clothes." "Fine, I have a few errands to take care of and I'd like to clean up too. When I'm ready I'll be by to get you." "Fine, I'll see you later." We left the bridge together and I went to my room.

When Kim showed up she had a little happy smile on her face. "What are you so happy about?" "I've thought up an ideal gift for Mr and Mrs Chi." "And what might that be?"

She said, "I'm going to allow them to say hello to their baby before it's born and believe it or not I've found a way to actually make it possible for them to communicate for a few minutes.

It's not like real talking but it is communicating and the baby will recognize them once born." "Wow, you can do that?" "Yes I can Mr Manning and here's a thought for you." I felt a rush; it was like adrenalin and could almost feel her naked body touching mine. "Do that again and we'll miss the party." We laughed and were on our way to the celebration.

The party consisted of Lin Chi, one very round Mrs. Chi and almost sixty guests. It was a celebration of life itself and the joy of bring new life into a new and exciting time for us humans.

After most of the guests had gone and things were quieting down Kim took Lin and his wife into a separate room. They were gone almost half an hour. When they returned their smile was so wide it barley still fit on their face. They explained what Kim had made possible to the remaining guests and that of course sparked a discussion about parents communicating with their children. All in all it was a wonderful evening and an interesting party.

Two uneventful days passed and the newly chosen ground crews were now ready to visit Copat. They'll be visiting as couples who are either married or about to be married. That should slow the sexual advancements of the

Lumy somewhat. They will visit the capitol first and then be given a tour of several cities.

Cpt. McCain has also invited several Lumy to visit the Enterprise. Quay-Matt has educated us in their customs and aside from sharing sexual favors very openly they are a lot like us.

I sometimes wonder if that is what helped them loose their natural and genetically driven aggressions and become the peaceful and friendly people they seem to be.

Their women are very pretty and move with the agility and grace of a cat. The men are equally graceful and I can imagine women liking their appearance and how they present themselves.

It will not be easy to maintain a segregation policy.

There's no sense trying to solve a problem that has yet to present itself.

Col. Vogel came to the bridge and addressed Cpt. McCain, "How much security is to be implemented on the visiting Lumy?"

Cpt. McCain said, "They are to be given the freedom to visit everything but class-A facilities." "It will be difficult to maintain surveillance" "I believe surveillance to be an exaggerated caution.

The Lumy are not the enemy, they are our colleagues and comrades and are to be treated with the utmost respect. That said I want to know if anyone of our people or theirs is somewhere where they shouldn't be." "It will be done, thank you."

Simlayar came over to me and said, "Mr. Barret has requested that you go to bay two on level seven. He said he'd meet you there." I thanked her and left for bay two.

Upon arrival I saw a colossal bulldozer with tracks so big that one link in it was fifteen feet wide and five feet long. The shovel was seventy four feet wide and was over thirty feet high. Everything had a coating of some strange rubbery looking substance.

Louis Barret stepped out of the cab and asked me to climb the ladder up to him. When I got there he said, "So what do you think of our dozer?" "Wow, that's quite a machine, may I look in the cab?" "Of course, come on in. I'll even let you take it for a spin around the bay if you'd like." "Really, yes, I'd like that a lot."

He showed me a joystick and an unbelievably complicated looking board computer. "All you have to do is tell it where you want to go, grab the joy-stick and push."

I said, "Right, I'll watch for starters and then I'll try."

He was very patient with me and after showing me the ropes he actually allowed me to drive it a short distance. It was a feeling of power, like you could do anything and conquer any task, all-in-all very exciting.

As we were finishing, there was an explosion just outside the bay door. On the viewing screen we could see the Freedom chasing another ship. Then several laser bursts were fired and the ship exploded.

Cpt. McCain came over the intercom system and announced that we had once again been challenged by the Palchek and once again they lost. It was as easy as that and then back to business.

I thanked Louis for everything and returned to the bridge as quickly as I could. Kim met me at the door. She said, "There were three of them, we destroyed two and the Lumy got the other as it passed on the other side of Copat. It seems they are quite capable of protecting themselves."

I asked the Cpt. "Did the Lumy say how often something like this happens?" "Yes, the Palchek seem to make an appearance about every two years. It's good that it was now before construction has begun. It would not have been easy to defend a construction site."

She contacted Cpt. Turner on the Adventure, "Good shooting Captain, how much of a challenge was it?"

"Not nearly enough, I can't imagine that was all of them. I strongly suggest we stay at full alert." "Point taken alert status will remain until we have reason to lower it."

Then she summoned Cpt. Cheedle, "I want one of your best students to take a shuttle to the edge of the solar system and send out long-range scanners to see if they can pick up any movement."

Jimmy said, "Cpt. McCain, may I be the one who....." "No, that is no longer your job and it is not some thing I'll discuss.

Do as I ordered and do it now!" "Consider it done." Jimmy chose one of his students and within ten minutes he was in his shuttle and on his way.

Cpt. McCain summoned Cpt. Zarka. He answered over the intercom system. She said, "Is your vessel ready for combat?" "Yes it is." "I want you to protect that shuttle as if your mother were aboard. You may however not advance. It must be from your present position." "Understood, it is secured."

As Kaito Akera, the shuttle pilot, deployed the four long-range scanners and they shot out into space one of them was immediately destroyed.

Before the flash was gone Cpt. Zarka had locked onto the source, which was most defiantly a Palchek vessel in hiding. He fired a torpedo at it and as we watched it travel through space toward its goal I almost felt sorry for whoever or whatever was at the other end.

The torpedo hit an asteroid which was about twenty five miles across and with a tremendous flash it was gone and I'm sure anything anywhere near it was destroyed.

The other three scanners were busy doing what scanners do when a beep was heard from one of them over the computer.

At the same time two more torpedoes were fired and an array of laser flashes surrounded the shuttle. It was an awesome sight and I'm sure Kaito was very nervous by now.

Jimmy said to him. "If you have a target, destroy it!" The torpedoes whizzed past the shuttle. Kaito began firing. Cpt. McCain said, "Cpt. Turner get out there and secure the area immediately after the torpedoes detonate."

That said, both torpedoes erupted into ultraviolet flashes and the Adventure was on its way. As it arrived at the point of detonation he radioed back to the Enterprise, "I believe Cpt. Zarka has cleared a path all the way back to Korant. There are no other life forms in this quadrant."

"And that's the way I like it," said Cpt. McCain. "Have Mr Akera load the shuttle into the Freedom and you may return." "What about the sensors?" "Leave them; I'm tired of being surprised by those bastards."

I want all Captains and able pilots in the ready room in one hour. Mr Berger, increase the shields to maximum power, nothing comes and nothing goes. The star ships Adventure and Freedom are to initiate maximum power on their shields before leaving them." We heard two "aye captains" and the spook was over.

In the ready room where Lars Kim and I had joined the captains and pilots, Cpt. McCain called the meeting to order.

There were no Lumy and no Ty present. She said, "Today we were put to the test and although one shuttle was damaged and a laser cannon did penetrate the shield on the Freedom, there were no casualties. As I watched the events unfold before my eyes I was very proud of my defenders.

We put on one hell of a show for the Lumy and I hope we didn't scare them. I also hope we didn't give them an opportunity to search for weak spots."

Cpt. Zarka said, "I wouldn't worry about that. There weren't any." "The entire battle was recorded and we're going to watch it right now, I hope you're right Cpt. Zarka."

The battle was played back via a 3-D hologram. It was stopped and replayed several times without finding fault in our defense.

Cpt. McCain, "If we can maintain this quality of defense during the next fifteen months we shouldn't have too much to worry about. Are your pilots good enough to advance to this level Cpt. Cheedle?"

Jimmy said, "Most of them are and the two who aren't will get better or be re-schooled in another discipline.

I would like permission to add an additional six candidates to our trainees." "Permission granted." "Mr Berger, do you have anything to say or to add to this meeting"

Lars said, "As you all know, the two new escort star ships will be modified. Construction is to begin in five days. If anyone has additional improvement suggestions, I'll consider them for four more days."

Cpt. McCain, "There will be no celebrations, no points for shooting down enemy ships and no advancements offered for you doing your jobs.

Although the Palchek are not human and although they find it necessary to fight and destroy us if they can, they are living beings. Their death is a loss to this galaxy and should we be confronted by them we will treat them with respect."

From all captains and pilots came an "aye captain". "You may return to your posts."

The meeting was over and I needed to go relax for a while. Kim looked at me and said, "No, I can't at the moment there's too much going on. You should go sit under our favorite tree and gather your thoughts. It is imperative that all this be documented properly.

I squeezed her hand and left the room. The tree sounded like a good idea so I headed that direction.

While crossing a meadow I met Eric Van Stahl. He said hello and asked if everything was OK. "Yes, everything is OK again, as you already know there was a battle with the Palchek which we, as you also know, won. It's a shame that they're so aggressive." Eric asked, "Are we going to hunt them down?" "No, quite the contrary, Cpt. McCain would like nothing more than to have them as friends. I'm afraid that that's not going to happen any time soon." "Well it's a noble intent." "Yes it is."

Then Eric asked, "Do you want me to saddle a horse for you?" "No thank you, I'm going over there and sit under my favorite tree and think for a while." "I'll ensure you are not disturbed, nice seeing you again." I thanked him and continued across the meadow.

A couple of hours later I felt a soft hand shaking my shoulder. It was Kim. She sat down beside me and asked, "Are you feeling better?" "I don't know for sure, it seems like yesterday we were contemplating the possibility of extraterrestrial life, then the possibility of meeting them. Then we find out that the galaxy is full of other life forms. Then we become a part of a galactic organization. Then we get attacked by real bad guys. It's as if I were stuck inside a science fiction film."

She said "There has been a lot going on and it doesn't look like there's going to be a pause any time soon. Hang in there, we need you."

I have a job for you." "What kind of job?" "Take me to dinner, I'm starving." "Now that's something I can handle."

She said, "I'm certain once you have documented the day's events and relaxed you will regain your equilibrium." "I hope you're right, I guess it's the fact that if those crazy Palchek were actually successful we'd be extinct that scares the hell out of me. And to stand there and watch a battle that is so important and critical is absolutely unreal."

"It's over for now and we need to concentrate on the new ships but let's talk about that later. I've not been with you for five days and I want a duck, some kind of chocolate desert and you." I said "I can make those wishes come true."

We had dinner and a wonderful evening and she did ensure I was alright. I said, "You know, I think I was about to have a meltdown." "You were, but then several of us were.

Cpt. McCain needed more help than you did. You're but a by-stander, she's the source. That's a hell of a lot of pressure for a mortal." "You're right. We sometimes forget that she's flesh and blood." Kim said, "She's the strongest person I've ever met and I'm certain she'll lead us to a fantastic future."

When we got to the bridge the following morning Chancellor Leo-May of the Lumy and his counselor were speaking to Cpt. McCain.

I said to Kim, "I wonder what they're talking about." "That's easy Mr. Manning. Go ask, it's your duty." She winked and I walked over to them and said good morning. They nodded and continued their conversation. The chancellor was saying, "We are sending several ships into deep space and would like to be reassured that they will not be mistaken for Palchek. The last ship you destroyed was over six hundred thousand of your miles from here. We were not able to identify it but we are hopeful that your captain did before he destroyed it.

Cpt. McCain said, "Although we do not owe you an explanation I would like to show you what my captain saw before he fired."

She turned the hologram on and played back what the screen on the Freedom was showing as Cpt. Zarka fired.

There was no mistaking. It was a formation of nine Palchek vessels headed this way. She said, "There was little to no time for second thoughts. Had they gotten within range we would have all been in grave danger."

Leo-May said, "Thank you for the demonstration. We will feel safer knowing you are here." "Please do not overestimate our capabilities. We can only see things like that when we are looking for them.

It is quite impossible to be looking all the time. I'm afraid your ships must look out for themselves." "Of course they will. We have been dealing with the Palchek for over a five hundred of your years. They have, in the past, caused a great deal of damage. We are now capable of fending for ourselves. I am here to ensure you do not mistake one of ours for one of them and remove it from the galaxy. Nothing more, nothing less."

Everything seemed to be in order so I decided to see how our excavation was coming along. A young lady scientist by the name of Rada Byko was talking to Lars about some of the titanium crystal samples. She was saying, "The samples have no impurities and even the by-product of the excavation is over 97% pure. We have very little to do to turn it into solid metal and that means we're ahead of schedule." "Very good thank you for the report."

She left and Lars walked over to me and said, "what-do-you-think?" "What do you mean what do I think?"

"You did see that beautiful woman just leave the bridge didn't you?" I looked at him in complete disbelief, "Why yes I did. Why do you ask?" "I find it hard to breathe when she's around and I get very nervous, I'm not at all accustomed to that."

I asked, "Does she know about your feelings?" "I don't think so and I'm afraid to say anything because she may not like me." "You're kidding me right?" He looked at me with a very concerned expression on his face.

"I believe the bug has bitten you." "What bug?" "The Bug. You are crazy about her, you must let her know."

Kim joined us and asked Lars if he thought she could help. "How do you know?" "You have a sign on your forehead that says you're in love." "Is it really that obvious?" We both said "Yes".

Kim said, "I really shouldn't say this because it's like tampering with nature but, she likes you too and wishes you'd ask her out."

I added, "Do not ask her out on a business dinner! Ask her out because you want to be with her. Do it or you'll be sorry you didn't when she goes with someone else." "OK, I will and thank you both."

I looked at Kim and said, "Our little Lars is growing up." We all had a good laugh; we wished Lars all the best and decided to go for a late cup of coffee.

When we got back to the bridge we noticed Cpt. McCain and Jerry Chapman at the conference table. We joined them and they continued as if we weren't there.

Cpt. McCain, "I'm certain we'll find a suitable solar system with one or two inhabitable planets in the near future."

Jerry said, "If we settle on a new planet it will inevitably become our home base and center of our culture." Cpt. McCain, "That's what I'm saying, I would rather you become the leader of our new start on a planet than have you shooting aimlessly through the galaxy.

If you insist on a commission I'll appoint you Cpt. of a star ship but I am inclined to keep them all much smaller than the Enterprise. In ten years it will have outgrown itself."

Jerry, "It would be an honor to initiate a new beginning. Who will I answer to?" "I am sure as hell not going to make you emperor but to be honest with you. You won't be far from it. You will need to create a system that actually works. Monetary objects will once again become important unless you find a way around it.

We have a good model here and I am hopeful you'll find a way to utilize it. I would like for you to build a group of advisors and prepare yourselves to inhabit a planet.

That will include building cities and securing food sources without destroying the planet's environment." Jerry said, "I'll do my best to be ready for it when the time comes."

I looked over at Bret Ambruse who I assigned to Jerry Chapman, "You're going to have your hands full my friend." "It sure sounds like it doesn't it?

Cpt. McCain asked Jerry, "Would you like to be the first to take a star ship on a reconnaissance flight?" "Do you have anything in mind?" "No, it's entirely up to you. Think about it and if you decide to do it, then consult with Mr Chi and Mr Berger and choose a route.

The goal of course is to find a planet to inhabit. Wouldn't it be something if you were the one to find it?"

"I'd like to give it a shot. Which ship will I have?" "The Adventure, Cpt. Williams has offered to assist Cpt. Cheedle in training our new pilot cadets. I'll give you two shuttles and a fresh crew. You can do some orientation flying if you'd like." "Thank you, I am a little rusty and could use some practice before we get started." Cpt. McCain said, "I'll expect to see a charted route proposal within seventy two hours."

They stood and shook hands and went on about their duties. I said, "I guess we'll have a supreme chancellor before too long." Kim, "We can only hope. He is for certain the right man for the job."

It was almost lunch time and Cpt. McCain called several engineers, Lars and two of his best scientists together for a luncheon so I decided to go along to see what she had planed.

During the luncheon she said, "Ladies and gentlemen we've begun work on two new star ships. I want plans for two more. They are to be double the size and I want artificial gravity throughout the vessels." That created quite uproar and many questions.

She said, "A few years ago we decided to try to save humanity by leaving our solar system. In order to do that a ship was built that was many times larger than anything ever attempted. Then we powered it with a power that had never been used, then we made a method of movement possible that was little more than theory. Don't tell me you can't do this, I know better. This is not a request, it's an order."

Lars, "Do you have other upgrades in mind?" "Yes, I would like the thrusters improved. The first ten seconds after initiation are not being utilized properly.

Engineers, I want a new design. These vessels are to be impressive and a little bit intimidating. I'll start accepting suggestions in two weeks.

On top of all that we're going to need twenty two new shuttles. I believe there's a bit of room for improvement there too."

Lars said, "I would like to suggest an actual fighter ship. It should be small and operated by one pilot. I would suggest ten per star ship and twenty five for the Enterprise."

Cpt. McCain, "Do you really find them necessary?" "Yes, I have observed them on Korant and Copat. They are capable of flight in an atmosphere and outside it. If they are the size of shuttles in mass they could be heavily armed and have an ample fuel supply."

Cpt. McCain, "I would like to see plans for battle ships as well. Cpt. Cheedle, I want you to produce instructor quality pilots; it looks like we're going to need a large supply of pilots in the near future. Mr Berger I expect to have a flight simulator program for the new fighter within ten days. I take it you have someone who can handle that." "Yes I do, it will not be a problem."

The meeting was adjourned and as we got up Jimmy looked at me and smiled. "I saw the look in your eye as she said flight simulator. When the program is ready and I've got the bugs out of it I'll let you know and you can take it for a spin." "Really?" "Sure, why not, it's not as if you could do any harm and you never know when knowledge like that could save your life." I thanked him as we left the room and asked, "Do you really think I could fly a fighter space ship?" "Absolutely, I believe you'd make a great pilot."

Kim said, "Boys and their toys." "You're jealous." "Right, I'd just love to have a thin piece of metal wrapped around me while traveling at half the speed of light dodging laser canons and who knows what other dastardly weapons might be out there."

"It's a flight simulator, nothing more." "Let's go have a cup of tea" We went to a café and relaxed over an Earl Grey and some really good cookies.

When we got back to the bridge there were Lumy representatives talking to Jerry Chapman about a number of stars with quality planets rotating around them. I asked, "What's a quality planet?"

Lumy representative, "It is a planet with the right size and atmosphere so can sustain life as we know it, the gravity is acceptable and the atmosphere possibly breathable. We have no interest in them as our sun is young and our planet is not over populated. Each of the three systems is more than thirty light years from here but that should not pose a problem." Jerry said, "I'm going to pick two of these systems to visit. If one would actually works out it would be a great start in the right direction." "I wish you luck."

I walked over to Lars who had already received a handful of sketches and model drawings of potential battle ships.

I said, "I see you're not going to have a problem with the battle ship concept." "Most of these are so hypothetical that they can not be considered. I'm hoping Cpt. McCain will accept mine."

"Oh, you've got one, please show it to me." He pulled a drawer open and pulled out a detailed blueprint of an awesome looking battleship. It was compact enough to put several in one bay, had a huge power source in reference to its size and was armed to the teeth.

I said, "Has she seen it?" "No, not yet." "What are you waiting for?" "It's only fair that they are all presented at one time. That's the way it is." "Well, I certainly wish you luck." He thanked me and left with the bundle still in his hands.

Kim was looking over some documents and I went to her and asked if she'd have lunch with me. "Yes, I'd like that, anything special in mind." "No, not really, any lunch becomes something special when you are with the right person."

Kim said, "I have an Idea, Lars hasn't asked Rada out yet and as you can see, he probably won't find the time unless pushed." I said, "So, what's the plan?"

"You go find him and have lunch with him at the Out-Look Restaurant. Rada and I will just happen to be there in forty five minutes." "I'll accidently see you in forty five minutes." That said I was off on a mission.

I found Lars in engineering going over the possibility of an afterburner for anti-material powered thruster with the newly appointed head of engineering Dion Svan, a tall blonde Swedish fellow. I politely listened in on the conversation and was totally amazed that they were speaking English and I was understanding absolutely nothing. I said, "Is it my translator implant or are there really that many words in the English language that I've never heard before?" They smiled and continued their conversation.

After about ten minutes I took Dion aside and quickly explained "the plan" and he said they were done anyway. He went back to Lars and spoke to him for another few minutes and then excused himself.

I asked Lars, "How fast are you going to make those things?" "They will be incredibly fast and agile. What are you doing here?"

"I had some errands to run down here and thought I'd check in to see what's going on. Why don't you show me some of that stuff over lunch, I'm starving." "Sounds like a good idea. I missed breakfast this morning.

We walked to the Out Look Restaurant and as we entered Kim who was sitting with Rada raised her hand. "Hello why don't you join us?" "We'd love to, thanks." Before Lars could comment I was seated next to Kim and he was next to Rada.

We had a pleasant lunch and some small talk then Kim and i excused ourselves and left. Kim said, "It's in their hands now and if Lars doesn't ask her out I'm going to kick him." We laughed and returned to the bridge.

On the way back I asked Kim, "Have you heard anything exciting from the crews visiting Copat?" "Yes I have, it seems the Lumy are primarily root eaters and that their vegetables grow very slowly but have an astonishing amount of vitamins and minerals in them.

They only have two meals per day and the vegetables are eaten raw or steamed." "I guess that's what keeps them slim and trim." "I guess so."

"What else is new down there?" "If you don't dote on the fact that they are not human, they are surprisingly normal. They haven't had a war amongst themselves for over nine hundred years." "That's definitely a goal worth striving for."

Once on the bridge Kim was summoned by Capt. McCain. "Can you pick up negative energy" "Yes, if something is being discussed with a great deal of negative energy it tends to stand out.

I must warn you though, I might tune in on conversations being held about a really bad meal or other harmless things."

Cpt. McCain said, "I want you to concentrate as best you can and if you find such energy zoom in on it and if the content is harmless disregard it and go on, if not I want to know the content." "Excuse me but without knowing what I'm looking for the whole thing sounds a little paranoid."

Cpt. McCain said, "There are rumors that the Lumy can have a negative effect on people if they wish to. That could create hostile thoughts and even induce acts of aggression. If it has taken place, I want to know about it. This will be done once every other day for a week. You may use my chambers for your meditation. Let me know when you find something or are finished."

Kim went to Cpt. McCain's quarters without further discussion. I asked Cpt. McCain, "Do you suspect any of the Lumy?" "No, of course not and I hope I'm simply wasting Ms. Lien's time. But at the same time I will not risk it happening without my knowledge."

"Tell me Mr. Manning, are you keeping up to date with everything?" "No, not at all and I don't think I'll ever catch up. I am getting most of it and I hope that it is adequate for our university's history lessons."

She said, "I'm sure it will be. I hear you're going to be put to the test as a fighter pilot." "Hardly, I am to be allowed to try the flight simulator once the program has been written." "As you showed a little interest I have arranged a little additional training for you, that way, as Cpt. Cheedle put it, should you need the expertise you'll have it."

I asked, "Has Kim been giving you lessons, how do you know all this stuff?" She smiled and said, "Cpt. Cheedle talks a lot and he likes you very much, you're a kind of hero for him, and yes,... I'm psychic."

I said, "That's astonishing, that young man is a mathematical genius who can probably out fly anyone in this galaxy. He is well schooled in all the duties he has ever had and I am his hero?" Cpt. McCain said, "We all have our heroes. That's what keeps us modest. Enjoy the instruction phase and don't crash my shuttle or my battle ship." She smiled, turned and walked away. "Wow, I get to fly both?"

After an hour Kim returned to the bridge and walked toward the captain. I joined them as I was interested in the outcome of the mental scanning. Kim said to Cpt. McCain, "Other than Mr. Svan being upset with one of his colleagues for miscalculating the heat needed to melt fifty tons of titanium ore in ten minutes (it was eleven degrees too hot) and Mr. Barret being upset because a track on his bulldozer got stuck, everything seems to be in order."

Cpt. Mc Cain said, "Thank you counselor Lien, we will be leaving for Copat in twenty minutes, we'll be there for about five hours. Mr. Manning, you will be joining us. We'll meet in bay 22."

The pilot Kaito Akera met us in bay 22 and helped us board the shuttle. He then asked Cpt. McCain for the exact location and we were off.

On the way she explained that we were invited to a luncheon. They want to thank us for the titanium ore and negotiate using some of our equipment or technology, she didn't know for sure, possibly to excavate other materials in other locations.

At the luncheon we were introduced to several other Lumy who were responsible for excavation and construction. They were all a little surprised that we came as such a small group.

Cpt. McCain asked them to explain exactly what they wanted and what they wanted to accomplish.

It seems their scientist Jodan Borko was very impressed with the impulse canon and would like to have a version of it. Cpt. McCain said, "I'm sorry but that is technology that we are not yet willing to share.

I will send a pilot with a shuttle to wherever you would like to assist with excavation. The pilot will however be alone in the shuttle, do his work and return to the Enterprise. I'm afraid that's the best I can offer at the moment."

Chancellor Leo-May asked, "Is it a matter of trust?"
"Yes it is. We have made many new friends very quickly, too quickly for us to have established a relationship based on trust.

Just as you have areas where our scientists are not allowed, we have things that we do not wish to share at the moment.

I am eternally grateful for the huge contribution of titanium and am happy that we can mine it for you as well. Your workers are very efficient and highly skilled and they are saving us thousands of hours of labor.

I am hopeful that one day soon we'll know one another so well that all secrets can be shared. It is an honor to know and be associated with you and your people."

Leo-May said, "Our engineer Tauchin who has been assisting on the Enterprise praises your work and methodology. He has not been so generous with praise for a long time. We have no intention of overstepping our boundary and we too are honored to have such warriors as friends."

Cpt. McCain had no intention of telling him that our vast experience as warriors consisted of blowing up three large asteroids and a skirmish with the Palchek near Korant.

She said, "We do not seek disputes, battles or war but we are capable of protecting ourselves and when necessary sending a message to others who would consider challenging us. I do hope the Palchek will think twice before they try again."

"I'm sure they will." Said Leo-May, "And last but not least on our agenda today is to ask for assistance in producing a single piece of titanium two kilometers long thirty centimeters thick and twelve meters wide. We need it for a bridge we are building and our engineer Tauchin who is working on the Enterprise believes you may be able to help. We have nothing here on Copat that could do it and certainly not in orbit." "I'll ask our science officers if they can do it. If yes then we'd be happy to help."

The meeting was over and we went back to the shuttle for the flight back to the Enterprise. Ambassador Quay-Matt asked if he could come along and spend some time with us. Cpt. McCain looked at Kim then at Quay-Matt, said yes and we were on our way.

Kim asked Quay-Matt if the procedure used with us was typical of all meetings with non-Lumy visitors. He hesitated and said it has always been our policy to demonstrate our power to visitors. Not aggressively and certainly non-threatening. Just to ensure that they know we are a powerful people.

For the first time, this was not possible. We did not see the Palchek coming and they would have most certainly caused considerable damage had you not been there.

You of course were only protecting yourselves and you had every right to do so. None the less it was awkward for us." Kim said, "You realize that it was quite awkward for us as well, especially for Cpt. McCain. She honors all life and did not kill the Palchek simply because she can. She did it to preserve the human race. We need for you to understand that."

Cpt. McCain joined the conversation and said, "I don't know how strong or powerful the Lumy are. I do know they are capable of fighting the Palchek and winning. That speaks for itself. I don't want to know how strong you are because I never intend to fight the Lumy. If you ever need our help you will have it and I would be grateful if I could depend on yours if needed."

Quay-Matt said, "You have earned our gratitude and we will be there when called to help." "Thank you." She therewith tactfully ended the conversation.

Kaito asked that everyone prepare for landing and no sooner said than done, she flew through the hatch of the Enterprise, we were attached to the bay and the hatches were closing.

We exited the shuttle and the Cpt., Quay-Matt and Kim headed for the bridge. I stayed and asked Kaito if he'd give me a tour of the construction site where the star ships were being built. He in turn contacted Jimmy Cheedle for permission. Jimmy gave him two hours and we were again under way.

I asked, "Where are they? I thought they'd be close so we could protect them." They're over there between those two small planets. We've got robotic cannons with 360 degree lenses on both of the planets.

Bad guys would do well to stay very clear of that area. Each and every vessel that is allowed to be there is registered in the gun-station's computers. Any unregistered vessel will be destroyed.

As we got closer I could see caravans of vessels transporting huge sheets of titanium for the outer hulls of the vessels. Two star ships and four shuttles were being constructed simultaneously. The construction site took up hundreds of square miles.

"Now that's what I call impressive." "Yes sir, and if you look right through the middle you'll see an array of hangers ready to begin construction on the battle-ships. I have hopes of earning the title of squad leader one day." "I'm sure you will if that's your goal. Have they decided on a design yet?" "Yes they have and in three days construction can begin. It should only take four weeks to complete the first of them and in six weeks we'll be flying them." I asked, "Do we have that many pilots?" "Yes sir, we do."

We circled one more time so I could see that over nine hundred vessels were coming and going twenty four hours a day and soon an entire fleet would appear.

"Who has control over the defenses?" "No one, they're programmed and can be altered if necessary.

It was the only fair way to do it. In six months it will shut itself down. Then it can be inspected to ensure everything is functioning as it should."

I asked, "What if we flew over to it?" "It would register our presences and allow us to advance within five hundred feet then it would warn us and under five hundred feet it would destroy us.

Both stations are being monitored from the Enterprise and from Kotar. It's pretty much fool proof." "Kotar can monitor this in his absence?" "Yes sir, he can."

We finished the second circle and returned to the Enterprise. It never ceases to amaze me just how much was going on in and around the Enterprise.

As we returned I saw that there were many work crews on the exterior of the Enterprise.

I asked, "Are there always that many people outside working on the Enterprise?" "No, they're taking advantage of the fact that we just fought off the Palchek so it's not likely that we'll be attacked any time soon and we're not traveling.

It's a perfect time to make sure everything is working properly and filters are exchanged."

Kaito asked, "Is it all right if I drop you off at dock 34? I need to pick up a construction crew." "No problem at all, that's near a café I like to visit occasionally." He docked, I thanked him and left to get a cup of coffee and document the days' events.

At about 22:00 there was a knock at my door. When I opened it there was Lars. He said, "OK it's all your fault so now you have to help me."

I asked, "What's all my fault?" "You two left me stranded with Rada." "Stranded!?" "Well, alone with her and I didn't know what to do so I asked her to go for a walk in the meadows."

"That's great did you have a good time?" "Yes, kind of, well at least till that horse ran by." "What horse?" "I don't know what horse, it was just a horse.

Then she asked if I liked to ride and I didn't want to seem un-sporty so I said yes and then she went on to say that she knew Eric Van Stahl and could arrange for us to go riding."

"Wonderful." He said, "It would be if I could ride!" That was it, I couldn't take any more. I burst out laughing and pulled him into my quarters.

I got us a beer, wiped the tears away from laughing and said. "I'll go riding with you tomorrow at day break. Eric can probably go with us and within an hour or so you'll be a pro." We laughed and drank our beer.

I said, "So tell me, is she the one?" "Yes, I'm sure of it. I even dream about her." "Go riding soon and make sure she knows how much you like her and I promise, everything will come together perfectly."

The next morning we met with Eric and told him what was going on. He actually laughed so hard he had to sit down. When he finally got his breath he said, "Yesterday evening Rada came to me scared half to death and begged me to teach her to ride on-the-spot.

She said that her life depended on it." Then Eric and I started laughing and could hardly stop. Poor Lars just stood there and didn't know what to say or do.

Eric said, "Mr Berger, you don't need to learn how to ride a horse, it serves no purpose." "What should I do?" "When you meet with her you look her right in the eye and tell her you don't need to be on a horse to know that you love her. Then you kiss her. That's pretty much all you need to do."

"If you two want to be around horses at a later date I'll hook up the carriage and take you for a ride in style." I said, "How about we three go have some breakfast?" They agreed and we went to the Out Look.

Later on the bridge Lars said, "First of all, thank you and secondly, Cpt. McCain just approved my plans for the fighter." "Congratulations now you've only got one more thing to take care of today. Do just like Eric said and you'll be a happy man for a very long time." He smiled and left the bridge.

I told Kim and the Captain what was going on and we all had a good laugh and hoped it would work out for them.

When Lars came back he seemed to glide across the floor and he had a very happy look on his face. I caught his eye and he smiled and said, "It worked, it really worked and we're a pair and will be seeing a lot of one another."

Cpt. McCain came over and congratulated him and then asked for the figures on the proposed trip that Jerry Chapman was going to be taking.

Lars face lost all expression, he pushed two buttons and the entire trip appeared on screen. Cpt. McCain said, "I am very happy for you and most pleased that it has not distracted you." Then she turned and went back to her station.

Kim gave him a hug and wished him well. By that time everyone on the bridge knew and they all came to give their good wishes.

Victor Kofi said, "It's about time you got yourself stabilized." "I'm stable." "Now you are and we're very happy for you."

The engineer Louis Barret came on over the intercom and said, "I need help quickly, this planet is extremely unstable. We've been removing thousands of tons per hour and didn't realize how small this moon has become.

Cpt. McCain asked, "Is it possible to place an electro magnetic field around it and squeeze it together?" Lars answered, "I'm afraid that that's not an option.

Science officer Jodan Borko said, we can create a mass that could cover the planet and then you could dig through it."

Cpt. McCain said, "How would it work?" "We would surround the planet with eight or nine bombs, then we will detonate them all at one time.

The mass will cover the surface. Then it will melt a little and will fuse. There will be no flame as it is a chemical reaction."

Cpt. McCain, "Does that sound doable to you Mr Berger?" "If they have such a chemical, yes." "What do you think Mr. Barret?" "Sounds good to me, let's try it." "Alright Mr. Borko, I want it to take place in two hours. Mr. Barret, get your people and machinery off that rock at once."

A Lumy fighter was summoned and shortly thereafter appeared, shot toward the little planet and fired a series of nine objects into orbit.

A voice said, "The bombs will be in position in four minutes." Cpt. McCain said, "Let the count-down begin so all can hear it. I want all vessels out of harms way."

The time went by quickly and the bombs detonated. The substance went exactly where it was supposed to and then we realized that it had to be one of the Lumy's weapons.

When it hit the surface a cloud was produced from the effect, then after two hours it cleared. The planet was stable.

Borko said, "It will not be easy to penetrate the surface but the solid part is only about fifty centimeters thick."

Cpt. McCain addressed Ambassador Quay-Matt, "That's quite a weapon you have there." "Thank you, he said, not as impressive as yours but none the less very effective."

Cpt. McCain said, "I have no doubt of that. If struck by metal will it produce a spark?" "Yes, I'm afraid it would, the only mineral harder is a diamond."

She said, "We'll give it a tap and see what happens."

She paged Jimmy Cheedle, when he replied she said, "I want you to hover ten meters over that rock and fire a minimal pulse that is no wider than fifteen meters at the surface. Put the video cameras on the point of contact so we can see exactly what happens.

Cpt. Cheedle, your shields are to be at maximum." "That may influence the pulse." "I'm aware of that."

He flew over to a large flat surface hovered and then fired a pulse wave at it. A hole was created and the surface cracked in a star form, a lot like glass when a bullet goes through it.

Jimmy, "I'd call that a success, Should I put two or three more beside it?" "Cpt. McCain, "One on either side of it making a row of three will do nicely thank you."

Lars had not been forgotten in all this, Jimmy said, "With your permission Cpt. McCain, Lars this is for you and

Rada." He fired what looked like a very small torpedo into space. It detonated and created a large one dimensional disk of white light that was at least twenty miles across. Then it went three dimensional and into every color of the rainbow and faded.

Jimmy said, "Mr. Berger designed that in his third year at The University of Heidelberg. He had announced that it was to be used on very special occasions." We all applauded and Lars thanked him.

Ambassador Quay-matt asked me, "Is it typical to have such a celebration when two people announce they are a couple?" "No not at all but Mr. Berger being our chief scientist and one of the busiest people among us has had little to no free time since our journey began.

We are happy for him that he can share in what we term normal life."

"I see, does this include sexual favors between them?" "That is something we do not normally talk about but I would think the answer would be yes.

We humans are not nearly as sexually advanced as the Lumy."

Quay-Mat said, "That is not at all the case, we have advanced in this manor and you in another. We are not more or less, simply different." "Thank you, all this is still very new to us and I'm afraid we'll need quite a bit of time to fully adjust."

"That is exactly how we felt when Kotar found and confronted us. That was only two hundred years ago. I'm certain the human race will make its mark."

Victor Kofi joined our conversation and although inevitable I felt uneasy when the Ambassador asked if we were the same species.

Victor was quick to answer, "When we were a very young species we were in a warm climate. All humanoids or Homo sapiens were black; at least we believe they were.

Then some of them migrated into colder climates and began to cover themselves with skins of animals they had killed to eat. The less light they were exposed to the lighter the skin became. It was simply a part of our evolution.

Our brains developed pretty much the same regardless of the climate." "I see, we must seem monotone to you as we are all a pale brown." "No not at all and I'm certain it helped avoid conflicts about who is better or more advanced.

We had problems like that and it took a long time to overcome them but it was long ago."

Quay-Mat said "I thank you for the conversation and now I must report back to the high counsel on Copat. I wish you both health and happiness."

After he was gone I said to Victor, "That was a great explanation. You made the whites look better than they were." "He said, "All that was truly long ago."

I asked, "How's Kikuyu and the wife?" "Doing fine thank you, she's growing fast and asking many questions. It's amazing to watch her develop. When are you and Kim going to get serious?"

"No idea, we have talked about it but the everyday life simply does not allow it but we're very happy the way it is. I asked victor, Tell me, what's going on worth writing about?" "Thank goodness nothing, we've been stationary long enough for my crew to renew and clean the systems on the Enterprise, Freedom and the Adventure and it'll be another four weeks before we can begin installing systems in the new ships."

I asked, "Have you come up with anything new and improved?" "Not really you can't beat the good old combination of 72% Nitrogen, 28% Oxygen a little H2O and a splash of argon." "I thought we had something like 78% Nitrogen and 21% Oxygen." "That's ancient history, I suppose you'd like me to throw in a few tons of pollen and dust so we have a nice sunset?"

"Can you do that?" "Of course I can but think about it, when is the last time you sneezed?" I thought for a while and was absolutely amazed "I can't remember for sure but I have no recollection of ever sneezing while on the Enterprise."

He smiled and said, "You're welcome." "You know I never thought of it in such detail before. You're a wizard." "Finally somebody who recognizes the beauty of what I do." We both laughed.

"How much air do you filter in a day?" "Let me say it differently so you can make a mental picture.

Alone on the Enterprise with it's five hundred filter systems and two hundred stations dispersing gasses; every hour two million cubic meters of air are filtered and altered to be composed of exactly 72.34% Nitrogen, 27.66% Oxygen with 53% humidity, inconsistent traces of argon and all that at 14.696 PSI. It is scanned at three hundred locations every eleven seconds and fluctuations are almost always less than 0.001% across the board. You're breathing pretty good stuff."

"If you think I'm going to remember that you're crazy but it is pretty damned impressive." Victor said, "I've found that people don't want to know the how it works. They just want to know that work." "Yes, I guess you're right."

Chapter XI

Jimmy Cheedle came to the bridge, spoke briefly with Cpt. McCain and motioned for me to come over to him. I thanked Victor for his time and information and walked over.

He said, "Are you ready to become a pilot?" "Well I'm certainly ready to give it a try." "Let's go to the training center." I looked at Kim, she smiled and waved and Jimmy and I left.

"Do I need some kind of super clothing for this?" "As a matter of fact you do. I had it made two days ago and it has been activated." "Activated?" "We need to know how you are doing and the suit itself is a pressure suit so as to make the flight as comfortable as possible."

When we got to the training center, I changed clothes and Jimmy showed me pictures of the battle ship and explained that once in the flight simulator there would be very little difference than flying the real thing.

"I can't just get in and go. I don't know what I'm doing." "No problem, I'm going to down-load the basics into your memory bank." "You're going to implant instructions into my brain?" "Yes sir, it's harmless and painless, relax."

He hooked me up to a machine with electrodes going to several locations on my head. He said. "You need to relax. It won't kick in until you do." I did my best to relax and in only a few minutes I theoretically knew how to fly. He unhooked me and led me to the flight simulator.

He said, "I'm going to take you for a very short and basic flight so you can get a feel for what is going to happen when you push the throttle."

We climbed up and into the box. From the inside it looked exactly like the pictures he had shown me. I sat beside him and we strapped ourselves in.

He said, "So as of now everything I say and do is dead serious and our lives depend on doing everything right. Trust me, it is not fun crashing this thing, I've done it and it is very realistic."

He looked at me and said, "Ready?" I nodded yes. He placed his right hand on the small joy-stick and gently pushed down. With a roar the thing came to life.

He looked at me and said look forward. When I did he pushed the throttle forward and we lunged at an incredible speed.

He said, "This thing has two speeds, really fast and Yikes! You need to stay away from anything you feel you could run into.

Objects will pass you and/or you will pass them with incredible speed. Remember speed is relative some objects will be traveling the same direction as you, they move slowly, others toward you, they move quickly and others will cross in front of you like the one in front of us now. It's going to my left so I steer to the right. Understand?" "I think so" "Good, take the throttle. Don't move it, just hold it till I give you instructions."

After a few seconds he said, "Move the throttle gently to the right." When I did it the ship lunged to the right and I was in the process of flying in a circle. "That was a bit too much. Straighten it back out and we'll try again."

He let me fly for about ten minutes which I interpreted as about an hour. I think I was actually sweating.

He took the throttle and landed safely back aboard the simulated Enterprise.

Jimmy said, "I guess you are going to need a little more practice before we actually take one for a spin. Let me know when you have the time and we'll do it again."

I thanked him and staggered out of the simulator. "Are you really willing to let me do that again?" "Sure, you didn't crash and I'm betting at least three of my cadets will. When you are at the throttle you are not driving or flying, you're on a mission of life and death. The ship is merely a means of getting there and doing a job.

After you've flown the simulator three or four times and crashed at least once you'll understand."

"Well, that sounds like fun." "I'll bet when we're done you'll enjoy it." "That would be nice."

I asked, "Do you want to have some lunch?" "I'd love to but I've got a class in ten minutes and then people to trade out at the construction site. Hope to see you again soon."

I left the training area and walked toward the woods. On my way Dr Khan saw me and asked if he could speak with me.

"Mr. Manning I realize that you are expected to be everywhere and document everything and that takes a lot of your time however if you don't start a training program and hold to it you are going to have a heart attack."

"I thought you fixed all that." "I put a cloned heart into your chest. It has the same problems the first one had in its early stages. You had neglected it and it quit on you. If you would like for me to grow another one and do it again I will but just because you had no pain doesn't mean that your body enjoyed me prodding around in it.

If you would kindly do the exercises in the brochure we gave you this conversation wouldn't be necessary. By the way, just in case you think I'm kidding, I'll give you twenty four hours to begin and if there is a single day you fail to exercise I'll report you to the Captain.

You are a very important person and it will not be my fault if something happens to you. Do we understand each other?" "Yes Dr. Khan, we do." "Now instead of eating, go exercise and I wish you a long and happy life." He turned and walked away.

I was a little bit stunned by his means of getting a point across but it was certainly effective. I went to the gym, down-loaded his instructions in the virtual trainer and got busy getting healthy.

Later on the bridge Eric Van Stahl asked me if I'd like to join him on a plant and animal orientation on Copat. I said yes, cleared it with Cpt. McCain and was about to leave when Kim said, "I'm glad you're doing your exercises." "Do things happen that you don't know about?" She said, "No" and gave me a kiss and said, "Go."

Eric and I went to bay 24 to catch a shuttle. I asked. "Where are we going down there?" "To a town called Sheetau which in English means Morning dew. I thought it would be the perfect place to begin since we're getting there at day break."

"Wonderful, off to Sheetau, now, where is it?" "Good one, it's near their equator so the vegetation will be of tropical nature I presume. I have no idea at all what kinds of animals await us."

"That's different. You usually have 95% of the answers before the questions are asked." "I did my best but they said they'd like to surprise me so I kept the research to a minimum." "What does that mean?" "I know we need high boots and a canteen of water." "I guess you could call that a minimum."

When we got to the bay we saw that they had delivered other clothes, boots, canteens, a few gardening tools and bags for specimens.

We changed our clothing, grabbed our back packs and boarded the shuttle.

A woman pilot by the name of Dakota Dryden welcomed us on board and helped us store our things. She's a beautiful young woman about 5'8" with red hair. I said to her, "You're Scottish aren't you?" "Aye she said and I'm proud to have such distinguished guests on board."

Thank you, are we really that distinguished?" "You are and that guy over there is my man." Eric blushed and said, "I'm sorry, I should have introduced you."

"If you two gentlemen will kindly be seated we'll be on our way." We did, she detached and we sped off toward Sheetau.

"So tell me, how long have you been married?" "Let me see, almost six wonderful years." "Oh did you marry while you were on earth?" "Yes, it was a last wish of her parents." "I understand. That must have been very difficult for everyone." "No, not really, they were happy and we honestly don't know that they aren't still happy today.

We can't change our fate, if something is meant to be then it will be. We can accept it or be crushed by its effects.

Life is good to us and we are even allowed to have children whenever we wish. Dakota has chosen not to train on the battle ships and has asked to specialize on shuttle flight and will one day be an instructor. Then we'll see about having some children." I said, "I hope some day to have the time and opportunity to meet your wife properly." "We'll make it happen."

A voice came from the cockpit, "Prepare to enter the atmosphere, it'll be a little bumpy." Shortly after that we were safely on the ground and saying our goodbyes to Dakota.

Two Lumy approached us, they introduced themselves as Gee Lamoo, botanist and KayCyto Bin, veterinarian.

We in turn introduced ourselves and we were led to a Lumy version of a barn. It was a huge two story building with an extremely high ceiling and very good ventilation. The animals were what we imagined that dinosaurs would have looked like.

KayCyto said, "These animals are our main source of meat. They are brought here for processing. This animal is seven years old and using your weight measurements weighs 4.2 tons. It is an egg laying half-mammal half- reptile warm blooded plant eater.

We eat very little meat so it is not necessary to hold these creatures as live-stock. They are free until we decide to harvest them." He gave us a tour of the rest of the building where they held several types of mammals, reptiles and other types of dinosaurs.

KayCyto said, "On the first planet that we inhabited we learned that we should not alter live-stock to meet our needs.

Our entire ecosystem suffered and the meat we harvested became bland and had very little nutritional value.

Here we work together with nature and it provides for us." Eric said, "That's a lesson we still need to learn."

Then we were led to another smaller building where men and women were preparing a meal for us on the terrace.

Gee said, "We have prepared small portions of many of the food items we utilize and are prepared to explain each of them if you wish."

Eric was now not only filming everything. He began recording it too. He asked, "Is everything on the table regular every day food or do you have exotic things among them?"

Gee said, "Everything you see here is a regular part of our diet. The small table holds the meat items and the large table the fruits and vegetables. You will note that most of our vegetables are harvested for their roots.

Beside every dish is the fruit or vegetable in its natural form." It was a lot and we tasted and asked questions for over three hours. As we were finished I said to Eric, I can't believe I just ate a dinosaur."

He laughed and said, "You didn't. It was just a bite of one. I hate to say it because it sounds so silly but it tastes like chicken." We both laughed and agreed it really did taste like chicken.

KayCyto asked if we would like to take a tour through the forest and grass lands to look at the wildlife. We both said yes then we looked at KayCyto. He smiled and said, "You will not be attacked and eaten. We have created ways of keeping them from harming us.

Some of the larger and fierce meat eaters still try but our defense is more than enough to repel them without hurting them." I said, "All right, we'd love to see your version of free nature."

We were seated in a hover craft that made almost no noise at all. I said, "This is very nice. Is it your regular means of transportation?" "KayCyto said, "No it is too costly to reproduce on a large scale.

These transporters are used when security is an issue." As it started to move it hovered about a foot above the ground. It was silent and fast.

We would occasionally stop and look at various plants and animals. The forest was not thick and the grass lands were very big. Then we saw a herd of the four plus ton dinosaurs. It was the kind they use as a food source. We approached it. As we did a monster of a dinosaur jumped out of the trees just a few meters from us and charged.

As it was about to eat us it was stopped by a force field. I heard myself yelling, "Good God we're being attached by T-Rex!" Gee said, "That's the same force field that gives us lift. It is virtually impenetrable." "Eric said, "And I'm grateful for that!" Slowly but surely I got my breath back.

I asked, "Are there a lot of those things on Copat?" "No there are less than five thousand of them. If they become too plentiful they kill each other in order to have enough food. The territory utilized by one family which is never more than two adults and two or three juveniles is often over one hundred square miles.

We imitate their markings which helps keep them away from populated areas." "Do they ever enter populated areas?" "I must admit, it does happen once or twice per year but they very seldom harm anyone and they are never killed for doing it. After all, they were here first."

Eric, "How do you convince them to leave an area?" "That's no problem. There are many sounds that they do not care for. We simply play the sounds so loud and so long that they leave and they seldom come back."

We continued through the grasslands and came upon a huge sea. I asked if we could get out but was told that it would not be safe.

Their equivalent of our lions was more like raptures. They were about two meters high and about three hundred pounds of teeth and muscle. We could see several of them about four hundred meters from us.

Gee said, "If you open the door and get out they'll be here in less than a minute. Unlike the big ones we really fear them as they are fast and smart. We are most grateful that they only populate this area."

I asked, "Do you have areas that you reserve for yourselves?" KayCyto said, "Yes of course we do, we have parks. Some of them cover many square miles. We have elaborate fences to keep the population from bothering the wildlife. The barrier complex is usually at least two hundred meters wide in order to ensure creature safety."

I asked, "Who takes care of Lumy safety?" "We are the most advanced species on this planet. We have the responsibility to take care of ourselves and secondly ensure that others around us are not endangered by our actions.

Our ancestors spent their time trying to be better and have more personal belongings than others around them. We actually destroyed an entire planet before we learned the importance of the things and life forms around us.

We have only been on this planet for two hundred years but during that time no animals have gone extinct due to our actions. And there is no pollution. We are very proud of that."

Eric, "We hope to have as much luck as you and find a planet we can inhabit. You have done many really good things here and I hope we are wise enough to learn from them."

Gee spoke briefly with KayCyto and KayCyto asked us, "Would you like to see one of our parks? We could do it on the way back to our station if you'd like."

Eric and I looked as each other and I said "Yes we would like that very much."

We drove to a park that I would estimate was over ten square miles. It was secured with a deep trench around it and obstacles on both sides to ensure that Lumy from the one side and wildlife from the other didn't fall in. The roads to the park were also protected by trenches and every now and then a wide bridge across it allowed wildlife to pass from one side to the other.

The park had huge parking lots, lakes for swimming, picnic areas, trails and playgrounds. Very much like our own and the people all seemed to be enjoying themselves.

We circled it once and then returned to the big barn where we had met them.

Upon arrival we could see the shuttle in the distance on its approach.

Gee said, "We took the liberty to summon your shuttle for you. I hope it is all right. I said, "Yes and thank you both for a very educational day.

We said our goodbyes just as Dakota landed. We boarded and were on our way back to the Enterprise.

On the way Eric and I discussed different options to make the ways of the Lumy known.

Eric said, "We are a different people and what works for them may not work for us but so much of what they have done is good and beneficial to all creatures and the environment that it would be a mistake to overlook it."

"OK, I said, my writings are read by many and I'll speak to the captain personally. You should broadcast your documentation and those who want to visit and see these things for themselves should get the chance." "I can speak to my colleagues and a large portion of the food producers. It will at worst create an awareness."

Dakota said, "It sounds like you two are plotting something, don't you dare leave me out." Eric said, "Honey, when I tell you what we did and saw you won't believe it, thank goodness I documented it."

She said, "We'll talk tonight in our quarters. I need you two to prepare to dock with the Enterprise."

Dakota docked and we went on our way full of new and exciting ideas about how we could create a better world for ourselves, once we find one.

I went back to my quarters and began documentation. The more I wrote, the more I thought about earth. What's going on there right now? Are there survivors? Will we ever return?

Had time and space changed for us due to the leaps? Could earth be re-inhabited?

I checked some of the files Lars had created, in reference to the effect the "Leaps" have had on us. It seems we do not distort time at all by leaping. That means the earth has been without us for four years two hundred and thirty four days. Hardly enough for it to have corrected itself and we have nothing to offer survivors, at least not at the moment.

That gave me even more reason to document the day and let others know how things "could" be if we find a suitable planet and populate it properly.

The next morning on the bridge I talked to Cpt. McCain about what we had seen and asked that she send crews to observe and document in more detail.

She was impressed but told me that Jerry Chapman is the one to speak to as it would be his opportunity and responsibility.

I thanked her and asked Simlayar to contact Jerry, who was on the Adventure for orientation. She was to make an appointment for us to talk. I also asked that she ensure Eric Van Stahl was at that meeting.

Kim came over to me and said, "Let's go have a cup of tea and talk about your trip." "That's a very good idea I'm thirsty and could use a breather." We went to the Out Look and ordered a cup of Earl Grey.

She said, "You seem to be very enthused about what you saw?" "I am. It's not exactly what the Lumy do that is so fascinating. It's their goals and their way of addressing their problems.

I have hopes that we can and will learn from them instead of finding a new home and making all the old mistakes all over again."

She asked, "May I see what you saw?" "Of course, we'll make an appointment,... "No, that's not what I mean.

May I read your thoughts and share your memory?" "Sure, you can do that?" "If I told you everything I can do I think I'd frighten you."

"OK, what should I do?" "You don't, I do.

Just close your eyes and remain calm it'll feel like a little shot of adrenalin and not at all unpleasant. Just try to stay relaxed, the whole thing will take about fifteen seconds. Ready? "Yes."

I closed my eyes and I felt a warm comforting feeling. It was like being in a very special and safe place. Then it was over. I said, "So what do you think?" Kim said, "I think you and Eric should weigh two or three pounds more today than yesterday." "You did the food thing too huh?" "Everything."

So what's your opinion?" "You have a point, they seem to have blended in with their environment instead of changing it to fit their needs." "Worth striving for?" "Yes, worth striving for."

"I have a meeting with Jerry tomorrow and would be grateful if you were present." "Alright, I will be, let's go back to the bridge before we're missed."

The Meeting with Jerry went very well and he promised to get more detailed information and archive it for future reference.

The weeks passed very quickly, Jerry left on his exploration trip, the construction of the star ships, battle ships and shuttles was coming along nicely. We and the Lumy have become very good friends and my pilot training has almost been completed.

Simlayar said to Cpt. McCain, "We are being hailed by the Ty ship Simu. It's Cpt. Kotar." Cpt. McCain said, "Put him on the main screen and overhead." The voice came in loud and strong, we have detected your scanners, and we are within thirty minutes of your position, we would like to de-cloak." Cpt. McCain said, "Please do and thank you for announcing your arrival."

The Simu de-cloaked and the detectors went off. I wondered how long it would be before we discovered how to cloak ourselves.

Kotar said, "We would like to know how you are progressing and exchange some items with the Lumy." "When you get here please do come aboard for a cup of tea, we would be honored."

Kotar said, "Thank you, may I bring guests?" "Certainly, your friends are our friends."

They came into view twenty minutes later and within the hour Kotar had boarded the Enterprise with his counselor Timlayar and two other members of the high counsel who were from the planet Zembra.

They introduced themselves as Tobago and Arawak of the people Becoua. They were similar in size with very dominate facial structure. Cpt. McCain greeted them formally and we followed suit.

As always Cpt. McCain took control of the moment. She said, "Welcome aboard the Enterprise, to what do we owe the pleasure?

Tobago said, "We would like to look at your vessel. We're planning a deep space voyage and will need something of this dimension." Arawak added, "We are not looking for a power source or weapon technology. What interests us is that you maintain such a large vessel without support."

Cpt. McCain, "Let us be seated at the conference table and I will have my science officer and Life support specialist join us."

They were seated and I asked an orderly to have coffee, tea, fruit and cake delivered, Kim asked Lars and Victor to join them and then we joined them as well.

Kotar said, "First I would like to thank you for your friendship and willingness to help others." Cpt. McCain nodded to Kotar and then had the two Becoua explain what they were here to learn and why they needed such large dimensions.

They were about the same size as we are and were, like us, not accustom to weightlessness. The possibility of having the entire vessel rotate and still function properly seemed like the most logical solution.

While Lars and Victor explained how most everything worked I wondered why the captain was so open and accommodating.

That was not necessarily her nature.

When they left for a tour of the vessel I asked Kim.

She said, "Several months ago I found a way to scan people and discover what one could call the intent for deception. Cpt. McCain and I worked out an undetectable system for me to clear the individuals so she knows if she is dealing with people who possibly have less acceptable motives."

"So you prequalify them as safe or unsafe?" "Correct." "How reliable is something like that?" "As Lars would say, there is no 100%, so I would say 99.9 into infinity %."

"Pretty sure of yourself aren't you?" "Yes I am Mr. Manning just like I'm sure you're taking me to dinner this evening." "I could have told you that." "That's what I've been saying, you already did."

Two hours later Cpt. McCain and Lars returned and said that they had sent them on with Victor as life support was their primary concern.

Lars said, "If they don't have a wireless power source they are going to have problems." Cpt. McCain, "They are going to have problems any way just like we do and a certain amount of them they'll just have to conquer on their own."

Cpt. McCain said, "I want a report from Bianca Lambert on how life is aboard Cpt. Kotar's Simu. Simlayar, please contact her and have her come over here for dinner.

If you would like to spend some time on the Simu you may provided Kotar approves." "Thank you and I'll contact her immediately." "You will of course come to the dinner as well." "Thank you again, I would like that."

Cpt. McCain announced she would be on Copat tomorrow with Kotar. She said, "Mr. Berger I would like to have a scientist with me tomorrow and I'm putting you in charge of the Enterprise in my absence. Do you have someone for me?" "Yes, I'll summon one of our graduates. Would Rada Byko suffice?" "Yes, thank you, she is to be here on the bridge at 08:00.

The day was coming to an end and Kim asked if she could be excused. Cpt. McCain thought for a moment and said, "I'll see you here at 07:30, both of you." We smiled and took our leave.

We went to the Look Out and had a steak. The meat had been delivered from Copat and was almost definitely dinosaur. It was very good.

Kim said, "Do you think Eric will still allow us to ride horses or is that considered unfriendly to inferior beings?" "Let's go ask him."

We walked across the meadow and through a wooded area to the riding stables. Eric wasn't there so I called him over the intercom system. When I asked about riding he said, "That's an easy one, go out to the pasture and get the horses. If they go with you it's because they want to.

Have a good time. I'll see you soon." We walked out to the horses, petted them and turned and walked back to the stables, they followed. Then we saddled them and put on bridles without bits and off we rode. Later we went to Kim's and had a quiet and wonderful evening.

The next morning we all met on the bridge. Kotar is on his way to pick us up in his shuttle. We will all go to deck 24 for departure.

He arrived just after we got there. We boarded and started our trip to Copat. I noticed that we had two more shuttles and an escort of five battle ships. They stayed with us until we entered the atmosphere. Then they returned to the Simu and we proceeded to the capitol city of Surat. It is a city of over thirty million Lumy and at least a dozen other species coexisting with them, all in all an exciting place to be.

Upon arrival we were met by politicians and business owners. Kotar asked Timlayar to handle the business and then asked the politicians to take us to their department of defense. We all looked at each other in surprise and said nothing.

We entered a large building with no windows. The security here was very high. We were led to a large room where over thirty Lumy were assembled to greet us. We were formally greeted and asked to sit down.

Chancellor Leo-May stood and thanked Kotar and Cpt. McCain for coming.

He said, "We are thankful for the help the Ty have given us over the years and the assistance the humans have given us with mining the titanium planet. We have however put ourselves in a very vulnerable position. We neglected to calculate the long term effect of not having the black sphere, as we have come to call it.

According to our scientists our beloved Copat will change its orbit within the next one hundred years. We will then enter an ice age. We are asking for your combined help to solve this most unfortunate problem."

Kotar said, "Why would you call the Ty? You and the humans have created this problem and we would like to believe that you can solve it."

Cpt. McCain nodded to Rada and she stood, introduced herself and addressed the group, "We have never attempted something like this and as you know our own planet is in a global white-out.

We have studied it in detail and will attempt to adapt a hypothesis to the dilemma with Copat. We would however be grateful for the expert opinions of the Ty."

Kotar, "Who is this person who speaks for the humans?" She said, "As I said I am an able scientist and physicist with the support of my captain and my people." "Alright able physicist, please show us how you propose to solve such a problem."

She activated her communicator and asked Lars to program the theoretical solutions for corrections of the planet's orbit. She had a pocket size hologram with her. The download only took a few seconds. She presented past, and present orbital information on the planet then showed how it could be altered with solar wind sails. "It is a very gradual change but change it will.

Lars Berger is also working on the possible use of tractor beams. It may be possible to install them on satellite vessels and drag the planet into a projected orbit. Again, the expertise of the experienced Ty would be most gratefully welcomed."

Kotar said, "I believe this problem could be solved without our help but we will naturally assist where wished.

Cpt. McCain you have a very talented scientist, we would be willing to offer her additional training if you wish." Rada looked very concerned, Cpt. McCain said, "Thank you very much for the compliment but it would be quite impossible for me to do without her." Then she looked at Kim and Kim telepathically told Kotar of Rada's connection to Lars. He smiled and said to Rada, "I look forward to working with you on this project." She thanked him and it was settled.

Kotar stood and said, "Please excuse me but the Becoua and I have some bartering to do and I would like to arrange for some sight seeing tours on your beautiful planet. Those warm blooded reptiles fascinate me."

We all stood and he took his leave. Leo-May walked over to Cpt. McCain and said, "Please do not be angry with me. I acted in what I consider our best interest." "Of course you did and between you and me I'm glad we'll have the Ty here to help us.

Please be so kind and have Mr Jodan Borko work with Mrs Byko and Mr. Berger on this problem. It would probably be best if he could stay on the Enterprise for a few days. He may bring his mate if he wishes." "Thank you he will be able to return with you if you wish." "Yes that will do nicely."

Cpt. McCain asked, "May I join Cpt. Kotar on his site-seeing tour?" "I don't know but I would be happy to ask. I'll get word as soon as I have it."

Cpt. McCain, "I have sent for a shuttle please have Mr Borko meet us on the landing pad as soon as he can." I looked at Kim and asked, "When did she order a shuttle? I've been here the whole time and I missed it."

"I'd tell you but then I'd have to kill you." "Oh really! So how did it happen?" "We have a code and I have a code with Jimmy.

He can be summoned from virtually anywhere." I said, "So if he's properly armed he's our James Bond?" "She smiled and said, "Now you're talking ancient history, he's simply our guardian with a means of getting us out of an area independently.

We should not be having this discussion." That's when I realized that it was really real and that Jimmy really is our guardian.

We said our goodbyes' and departed for the landing pad. When we got there Jimmy had already landed and was talking to one of the Lumy pilots.

As we approached he opened the hatch and reported for instructions. Cpt. McCain explained that we'd be waiting a few minutes for an additional passenger.

Ten minutes later the Loomy appeared with a small suit case and explained that it was Maylar's and his mate's clothing and belongings. Jimmy had him open it and place it on a table far from the shuttle and instructed him to wait for Maylar. He did so without comment.

When our two guests arrived they went through their belongings with Jimmy then sealed the suit case and boarded the shuttle.

Jimmy then excused the man who had brought the suit case. It had been years since I had witnessed any kind of real security and I secretly hoped I wouldn't see it again. I guess I'm a little naive and tend to trust everyone.

Jimmy closed the hatch and asked everyone to prepare for departure. Cpt. McCain looked at Jimmy and said, "Impress me." He nodded and took his seat.

The shuttle started and raised vertically about three hundred meters then with no warning we went from a dead stand still hover to leaving the atmosphere.

Lars had created an electromagnetic impulse engine that was good for short bursts of astonishing power. As we entered space Jimmy fired the anti-matter pulse engine and we were at the Enterprise in less than ten minutes. When you consider that the Enterprise is about as far from Copat as Saturn is from earth that's pretty astonishing.

Jimmy docked and as we departed. Cpt. McCain smiled and said, "I believe you just set some kind of record." "I'm sure I can improve." "I'm sure you can, thank you and bring me the details on that flight."

"They are already on Mr. Berger's computer." Cpt. McCain left the shuttle and we all went to the bridge.

She said, "Mr Berger I want you and Mrs Byko to work hand-in-hand with Mr. Borko and Maylar to solve this problem. Mrs. Byko will fill you in on the details and then Mr Borko can show you two his calculations on how and why Copat will change orbit. I understand that it is a complex matter but I want it addressed, solved and off the table in seventy two hours."

The four of them sat down and began their research. In our absence Jerry Chapman had reported in. The first solar system they had encountered had no planets near the size of earth and although two of them had suitable atmospheres the problem of high gravity due to their size could not be overcome. They are now in transit to another possibility.

Jimmy Cheedle approached me and said, "Are you ready to go chase a comet?" "Are the battle ships done?" "Done, tested, armed and ready for duty. Well at least six of them are.

We'll only be a couple of hours but they will be intense. We're going as a ternion force." "What's that?" "Sounds impressive don't it? It's simply a group of three and you're the lead dog."

I looked at Cpt. McCain and she nodded and said, "I'll expect a full report and don't wreck my new battleship." I said, "Yes mam", saluted and Jimmy and I left the bridge.

We went to an area I had never been. I said, "I thought this was a storage area." "So does everyone else. It's actually a kind of test ground for all kinds of gadgets and some of them are big and powerful.

It's completely screened and has its own life-support and force-fields. The exit cannot be detected from outside which is strategically important." "Exit?" "This is the bay that will contain the twenty five fighters for the Enterprise. We will need a door." "You aren't going to make me fly that thing alone are you?"

"Cpt. Manning, I'm sure you'll do just fine." Suddenly I felt ill.

We walked over to a wall with a light sensor, Jimmy said, "Put your left hand on that glass plate." I did so and a huge door opened about a meter.

We walked through and it closed. "You are one of the very few who are allowed here. We are not withholding information. We are protecting strategically important objects and personal."

We walked over to the group of six fighters. One other pilot was present; she greeted me and gave me a flight suit.

After we were dressed we were seated at a table to discuss the planned operation. Jimmy said, "Mr Manning I'd like you to meet pilot Emily Preston she has over ten real flight hours on these new battle ships and is very reliable and competent. She will be positioned on your left and I will be on your right.

The course is predetermined and can be seen on your screen. Once we get to our destination you will choose an object that is from five hundred to a thousand meters across and declare it hostile.

When that happens, Mrs Preston and I will attack. You will be our guardian and protect us from being attacked from the rear.

From the time you have designated an object as hostile to its elimination should be less than three seconds but as we have had no real training it could take four. Things out there are going to happen real fast and there is no room for hesitation or indecisiveness. This is going to be real Mr. Manning. Do not falter."

We boarded the fighters, it was amazing, and I felt comfortable and knew exactly where everything was as the flight simulators were a perfect replica.

I heard Jimmy's voice say, "As of now Mr Manning is number one Ms. Preston number two and I am number three, no names.

Take us out number one the escape hatch is white just head for it and it'll open automatically." I remembered, no hesitation so I started the engine did a 180 degree turn and accelerated. Although I was doing several hundred miles per hour by the time I got to the door it was open and I found myself in outer space. Just as I was about to get nervous because I was alone they showed up at my side. The exiting and formation building maneuver took less than four seconds.

I said, as I had been instructed, "Initiate plan C", with that we all entered the letter "C" on the console and a laser plotted our path and I said, "Initiate! We accelerated to 0.2, which was one fifth the speed of light. Number two and three were right beside me as if we were connected.

The shields reflected small objects such as debris and the a. i. located larger objects and guided us around them without actually changing our course.

As we neared our goal I said, "Initiate impulse". I waited three seconds as I had learned, and then said, "initiate". There were a number of objects before us, I chose one, marked it with a laser and declared it hostile.

When I said the word hostile the two ships beside me simply disappeared and the object exploded. It was amazing to see just how lethal these fighters really are.

We repeated our attack method eight times and then Jimmy said, "Just when you no longer expect it a bonus appears. Number one, there is a hostile object approaching and number two and I have both lost power, help!

I spotted the comet and lunged toward it at .32c. As I passed the comet I shot a photon torpedo out the back of the ship at it. A second later it was but a memory and I was trying to out-run the shock wave.

I returned and took my place between the two of them without comment.

Jimmy said, "I believe we can return to base now." I gave the order and we were on our way. After we returned and had docked we went to a debriefing.

Ms Preston was congratulated and then received the very first title of Fighter Pilot. Then Jimmy said to me, "You did well out there and I would not want to be your foe." I thanked him and said, "I hope I never have the chance to use that knowledge." "We all hope for that.

Your report will be in the captain's hands before you get to the bridge." As I took my leave there were several other pilots admiring the fighters and I couldn't help but feel very safe knowing the capabilities of the fighters and the commitment of their pilots.

I returned to the bridge and was greeted by the captain. She said, "Jimmy filmed you on your maneuver. You did very well, would you like to see it?" "Yes I would. I know what it's like in the cock-pit but have no idea what it looks like from a distance."

We watched it and I was astonished that it was me in that thing.

Cpt. McCain said, "I want you to take a short orientation flight no less than once a month. You should trade off between shuttles and fighters." "I've not flown a shuttle." "I'm sure you'll do just fine."

I walked over to Kim and asked why I was getting all this training. She said, "Stop and think about it. You are constantly on the road and when there's something new and undiscovered you usually get there ahead of half the scientists.

If something should go wrong and a pilot is needed in an emergency situation it would be more effective to have you fly out with whoever needs help than to send more people into a potentially dangerous situation.

It's a matter of solving a problem before it happens and you get to play with the big boys toys." "It sounds a lot better when you put it that way"

Bianca Lambert entered the bridge. She's been aboard the Ty ship Simu since we left Korant. We all greeted her and then Cpt. McCain said, "We're having dinner this evening and discussing her stay aboard the Simu. Whoever would like to come along is welcome."

I looked at Kim and she said, "I have to be there anyway and I hear we're having some rare treats from Suboro. You're coming aren't you?" "Of course I am but first I'm going to find out if our master-minds are close to solving their problem."

I walked over to Lars and asked if they were making progress. He said, "Progress, well yes, I guess you could say that. We know what the problem is. We know what has to be done to solve it and we have three methods of doing it.

Personally I believe my way to be best but then so does Jodan and last but not least so does Rada. We entered all three methods into simulators and now we're waiting to see which of the three solves the problem most efficiently and if the problem will stay solved." "Well that sounds easy. I reckon you'll all be coming with us to the dinner this evening." "Dinner, what dinner?"

I told him that Bianca was back for a visit, they had been so busy with their project they had not heard or seen anything. "Of course we'll come. We're not going to have any real results before 21:00."

At dinner Bianca told us about several adventures on the Simu. On one such occasion, while visiting a planet with early stage advanced primates which were a lot like our Neanderthal, they were actually treated like Gods.

She said, "I guess for them we were Gods. Kotar tried to explain that we were interested in their future and that their life would get better if they worked at it.

He showed them minerals in the ground and taught some of them to harvest it and others to refine it. The rest was left up to them." I said," I wonder if his great grandfather did the same for us." "Indeed" said Cpt. McCain, Could the Ty be the source of our spiritual beliefs and if so why did they allow it?" Bianca said, "Kotar never presented himself as a God but as an advanced being who was interested in these peoples future." I said, "We humans tend to see what we want to see and stories handed down through the ages always get modified and distorted."

Bianca said, "Thousands of years ago when the earth was first visited by the Ty they used individual flying units. Kotar believes they may have been misinterpreted as wings."

Kim didn't want the conversation to wander into a religious debate so she asked, "How do the Ty foods agree with you?" "We only have meat twice per week and then only a small portion.

216

When we're very busy we have food supplements in the form of pills. They have all the nutritional value we need and balance the stomach acids so there is no hunger. It even works on me without having to change its contents."

Victor said, "Something like that would be good to have on the shuttles." Bianca said, "I was told its all natural products reduced and dried. We can do that can't we?" I said, "I'm sure we could and I'd welcome having synthetic food banned."

The small talk went on till almost 22:00 and then I decided to check back in on the bridge to see who of the three scientists had the better idea about stabilizing Copat.

When I got there they were still there and still hard at work. I said, "I thought the answer would be waiting for you after dinner." Rada laughed and said, "So did we, it seems that tractor beams are most efficient but are only a quick fix. Solar sails are a permanent fix but very slow and an ion propulsion unit would cause vibrations." "That's easy, fix it with a tractor beam and stabilize it with solar sails." Lars said, "I was just about to say that." We all laughed and decided to call it a night.

The next morning preparations were being made to install a satellite with a tractor beam attached into geo-stationary orbit around Copat. Maylar and Jodan were having the solar sail fabricated on a Lumy workstation orbiting Copat.

New shuttles and new battle ships were buzzing around the Enterprise and Cpt. Zarka just arrived to inform Cpt. McCain that the new star ship was ready for its maiden voyage. She would naturally be on board for the flight and festivities. She said, "Mr. Chi, Mr Kofi I want to see your last reports on the installations and deficiencies."

She read the reports carefully and asked Cpt. Zarka, "Have you had the power on?" "Yes, it was on all night with no variations and no discrepancies.

Cpt. McCain, "The maiden flight and christening of the Horizon will be at 13:00. Mr. Berger, Mr Chi, Ms Lien and Mr Manning will accompany me.

Jimmy Cheedle flew us to the Horizon which was about a hundred and twenty thousand miles away. Even at impulse it took but a couple of minutes to get there. We were all issued what we had come to call star-ship shoes. They were magnetic and kept us from floating around.

We landed in the bay of the Horizon and exited the shuttle. We were greeted by the first officer and taken to the bridge.

It had been weeks since Lars had received the order to create artificial gravity and since so much had been going on no more was said about it.

Before the festivities began Lars asked for everyone's attention.

He said, "As you know this vessel is to be something above and beyond what we have created so far.

I would like to take this opportunity to add my own personal touch." He placed a pen in the air in front of himself. Then reached down and pushed a button and suddenly the pen fell to the floor and I weighed 300lb, and then it stabilized and we had normal gravity.

The happy look on Cpt. McCain's face was priceless. She said, "You never cease to amaze me Mr Berger." "Actually I had help. I was very close to the solution but couldn't seem to dot the i and Kotar allowed his science officer Maylar to help me."

Kotar was present. He stepped forward and said, "We simply accelerated the end effect. Lars had the answer in front of him but had not yet recognized it.

All Maylar did was point. It is a human triumph not Ty."

Cpt. McCain, "We are most grateful for the point that made it possible and I am very pleased with my science chief officer. How much of the ship has gravity? Ninety eight percent 24/7.

She made her speech and christened the ship. Then gave the order to launch the Horizon.

As it slowly moved forward she said, "It gives me great pride to put this great ship in the able hands of Cpt. Zarka."

He stepped forward, thanked her and took his seat in the captain's chair. She nodded to him and he gave the command, "Ahead .5" and the Horizon leaped into action.

We toured for about fifteen minutes then circled the Enterprise. When on board, the Horizon felt spacious and big, but as we flew past the Enterprise it was clear, compared to its mother ship, the vessel was quite small but agile.

We returned to the bay and noted that the hatch was open but we were not decompressing. I asked about it and was told that it has a force field that can seal an opening for up to forty five minutes.

We boarded the shuttle and as we got to the shield it was deactivated just long enough for us to pass through. We circled the Horizon for one more look. It is truly a work of art. Then we returned to the Enterprise.

As we walked toward the bridge Kim said, "Jerry Chapman is due back tomorrow. We're all curious to hear about his trip." I said, "We would have heard if he had found a suitable planet wouldn't we?" "Yes of course but he did see a lot and checked out four solar systems. He'll be happy to feel real gravity again." "That's right, I didn't even think about that."

I asked, "Are you working late today?" "Yes but I'd like to visit you when I'm done. Will you be awake?" "Yes, I've got some writing to do." "Then I'll see you around 11:00 I've got to go down this corridor, bye." I said bye and she disappeared around the corner.

Dr Khan walked up behind me and said, "How have you been treating that ticker?" "Hi doc, good I promise."

"It's not for me Robert it's for you. If you're going to the bridge I'll walk with you." "Someone up there sick?" "No, the Adventure is due back in a few hours and I'd like to discuss examination procedure with the captain."

I said, "I didn't know there was one." "Of course you didn't and that's because there isn't one. Until now we simply relied on implants and clothing for information and cures. I want a close-up look at a few of those people."

I asked, "Any special reason?" "They went off with nothing more than scanners and basic remedies. If something had gone wrong they would have had no choice but return. A doctor should always be on board and I'm going to see to it that there is." "That's a good idea, you've got my support."

When we got to the bridge Dr. Khan made a bee line for the captain and I wandered over to Lin Chi and asked about his family and the baby.

He said, "The doctors tell us that she's developing perfectly normal. There are now over one hundred eighty children that have been born on the Enterprise and not one has had something critically wrong with it.

It seems that our improved food, eating habits and also the fact that we're all required to maintain a certain amount of fitness has had a positive effect on our offspring."

I said, "I'm very happy for you, when are you going to have number two?" "Actually we're hoping to have one more by the end of this year. That way they can grow up together." "Good idea, give my regards to your wife." He said, "Thank you, I will."

I walked over to Lars to see how their project is coming along. Rada and Jodan were at another station working on the final details while Lars was busy with Cpt. McCain preparing for the return of the Adventure.

I asked Kim what the big deal is about the return route. She said, "They're being followed but they don't know by whom. Lars is working on a 1.5 second Leap.

If the Adventure misses it by a fraction of a second it could end up in a different universe or in a different time, if they make it longer they could be followed."

I asked, "So how do they plan to do it?" "Lars is planning to have them initiate the Leap ninety five degrees to their right. When the time comes the Adventure will accelerate to maximum speed, induce the Leap and then turn into it. That should be a maneuver that cannot be followed."

I asked, "Can Jerry do it?" "Good question, we certainly hope so. It's not going to be easy." "So how are they going to get this information to them without it being intercepted?"

She said, "I'm going to implant it in Jerry's mind. This is going to be a first and I hope more than ever that time and space are truly irrelevant because we won't know if it worked until he's here."

Lars called Kim over, he placed a thing that looked a lot like a head-set on her and initiated a download into her mind. She in turn seemed to fade into a trance.

Cpt. McCain initiated a full alert. Everything we, the Lumy, and Kotar's ship had to offer is at the ready.

If whatever is following him makes it through the Leap with them it had better be ready for one hell of a reception.

Kotar's ship the Simu, which means defender and is undoubtedly the greatest power in this galaxy has moved out into deep space and has been cloaked. All the other vessels have created a semi circle where we expect the Adventure to appear.

Kim slowly opened her eyes, she looked very tired. She said, "He will be here within thirty seconds." We stood in silent anticipation watching the screens and waiting.

Suddenly there was a bright flash exactly where Lars had calculated they would appear and Jerry shot by us with enormous speed.

Then he made a circle and returned. Nothing followed him and it seemed safe to assume that all was well. Kotar placed additional sensors in the area and then came back and stationed his ship near the Enterprise.

Several shuttles were dispatched to pick up Jerry Chapman and relieve his crew. Thirty minutes later he was on the bridge.

He asked that his scanners and board computers be evaluated in order to attempt an identification of whom or what had followed him. Lars said he'd get on it and Jerry asked for a debriefing.

Kotar asked if he could be present and Cpt. McCain said, "Yes, please join us maybe you'll be able to recognize them."

We went into a conference room and Jerry told us about the entire trip which for the most part had been uneventful.

It seems that long range sensors can not retrieve enough information for us to determine if a solar system has an inhabitable planet or not. We need to check each and every one first hand and it is looking like it is going to be very time consuming.

Then he said, "At 14:30 yesterday our sensors picked up an object moving under its own power. At the time it was several million miles from us but it was obvious that they had seen us as well.

It stopped and maintained its position for over four hours. For a moment we thought we had made a mistake. Then it launched an exploratory unmanned vessel in our direction. We immediately did the same. As they were within a thousand miles of each other their probe fired on ours and destroyed it. I then destroyed theirs with a laser burst.

After an additional two hours they launched a second probe and again we did the same. This time they passed each other unscathed.

As they turned theirs on so did we. They again fired and destroyed ours and so I again destroyed theirs.

Then I fired a photon torpedo in their direction. As it was half way between us I detonated it. They backed off another two or three million miles, just barely within tracking range and followed us. That's all I know.

Cpt. McCain, "Thank you #1, I would have reacted similarly. Do you have a hypothesis Kotar?"

"There are life forms out there that we have yet to encounter. They seemed to be curious but unwilling to allow Cpt. Chapman to scan them, it is a pity you could not make contact. It may be a thousand years before we meet again. I would suggest a slow approach the next time. You should keep up your guard but be confrontational in a non-hostile form."

Jerry said, "Point well taken thank you."

Cpt. McCain said, "Finding a suitable planet will not be an easy task and it looks like we'll have to be prepared to meet others out there.

We will now allow Cpt. Zarka to have a go at it perhaps he'll have more luck. Mr Chapman please give him any information you feel could be of help."

"I will, is he on board the Freedom?" "No, he's now captain of the newly christened Horizon." "So it's up and running?" "It is and it's ready for it's first test."

We left the conference room and Kotar said good-by as he was on his way back to Korant with his guests.

Cpt. McCain said, "We would like for you to come back in fourteen days as we will be celebrating the first five years of our journey.

Until our ship construction is finished we can not travel. Please bring whoever would like to celebrate with us." Kotar said, "Thank you I will announce it before the senate and extend your invitation."

I was amazed that she had found time to even remember that it was coming up. Kim said, "You underestimated her didn't you?" "Yes I guess I did. It's hard to believe she can do so many things, keep everything straight and then remember such a trivial thing as an anniversary."

Kim asked, "You are taking me to lunch aren't you?" "I'd like that. When will you have time." "I'll meet you at the Out Look at 12:30." That said she disappeared down the corridor with Cpt. McCain. I decided to get some time in on the flight simulator and went to the training bay.

Jimmy was just finishing a class as I got there and he introduced me and actually showed them my flight and my attack on the comet.

He asked the group, "What made the execution of this maneuver strategically valuable?" One of the cadets answered, "The approach was varied in speed and direction making him a difficult object to lock on to and the torpedo was fired at the earliest possible opportunity." "Bravo, you hit the nail on the head but now comes the hard part to grasp.

Mr Manning had absolutely no combat training and simply did what he was told to do the best way he knew how. Ladies and gentleman, instinct is what is going to save your ass out there, not calculating this and approximating that. Go in there, do what you went there to do and get the hell out before someone or something has time to ruin your day.

That's exactly what Mr Manning did and it worked extremely well. I'm going to give you all the opportunity to show me what you are capable of some time between now and 6:00. Until that time you are on alert. Dismissed." They rose and scurried away.

Jimmy said, "Hi, what can I do for you today Mr. Manning?" "After that praise I'm not sure. Did I really do that so efficiently?" "Yes you did and we were all very impressed. You nailed that thing as if your life depended on it." "Well, when you send someone out to do a job in a machine like that, I would think a mistake would be fatal, wouldn't it?" "Yes it would and I hope my cadets get that into their heads before they get put to the test.

Now, why are you here?" "I'd like to fly the shuttle simulator before somebody decides I know what I'm doing before I really do.

You do realize that I have no formal education in being a pilot and that anything I do right is purely coincidental?" "You're too modest. Come with me." He took me to a flight simulator, handed me a manual and said, "I'm sorry but I've got some work that must be done. I'm sure you'll have no major problem with anything. If I can answer something in my absence please call me on my communicator." I thanked him and he left.

I spent an hour going over the manual and instrumentation and another hour flying. Then it was time to go get cleaned up and ready for dinner.

At dinner Kim told me that the mining of the titanium planet would be complete in two months and the ships being constructed would be complete shortly thereafter.

She said, "That means we need a place of our own sooner than we had anticipated. Cpt. Zarka is next to take a shot at it and then Cpt. McCain wants to give it a go.

I am against her leaving her command for such a trip. I fear if she didn't return we would all be lost.

I need your help." "How do you want me to help?" "We have to corner her and discourage her." I said, "You could do that and she wouldn't even know it." "I will not manipulate my superiors.

Her decision is law and I will die for her if I must but that does not mean I must always agree with her." "Is it really that serious?" "Yes, I'm afraid it is. She is our leader, our strength and our future and it is a great burden for her.

I'm sure she would love a short break and would use the opportunity to unwind and relax a little. We need to find a way to make all that possible in a controlled environment."

I said, "I have an idea, KayCyto Bin and Gee Lamoo took Eric and me on a tour in an automobile that was virtually indistructable. We could possibly arrange for her to have that safari that she wanted to take with Kotar.

The auto holds up to eight people and I'm certain they have safe houses for overnight excursions. She can take two or three people with her and they could take her on safari. What do you think?"

"That will be perfect after we have spoken to her and made it clear that a trip in a star ship to unknown systems would not be a good idea."

I said, "OK, when are we planning to talk to her?" "How about right now?"

We finished our desert and went to the bridge.

Cpt. McCain was calculating the distribution of weapons resources and we asked if we could have a few minutes of her time.

She agreed and we sat down and told her our thoughts and asked if she would consider a wild safari on Copat as an alternative. She was visibly moved that we were so concerned about her and her well being. She told us she was honored that we considered her so vital to our mission.

She said, "I'd like very much to go on safari. You two will of course join me. I'd like Mr. Vogel to join us as well, could you arrange it? Andrew Vogel is head of security and I saw no connection but I of course answered with a yes, "I would be happy to." "Then it's settled, a safari it will be."

Then she hypothesized, "Once we find a planet to live on we can put the Enterprise into geo-stationary orbit and utilize smaller vessels.

I'll have one made to suit my purposes and can explore as much as I wish.

Well now that that's settled, I'd like to take that safari shortly after our anniversary celebration." Kim said, "Are you sure you want Richard and me along on the safari?" "Yes, I'm sure. We'll leave our rank and titles on the Enterprise and enjoy a few days of pure R&R.

Later over a glass of wine with Kim I asked, "What's the deal with Andrew Vogel and the captain?" She looked at me in complete disbelief and said, "Do I really have to explain that?"

Oh, is it something serious?" "Well, let me see, are you and I something serious?" "Wow, I think I opened a can of worms."

"They're two people who enjoy each other and make the best of it when they can, nothing more nothing less. What I would like to know is how you slept through it."

"What do you mean?" "Well, they have been seeing each other for almost a year and you never noticed."

I said, "It's hard for me to accept that Cpt. McCain is just a person. For me she's like an all powerful, all knowing being who is leading the rest of us. I can hardly accept the fact that she's mortal."

"Trust me, she is. She feels, has wishes and fears just like the rest of us and every once in a while she needs to unwind and I believe we are all far enough along that we should insure she has her time off like everyone else."

"You're of course right and we really are stable enough to get by in her absence for a while. I look forward to seeing those dinosaurs again." Kim said, "Personally I think you've got a bolt loose." "If I didn't I wouldn't be me."

We ended the evening with another glass of wine and a lot of love.

Shortly after 5am Kim was paged to the bridge. Simlayar said, "We've lost contact with Cpt. Zarka, he was testing the thrusters on the Horizon. During an acceleration process the Horizon simply disappeared."

Kim went over to a sofa, sat down and closed her eyes. After about thirty seconds she smiled, opened her eyes and said. "He'll be right back. He inadvertently created a Leap of some kind and ended up over fifteen light-years from here. You should wake Mr Berger he'll want to be here when Cpt. Zarka returns."

I asked Kim, "What happened?" "It seems Cpt. Zarka created or at least entered some kind of vortex and then accidently flew into or through it and traveled 15 light years in a very short time.

Fact is, he has determined where he is and will be returning via a regularly induced Leap."

Simlayar asked Jerry Chapman if she should wake the captain. He said, "No, let her sleep, the excitement is over and provided Cpt. Zarka has a successful Leap Mr. Berger and he will have to find out what happened."

Jerry met Lars as he came through the door and said, "It looks like Cpt. Zarka tapped a worm hole. Get all the info you can from the main computer and I'll send him to you as soon as he gets here.

I said good morning as he walked by and he said, "Good morning and is there any coffee around here?" "Sure, I'll bring you a cup." Lars walked over to Kim and asked, "Can you tell me what happened?" She explained it as best she could and suddenly he was wide awake. "Are you sure of what you're telling me?" "Of course not, I only know what Cpt. Zarka gave me as telepathic information. It could be flawed.

At that moment Cpt. Zarka came on the screen, "We'll be there in four minutes. Jerry said, "As soon as you are in range, jump in a shuttle and come over here. I want a full report and you and Lars need to put your heads together and come up with a plausible reason how it took place. I don't want to be standing here with empty hands when the captain gets to the bridge." "I'll be there in three minutes."

The time went by quickly and a bright spot appeared and the Horizon appeared as it passed us a new modified shuttle shot out the side and was docked in less than one minute.

When Atilla Zarka got to the bridge, Jerry, Lars and Kim said in one voice, "What happened?" "I don't know for sure. We need to tap the horizon's computers, everything that took place is documented."

Lars logged on and began the replay. Everything seemed to be perfectly normal but when Atilla accelerated there was a small flash out in front of the Horizon. It really looked like he had inadvertently tapped into a worm hole.

Lars said, "I wonder if that could be repeated?" We all looked at him." I mean of course if we ever happen to see a worm hole drifting by." I asked, "Could he have done something to create it or make it visible?" Lars, "That's a real good question. I'll check the exterior censors for fluctuations.

Jerry said, "Cpt. McCain will be here in twenty minutes she'll want a report and I'd like to take a ride in that thing some time."

Lars and Atilla got busy trying to find a solution and Kim and I slipped away for a cup of coffee and some breakfast.

When we got back Cpt. McCain, Cpt. Zarka and Lars were leaving the bridge, Kim looked at Cpt. McCain and then said to me, "Good thing we had breakfast, we're going with them." "And where are they going?"

"There you go again, asking questions that you already know the answer to." "Do you realize that a worm whole, theoretically, reduces you to a molecular level and reassembles you at the other end?"

"Not just that, it does the same to the space ship and everything in it. Theoretically we could be reassembled as part of the space ship." I said, "Now isn't that a pleasant thought."

Cpt. McCain, "You know I don't really need you two along with us but I'd miss your witty comments. You must admit this is all pretty exciting.

Mr Manning, did you train on the simulator for the Horizon?" As I slowly turned as white as a sheet they all began to laugh. "Don't be alarmed, you won't have to pilot it this time."

We boarded the shuttle and flew to the Horizon. Cpt. McCain said, "Circle the Horizon before landing." "Aye Captain." We circled but there was nothing out of the ordinary. Then we flew into her bay and landed.

The Ship was minimally smaller than the Adventure but quite a bit more up-to-date. Almost every improvement suggestion had been implemented.

Cpt. McCain asked that everyone not directly involved in maneuvering the ship either be seated or leave the bridge.

Then she said, "Cpt. Zarka, bring us to the location where you were when you initiated the kick thrusters."

Kick thrusters were the end product of Lars's idea of an afterburner for a space ship.

Atilla ordered the flight engineer to proceed to the point where they launched their experiment. He accelerated and the Horizon quickly surged forward.

As we approached ground zero Atilla placed his hand over a blue glowing sphere and applied downward pressure to it. We shot forward with breath taking speed but not through a worm hole, just forward.

Lars said, "I believe that was what was supposed to happen the first time." Cpt. McCain said, "Bring us about, I guess this is going to remain a mystery for the time being."

We returned to the point of departure, took a tour of the Horizon and returned to the Enterprise none the wiser.

On the way back to the Enterprise we could see the final stages of the excavation of the small moon of titanium. I said, "It's hard to believe that we actually harvested so much of a moon for building material. It's little more than a big asteroid now." Lars said, "Yes it really is amazing but we most certainly did do it."

Once back on the Enterprise Cpt. McCain said to an orderly, "I would like breakfast served on the bridge. Does anyone else want anything?" Lars and Atilla ordered and then we all went to the Bridge.

I said to Kim, "What's the chance of getting some free time this afternoon and going horse back riding?" "That sounds wonderful. Can you arrange it with Eric?" "I'm sure I can, I'll let you know just after lunch.

I'm to be fitted for some updated clothing yet this morning." "That'll be fun, I got mine last week. They actually try out some of the life saving features, it's quite amazing." "Well, I've got to go this way, I'll see you around 1:30 or 2. Kim said, "Let's shoot for 4 OK?" "OK, bye."

With a little anxiety, I went to the fitting room which is near the main clinic. They scanned me from head to toe and created a 3-D image of me out of a kind of Styrofoam. Then they said I could leave for 90 minutes while the suit was created.

I decided to use the time to arrange for horseback riding and maybe a little picnic. Eric was a little hard to find but when I did, he readily agreed and said he'd have everything ready at 4.

When I returned to the fitting room two physicians were there waiting for me. As Kim had said, the process was not a lot of fun. Injections of Nano-robots were possible on the arms, legs and spine. Of all places to try it out they decided for the spine. That gave me an additional definition for pain. The suit fit loosely but tightens when the body needs support. Overall it was quite amazing. It's like wearing a life support system that keeps you warm when needed and cool when needed and has tracking devices that can be read hundreds of miles away and maybe even much further. I suppose it won't be long before they start implanting these gadgets into our bodies.

Chapter XII

The days passed and our fifth anniversary celebration was upon us. There were guests from over fifty planets. We, of course, had a fireworks show and something that resembled a parade using our shuttles and fighters. It was quite spectacular and was well received by our guests. The speeches were kept to a minimum and the parting maximized. The festivities lasted two days and we all need a rest once the last guests were gone.

The next several weeks passed with no major events and Cpt. McCain announced that we were far enough along with our construction that the rest could be completed in our absence. That meant we were moving on.

She had thanked all the peoples who had helped us over the past ten months. A space station had been built to house those staying behind to finish the ships and one morning she announced we were leaving the solar system.

That said, Lin Chi guided the Enterprise to a safe distance from Copat and their solar system. It was in then that Lars induced a Leap taking us back to Korant.

We picked up the crews that had been stationed there in our absence who now wanted to continue the voyage with us. They were replaced with new volunteers.

Hetshepsut Bonafrit who had appointed ambassador and member of the high counsel on Korant was very happy in her position and Cpt. McCain reappointed her. Once again we were off to new adventures.

Lars asked Cpt. McCain, "What course shall I plot for the Leap?" She pointed with her finger and said, "twenty Light years in that direction." It was clear that all our scientific plotting and planning had not helped us find a new home, maybe a shot-in-the-dark would.

Lars took a few minutes to ensure the path was clear and initiated the Leap. The three escort star ships were in formation beside us and in an instant we were in uncharted territory and a new adventure was about to begin. Cpt. McCain sighed and said, "I've missed this."

Lars scanned the area, determined that we were alone and Cpt. McCain sent the Adventure and the Freedom on scouting missions. We were combing the area for inhabitable planets, nothing more and nothing less. It was like a shot of adrenalin and it felt good.

Cpt. McCain said, "Mr Chi I'd like for you to head for the nearest star. Once we're close enough to determine if there is a possible planet for us in the system, I want it scanned. If it looks promising, let me know and we'll head for it. If not, note where it is, name it and head for the next one.

Each of the star ships is doing the same." "Aye captain." Then she addressed Lars. "Mr Berger can we average six Leaps per day, and if yes, how long can we keep that pace?"

Lars checked the computer and said we can do it for twenty four days if I take into consideration that there is a daily eight hour break where no Leaps take place." "Very well, inform the other ships that I expect two systems to be checked per sixteen hour shift for the next twenty days. When we leap, they leap with us. On day nineteen I'll determine where we'll meet. If something is found I or #1 should be notified at once." It was acknowledged by all and we were off.

Seven hours into the search Jimmy Cheedle came in over the communicator. "I'm being followed and the ship looks a lot like those that attacked us near Copat. I may have to defend myself." Cpt. McCain said, "Don't try to flee. They could lure you into an ambush. Stop and face them, help is on the way." Kim said to Cpt. McCain, "It is the Palchek and there's more than one."

"Cpt. McCain said, "Zarka!" and the Horizon disappeared. Then she told Lin Chi to follow him. As we arrived about twenty five seconds after the Horizon, we saw Cpt. Zarka in the Horizon facing one of the Palchek ships from about five miles. That had to be intimidating.

Jimmy had stopped and had launched four fighters and as we arrived Cpt. McCain launched an additional six fighters. Cpt. McCain said, "Mr Berger, how many of them are out there?" Six but three of them are in retreat or so it would seem." "Fighters 2, 3 and 4 stop their retreat. If you can do it without destroying them do it, if not you have permission to use any force necessary."

By the time she had finished her sentence they were half the way there. While we were watching them chase the Palchek who were trying to flee, the ship facing Atilla Zarka fired at him. That was a fatal mistake. He actually deflected their laser shot and fired an array of lasers back cutting their space ship into three pieces. It was over in the blink of an eye.

One of Jimmy's fighters shot out toward the rear of the Horizon. Then it turned and fired everything it had, just missing the Enterprise. We could feel the shock wave from the explosion that took place behind us.

We could see a battle on the long range scanners and knew that the Palchek had not surrendered.

Then there were three tremendous explosions. Two minutes later one of the fighters returned. Cpt. McCain said, "Number three, report!" "The voice at the other end was trembling when the man answered, "Number two and number four didn't make it. The Palchek were very well armed and had anticipated our approach, they're gone captain."

There was a moment of disbelief and shock and she said, "There are two more of them out there. They will surrender or die." Jimmy shot forward with the Freedom of which he was now captain and we saw the Palchek ship fire four shots at him just before Jimmy's torpedo reduced them to dust. The shots were deflected. The last ship was making a realistic effort at escaping. Without the captain saying a word Lars fired an enhanced laser at it and like an ant under a magnifying glass in the sun, the ship simply melted.

There was a long silence and then Cpt. McCain said. "Captains, back to work, continue your search, tomorrow at 1900 there will be a service held for our fallen pilots. For those who wish to attend the service, it will be held on deck #01.

We headed back to where we had left off. During the flight Cpt. McCain went over to Lars and said, "Nice shot." He answered with a simple "Thank you." And for the next hour not a lot was said.

During that time I checked on who we had lost. Pilot number 2, Edward Bowman twenty eight years old, a former U.S. citizen from Carson City, Nevada was a math scholar, nano-technician, and one of Jimmy's first students. Thank goodness he was not married and had no dependents on board the Enterprise.

Pilot number 4 was a woman named Amara Nistor, thirty one years old from the city of Resita in Rumania. She too was a math major and software engineer who finished her pilot training five weeks ago. She was to be married next month.

Cpt. McCain approached me and said, "I see you're already doing research on our two lost pilots. Who were they?" I looked at her a moment and then told her what I knew. She said, "Can such a loss be justified?" It was a question that could not be answered. I answered by changing the subject.

"Is the battle documentation public information?" "No that would be a breech of our security but there will be no cover-up. I will explain what has taken place, the orders that I gave and that they died following those orders. They truly gave their all as I had ordered."

I corrected her with, "They died protecting us from harms' way and that's how it will be documented." She nodded and she went to her ready-room to be alone.

When we docked with the Enterprise Kim whispered, "I'm sure you have things to do. I need to be alone with her, I'll see you later." I said, "OK" and went to my quarters to contemplate and document what had happened.

The search for a new planet was resumed and three hours passed. I decided to see if there was any progress being made on the bridge and if they had found anything interesting.

As I got I saw that all hell had broke loose. Simlayar was sending an emergency signal to Kotar and summoning any and all federation vessels that could be reached. It seems we had stumbled into a hornets nest. It looked like it was the home planet of the Palchek. Cpt. McCain initiated a Red-Alert throughout the entire system.

Kotar was the first to arrive and immediately came on board the Enterprise. He asked, "Do you have confirmation of your suspicion?" "Cpt. McCain said, "Mr Berger, on screen." We could see hundreds of vessels congregating and their emission foot-print was that of the Palchek.

Kotar looked on with concerned eyes and said, "We have to at least try to settle this without an all-out war." Lin Chi said, "Here they come and they don't look like their coming to negotiate." Kotar said, "I must return to my ship." Then he was gone.

By the time he got back to the Simu the Palchek were within firing range. They opened fire and Kotar's ship the Simu faded into a cloak. Then Kotar said, "I wish I didn't have to do this.

Attention all federation ships, defend yourselves." All our battle ships were deployed. Our escort ships were stationed around the Enterprise and by then another sixty or seventy other federation ships had joined us. Outer space became a light show with lasers and torpedoes flying everywhere.

Star ships were being torn apart by enormous blasts and debris was quickly becoming a problem. The Adventure took a direct hit and shuddered but the force fields held it together. We could only hope that the crew had survived.

Cpt. William Turner of the Adventure called over the overhead communicator. "Cpt. McCain, we've taken a direct hit and can not hold our station, it has been an honor." And therewith he accelerated, ramming one of the largest Palchek ships and they both exploded. The Adventure and its crew were gone.

In the distance I could see the planet being blasted but could not see the source. It was almost definitely the Simu.

The Enterprise was taking quite a beating but at the same time was firing a torpedo every thirty seconds and the Lasers were firing non-stop. The escort ships were firing torpedoes every fifteen seconds and had four laser cannons each firing non-stop. Almost all of them found their target and with the help of the federation which was very impressive, we were slowly overpowering the Palchek.

The battle went on for over seven hours and when it was over, fifteen federation ships had been destroyed and the Adventure was one of them. That meant we had lost almost two hundred of our people and who knows how many federation members in the battle.

The Palchek planet was so heavily damaged that there would be no recovering for them, and Kotar sent over one hundred thousand of his troops to the surface to ensure that they did not.

Cpt. McCain sent an additional five thousand. It would take some time but they had lost and were facing annihilation.

A few hours later the majority of the captains met aboard the Enterprise. Many of them had damaged vessels and would need help before they could continue.

Cpt. McCain thanked them for their help in our greatest hour of need and ensured our support and/or help to them and their people whenever needed. Then Kotar took the floor. He went over the events that had taken place and stressed how fortunate we all were to have finally found the source of their greatest problems.

He said, "This day is significant for all peoples, each and every nation should ensure documentation of the day that the earthlings found this planet and allowed us as a federation to help solve a problem that has been unsolvable for so long. It is of course their right to claim this planet as their own. I and the Ty whom I represent congratulate them."

The others rose from their seats and congratulated Cpt. McCain and Jerry Chapman. They were both still dumbfounded by what had just taken place and were unable to speak in whole sentences.

Kotar had taken it upon himself to ensure we have that which matters most to all peoples, a home of their own. He did it so quickly and efficiently that the others had no time to stake claims.

Slowly but surely Cpt. McCain and Jerry regained their composure and Cpt. McCain said, "Again we thank you for your help and are pleased that we have a planet that we can now attempt to make our new home.

Everyone knew it would still take weeks to flush out the rest of the Palchek. Who knows, maybe they will surrender and become a people we could share the planet with. Then again maybe that would be a little too optimistic.

Captains from the planets Korant, Copat, Zembra and Vook, another member of the federation, have offered to stay and assist us with ridding the planet of Palchek. They had brought troops in transporters that were nearly the size of the Enterprise. They almost seem eager to stay. I believe they have old scores to settle. Even the mild mannered soft spoken Lumy look fierce in their battle dress and their fire-power is amazing.

The Becoua from Zembra who we had recently met through Kotar, were very well represented. Their war ships are a lot like ours in size and they are a very courageous people.

The Koorak from the planet Vook had, like us, lost one of their battle ships and I don't think it was the first one they had lost to them. They were a fierce looking people almost seven feet tall and hair that resembled a Viking. Kotar told me they have an impressive culture and history and that their bravery was unmatched. They are truly warriors of the universe. I'm glad they're on our side.

Jerry Chapman guessed the number of peoples helping us at two hundred fifty thousand but we would still have to do most of the work from the air.

There was to be no pause and no rest until the mission was complete. The troop transporters were already in orbit around the planet and troops were being transported to the surface. I wonder what it looks like down there.

Kim came over to me and said, "I'm not sure this is a good omen. A new beginning for us at the cost of an advanced life-form loosing their right to exist." "Are you sure that that's the case? After all, they are constantly attacking other planets. They probably have more than one planet." Others heard what I had said and for a moment you could have heard a pin drop. I followed up quickly with, "I am of course not at all certain that that is the case."

Kotar radioed to his captains to ensure that all communication systems on the surface were destroyed at once.

Jimmy Cheedle said that if we put a star ship into the atmosphere and flew over the cities and settlements with Mach 9 it would most likely destroy all the structures. Cpt. McCain said, "You may try it on one large city. If it works, continue, if not return to orbit at once. And Cpt. Cheedle, don't let them destroy my ship." "Aye captain." Jimmy gathered his pilots and headed back to the Freedom.

I asked Cpt. McCain if I could go with him but without hesitation she said no and I had no intention of arguing with her.

Kim said, "Have you completely lost your head?" "No, not completely, I'm curious to see what it looks like down there and would like to know more about them and of course their technology.

We could possibly use it against them." Jerry Chapman said, "We'll find more than enough of their technology down there and we have one of their ships." I said, "Oh, we have prisoners?" "No, just the ship. The Koorak stormed it and they don't take prisoners." That was more information than I needed.

The task of ridding the planet of the Palchek went on for the next twenty two days. Although they were very advanced in warfare they had never made it to the point of being what we would call a civilized culture as they were anything but civil. Most of the dwellings and other buildings were more fortress than habitation.

They were either unwilling or unable to accept defeat in any form and choose to die rather than accept an unknown fate. This of course made it difficult for everyone. Instead of trying to pin a group down and wait till they gave up, which we would normally do, a strike-force would be called in and they would simply be destroyed. Then it would be off to find the next group.

We were exterminating an entire race and that was something we had vowed not to do. The Ty, Lumy and Koorak seemed to have no problem with it and worked fast and efficiently to get it over with.

Once it was finished and most of the peoples who helped us had returned home. Cpt. McCain sent for the one hundred thousand clones that had been created on Copat.

They were to be part of the initial inhabitants of our new home which we so lovingly call New Earth. It's nestled in a group of seven planets, one of which is a gas giant. And once again, we're the third rock from the sun.

It's a little larger than the earth, water covers 67% of it and it has four continents each a little larger than Africa. Amazingly two of them were not used by the Palchek, probably because one is in the north and the other in the south and both have moderate to cold climates. There are vast forests on all the continents and the air is 76% Nitrogen, 22% Oxygen and almost 2% argon.

New Earth has two moons and both are smaller than the one we knew circling earth. There relatively close to one another, one a little behind the other. The closer of the two is 225,000 miles from New Earth and with the gravity of both the tides in the oceans of New Earth are very similar to what we were accustomed to on earth.

Reconstruction and renovation of two cities is under way and they should be inhabitable within two to three months.

Cpt. McCain has placed a large number of long range sensors around the solar system to ensure that we do not get surprise visits.

The Ty and the Lumy have been very helpful and continue to assist us in preparation of moving a large population onto the planet.

Jerry Chapman has designed the governmental complex with an impressive state house in the center and the construction is almost finished. On his birthday, which was last week, Lin Chi and Lars jokingly gave him a throne from which he is to rule. I hope he doesn't want a crown.

All jokes aside, Jerry has been appointed chancellor and will appoint a temporary senate to help govern the planet. After one year the members of the senate are to be voted for and those who have proven themselves unworthy of their position will be replaced. Although Jerry will have the last word the country is to be run by the senate.

Jerry Chapman will remain in office until Cpt. McCain calls for an election to replace him. She is contemplating a ten year reign. I believe she has chosen the perfect candidate.

The clones, which we can no longer call clones, are to arrive over the next three days. They have been given names and memories and have not been told that they have been grown. They are equal to the rest of us except for the fact that they can not reproduce. The women can be artificially inseminated with fertilized eggs from our egg and sperm banks should they wish to have children. That will ensure that the next generation is of perfectly normal human beings.

There has been talk of a ship returning to earth to look for survivors. We are uncertain if those we left behind could handle the change in us as a people and question how much we still have in common. The answer has been put off until the government is up and running and the matter can be properly addressed.

Cpt. McCain has arranged for construction on her star ship to begin. It will be almost twice the size of the Horizon and even more advanced. I've heard that she's negotiating with Kotar to get the technology to cloak it. Then there would be two ships in the galaxy with that ability. It's not likely that he will be willing to share that kind of information. On the other hand I've underestimated Cpt. McCain before.

The new ship is to be ready for use in six months and shortly thereafter she wants to continue exploration of the galaxy. She has promised to keep her bridge crew intact and I'm hopeful I'll be a part of it as well.

Kim has been spending a lot of time with Agda Frykman, an enchanting Swedish woman whom she has chosen to be Jerry Chapman's personal counselor. On New Earth she'll be more of a guiding light for Jerry and will not necessarily be available to counsel others. Kim, it seems, has been and remains the stabilizer for all of us.

The Enterprise has become a very busy place. Ships from Korant have been coming and going bringing our new citizens. Once the new citizens have been unloaded on New Earth many of the captains stop in to say hello and offer to help.

The Lumy from Copat are also steady visitors and again have supplied a large force to assist with the building projects on New Earth and up here with the new space ship. It actually seems normal to be among the various species of humanoids and with the translators that the Ty have implanted into our heads all languages sound the same and are easy to understand. The peculiar part is that I no longer know what language they are speaking. Everything sounds the same and is comprehensible.

Kim came onto the bridge, checked in with Cpt. McCain and came over to me. "You're taking me to dinner this evening and I want to relax with a glass of wine." "Yes mam I'm at your service. Will 07:00 do?" "No, how about 6:00?" "I'll meet you at the Look Out and we'll take it from there." She gave me a kiss on the cheek and was gone again.

I went over to see how Victor Kofi was doing. "Hello Victor, how's the wife and your lovely daughter Kikuyu?" "Hello Robert, we're all fine but lately my wife and I have been talking about moving to land and I think I'm going to ask if we can move to New Earth.

We would like a more stable form of life for our children and my wife has set it in her mind that she wants two more. I have trained a fine young man to replace me if Cpt. McCain allows us to go." "When do you want to leave?"

"That's up to Cpt. McCain but I would think the perfect time would be when she changes command to her new vessel." "I'll keep my fingers crossed for you. I'm sure there will be no problems." I wished him a good day and my best to his family and went over to see what Lars was up to.

As I got there he was finishing a lecture with eighteen young physicists in training and looked very happy with how things were going. He introduced me and we all exchanged ideas for a while.

It seems that four are to remain on the Enterprise after deactivation and the other fourteen are to help develop New Earth. They were in their early twenties when we left earth and they are to get to work on New Earth to help develop a society without destroying its environment. I encouraged them as best I could.

I also suggested that they travel to Copat to study how the Lumy managed it. I said, "I have not yet had the opportunity to explore New Earth but I assure you that the Lumy have animals that resemble the dinosaurs that at one time inhabited the earth, some of them are fierce carnivores and yet they settled there without disrupting them or endangering their own people. I am hopeful we can do the same here on New Earth."

Lars said, "That's exactly what we've been talking about. The trip to Copat is a great idea. I'll see what Cpt. McCain thinks about it and until then I would like you all to consider agriculture on a large scale with little to no impact on New Earth and its inhabitants." Then he dismissed the class.

I asked him, "Have they considered doing a portion of the agriculture in, on, or around the Enterprise?" Lars said, "I'm hopeful they'll think of it on their own. It could even be a stand-alone agriculture station in orbit. I'm doing my best to inspire creativity."

"Speaking of being creative how are you and Rada Byko getting along?" "Very well thank you and although she's a gleaming star and Jerry Chapman wants her and her expertise on New Earth, Cpt. McCain has left it up to her to serve wherever she wants."

"You do realize it's a favor to you not to her, don't you?" "Of course, I'm not naive but she's the one deciding and it's nice to be wanted and needed and....." "Yes, it is. Do you know that Victor wants to move to New Earth" "I even know that Cpt. McCain has picked out a beautiful home for him on a lake with a huge garden.

It's her way of saying thanks and good-bye. She's planning to take him there next week when they go down to inspect a few systems that are being installed. She's having his wife and daughter brought down separately and making a bit of a surprise out of it." "I don't think she'll ever stop amazing me."

Kim joined us and said, "Speaking of amazing people, I hear you've gotten permission to go on an expedition on New Earth. You do realize that it could be dangerous down there don't you?" "Sure I do and I'm sure you know that it's Andrew Vogel's expedition." She said, "He's good but he's not invulnerable." I asked, "Would you like to go along?" "Only if Jimmy Cheedle flies directly over our heads with every weapon he knows how to fire."

"Where is this fear of yours coming from?" "They didn't get them all, there are still a few Palchek down there and I'm sure they are armed and have no intention of surrendering."

"I'll ask for a fire arm and I promise to be careful." "Please stay within the force fields until Andrew's people have checked an area for potential threats." "OK, I promise, I have no intention of coming back here with something blown off."

She gave me a kiss on the cheek and said, "I've got to go, got work to do." She waved to Lars and was gone. Lars said, "You know she's right don't you?" "Of course I do but you know as well as I do that Cpt. McCain is going to leave when she can and my position is on her ship and I wouldn't have it any other way but I would also like to check out our new home." I know what you mean, I'm going with you." You're kidding, you're allowed to?" "Sure, why not?" "Many of us consider you the most knowledgeable human alive. That's not something you put in harms way."

"That's why I've decided to create a force field around us. Don't worry, I think it'll work." "You think?" He laughed and said, "It works and will deflect anything short of a laser canon and I've been told there are none down there."

I said, "I hope whoever told you that is right. Will it fend off attacking wild animals?" "Yes, after your stories about Copat's attacking dinosaurs spreading throughout the Enterprise there is an increased awareness for personal safety.

We have a hovercraft with a force-field and it will also be armed. I'm in high hopes of seeing some larger animals that are new to us and possibly finding traits or immunities that could help us." "Did Cpt. McCain approve experiments with the animals?" "As long as we stay under 0.01% of the total population, but for now all I want to do is document and photograph the animals and show our scientists what's out there.

They'll decide if the human population will need protection or if they need protection from us. If the animals are so plentiful that a portion can be harvested we may end up with some new food sources."

"OK, I'll see you in the morning at 07:00. Have a good evening and my regards to Rada." I went to my quarters to document the day and get ready for dinner. I met Eric in the hall and he said he'd be leaving soon. He is to co-ordinate the growing and harvesting of all foods for New Earth.

I asked, "Isn't that a bit much for one person to attempt?" "Not at all, I already do it for the Enterprise and all I have to do is know the population, the raw materials and how much we want to store for how long. The big job right now is building farm equipment and making sure our plants don't harm the indigenous plants. I'm hopeful to find new vegetables and fruits on New Earth."

"Sounds like you're going to have your hands full." "Yes sir, I am and I'm real anxious to get started." "I wish you all the best and I promise to visit when I get the chance."

Later in my room I realized there were going to be a lot of big changes and there will be a lot of friends that I may never see again once New Earth is settled. Its part of the price that has to be paid but I'm certain it will be worth it.

The next morning I was up early and in bay 22 twenty minutes before the others, ready for our expedition. We were a party of seven and the hover craft was built for twelve so we had lots of room for equipment.

Head of security, Col. Andrew Vogel was in charge, he had two armed security officers with him. Then there was Lars, Eric Van Stahl, Cpt. McCain, and me.

I said, "Good morning captain, I had no idea you were going along." "No one else did either and I like it that way. I'm hopeful we'll have an exciting and eventful day." She opened a locker near the bay entrance and took out laser hand weapons for all of us. She said, "These are for self defense only. They're set at maximum power and will vaporize anything under three hundred pounds. For larger targets you may have to fire twice."

Eric said, "Do I have to carry one of those?" She said, "Yes you do and if one of us need help I expect you to be there. We are as strong as our weakest link." "I understand, sorry."

We boarded the modified shuttle that Jimmy Cheedle was flying. I said jokingly, "Have you been demoted?" "No, this little baby is equipped with a few new weapons and if you come across a stray Palchek we just may need one or two of them."

"You're coming along?" "Not exactly but I'll never be far away." "That makes me feel a lot better." He smiled and we were on our way.

Jimmy picked a large flat clearing with little to no vegetation to land on. As he sat the shuttle down he intensified the scanners to ensure that nothing and no-one who could pose a threat was anywhere near the shuttle when he unloaded the hovercraft.

He checked the scanners one more time via his remote surveillance, which looked a lot like a wrist watch and then motioned for us to exit. Andrew went first followed closely by Cpt. McCain then Eric, Lars me and the two guards. We boarded the hovercraft that Cpt. McCain had decided to drive, waved and were on our way.

The hovercraft is the size of a small bus and the top two thirds is of glass. The force-field is completely invisible and it's a lot like being in a sports car with the top down. We were about a meter off the ground and it maintained the one meter as the terrain changed. It was a little like a rollercoaster.

The motor was almost silent and only a little buzz is created by the force field, kind of like a cat purring. Cpt. McCain headed for a large lake. While on approach she asked Lars. "Will the sensors recognize the water as a solid or as a liquid?" He answered, "It will be recognized as a solid. If you want to go under water you'll have to turn it off, submerge and then reactivate it. Then it will register the water as it registers air." She said, "I'm perfectly happy above the surface for the moment."

After two hours and several miles of travel we had seen only a few small herds of reptile like animals that looked a lot like dinosaurs. Many of them are covered in bright colored feathers and those without feathers have astoundingly colorful skin. So far we've seen no meat eaters large enough to threaten us. The astounding thing was there seem to be no mammals at all on this planet.

While entering a clearing the hovercraft came to an abrupt stop. It actually knocked me out of my seat. I quickly got up, it was just in time to witness three Palchek walk up to the shuttle. It was apparent that they had stopped us and they believed we could not harm them. They slowly circled the shuttle observing us and occasionally stopping to stare.

They are covered completely with scales. Their faces are pale and seem to change colors as they communicate. The rest of their exposed parts are different shades of green. I guess they can change colors somewhat like an octopus. They are about seven feet tall and have three fingers and a thumb. They look very menacing.

As they stepped back from the shuttle and took aim to destroy us Cpt. McCain open fired on them. It was virtually point blank and there was very little left of them. It'll be a long time before I forget those faces.

It's good that we're out of danger but on the other hand, who is going to release us from the beam holding us in place.

Cpt. McCain called for Jimmy and within seconds he was here. He followed the beam to its source and fired at it. The shuttle shuddered but was still bound. Then he fired again, this time with what looked like a blue ray. The entire area was reduced to little more than sand and we were free. He said, "Well, I guess that did the trick."

Cpt. McCain thanked him and he was gone. She looked at Lars and said, "What was that weapon he just fired?" "It's a mixture of ions bundled in the ray of a laser and allowed to release their energy upon contact." I asked, "Is it radioactive?" "No, as a matter of fact it isn't, the only drawback is that there is absolutely nothing left after firing so there's no second chance for whatever or whoever you shoot at.

Cpt. McCain looked out the window and said, "That part is obvious, can you put power like that into a hand held weapon?" "I'll certainly give it a try."

We continued our journey and are now entering wetlands. It's a huge flat area with occasional shrubs. Although it looked as if the water was still, it was actually flowing. This must be a river delta. We could see snakes that were over fifty meters long. That's half the length of a football field. As we continued we could see an occasional head pop up from below the surface. Cpt. McCain went to two hundred meters altitude in order to get a look at what was surfacing. Andrew said, "Did you see that? If this thing can hover, stop for a minute." Cpt. McCain stopped and we could see many very large creatures below the surface. Some were the size of our hover-craft. I said, "Does anyone want to go for a swim?"

Cpt. McCain remained at two hundred meters until we were no longer over water. Then she headed for a clearing where we stopped to have a bite to eat and relax.

We scanned the area and had Jimmy make two sweeps with his scanners. When it was clear that we were alone we got out and in groups of two and three took a look around the area. I was with Eric and a guard by the name of Lee.

We were of course looking at the vegetation. Most of it looked just like the plants on earth and occasionally we would see one that was red or blue. Eric said that they were probably poisonous. Lee said, "We're getting too far away from the hover-craft, we don't have to take the same way back but lets head in that direction."

I asked, "Have you already spent time down here?" "Yes, I was in the first group that landed on New Earth." "That must have been a war zone." "Yes sir, it was and I'm glad so many of us are still here to talk about it." Eric said, "Did they resist or were they just eradicated?"

"Eradicated, what makes you think something like that? When we landed we had shields to protect us. We laid our weapons on the ground and backed away from them to show the Palchek that we didn't want to fight. They were like wild animals and charged firing with everything they had trying to kill us. Then Col. Vogel told us to prepare for battle. We did exactly that, the force field was disengaged and they died. It was a hell-of-a mess. Their blood was a fluorescent green and the stench was wretched."

Eric asked, "Do you think they can survive in this wilderness?" "Yes sir I do. I believe they have maintained enough of their primeval origin to survive indefinitely." I said, "I sure hope you're wrong."

When we got back the food had been placed on a make-shift table and we had New Earth's first picnic.

It was a beautiful day, the temperature about eighty degrees and we could see a thunderstorm forming on the horizon. The low pressure system was drawing all the moisture out of the air and that made everything so clear it almost seemed digitally enhanced.

As we ate and enjoyed the afternoon, a powerful white beam shot into the sky from the other side of a nearby mountain. It engulfed Jimmy's shuttle and for a moment I thought we had lost him. The burst lasted for almost five seconds. When it stopped, one of those blue beams came from the shuttle and there was no doubt, he wouldn't have to fire twice. The impact was so great that a glass that was on the table fell over.

Cpt. McCain called Jimmy immediately, "Are you alright?" "Yes mam, just a little shook up." "Get down here and pick us up. This expedition is still a little pre-mature." She looked at us and said, "Let's get the hell out of here." We put our stuff in the basket, folded the table, and Jimmy appeared over our heads. The shuttle exterior was actually wrinkled from the blast he had received.

We all jumped into the hover-craft and Cpt. McCain drove it on board the shuttle. Jimmy appeared at the doorway with blood coming out of both of his ears, his nose and one eye.

Cpt. McCain yelled, "Mr Manning, get us out of here!" I ran to the pilot seat and without so much as a thought, pushed all the right buttons and we were air-born with shields up. She said to me, "Quickly Mr. Manning quickly." I gave it all it had and we were approaching the Enterprise at an astonishing speed.

I called ahead for Dr Khan. Cpt. McCain said, "Robert, fly into the bay. We've got to keep this boy alive." I did as I was told and Dr Khan and his team were there waiting on us. They took Jimmy and we all stood there dazed by what had happened.

Cpt. McCain said, "Every human on New Earth is to activate their homing implant. I want this Palchek problem solved now!"

Back on the bridge she called Kotar, the Lumy, the Koorak and the high counsel and asked for help. She said, "This is my planet now and I will not tolerate these things any longer.

Kim went to her side, took her hand and closed her eyes. Tears appeared in both their eyes and I cleared their portion of the bridge. I had a feeling that the Palchek were about to go extinct on New Earth.

Lars was working on something and I asked him, "Is that a new device?" "No not exactly, if we can get one Palchek alive I can create a virus that will kill them all." "Please don't even think something like that. You'll end up killing half the population on New Earth. Get one and trace the DNA, you can trace DNA from a safe distance, once confirmed you can blow them to hell." OK, DNA it is, but I won't rest until it's over." "That's two of us."

I left the bridge and went to the clinic where Jimmy was being treated. After a four hour wait Doctor Khan came into the waiting room.

I looked him in the eye and said, "What's the deal?" "It's under control and I'll have him put back together and running around in a couple of days. That boy took a hell-of-a beating." "Would you please let Captain McCain know he's OK, she's very worried about him?

I'm afraid she took the attack on him personally. I certainly would not want to be a Palchek." Dr Khan said, "Of course I'll let her know, now go to your room and rest everything will be taken care of."

When I got back to my room I found Kim waiting for me. She said, "Are you OK?" "Sure, it's all been a little overwhelming but I wasn't really involved in it."

"That's where you're wrong, you got everyone out of harms way and did it like a born fighter pilot." That's when I first realized that I had flown the shuttle back to the Enterprise.

I looked at Kim with a blank expression and she said, "Relax, you have posttraumatic stress disorder and you need to rest. I'm going to talk to you for a while and then you are going to sleep. You will sleep very deeply and will feel refreshed and in control when you wake."

It seemed like she spoke to me for a very long time and then there was nothing. I woke thirteen hours later and felt great. Kim was there watching over me and said, "Feed me I'm starving." I took a shower and we went to the Out Look. We had a glorious Peking Duck with all the trimmings and a piece of chocolate cake with whipped crème.

I said, Thank you for whatever you did, I was feeling claustrophobic." "I know, you'll be OK, you're a hero you know?" "No, really?"

"It'll all come back to you in bits and pieces. It's easier for your brain to cope with it that way. Let's go to my place and

I'll give you the rest of your therapy." "Who am I to question the therapist?"

The therapy lasted all afternoon and into the night, she made me glad I was alive.

The next morning after breakfast we went to the bridge. Cpt. McCain was also just getting there and said. "I want to have a meeting of everyone working on the bridge plus Jerry Chapman and his crew at 09:00, Simlayar, make it happen." That gave Jerry and crew forty minutes to get here. If you consider that we're a hundred and sixty two thousand miles from New Earth. That's pushing it.

Kim said to me, "Would you have the café deliver coffee, tea and a little something to eat for the conference room?" "Sure, no problem." As I was leaving the bridge Jimmy was about to enter. We paused and I gave him a warm hand-shake and said, "It's nice to have you back." "It's nice to be back and from what I've been told I'll need to buy you a drink." "Any time my friend, any time.

I'll see you in a few minutes I'm on a mission for coffee and tea. We're about to have a meeting." "I know, that's why I'm here." "Go in and say hi, I'll be right back. I left for the café.

When I got back everyone was still gathered around Jimmy and I joined them. Cpt. McCain said, "Ladies and gentlemen, please follow me to the conference room. Jerry and his crew arrived and we went in and were seated.

First she allowed Jerry to give an extensive update of the progress being made on New Earth and then Lars updated Cpt. McCain on the progress being made on her space ship. It seems that both need another four weeks.

Cpt. McCain said, "After the latest vicious attack by the Palchek I have asked the high counsel for help. I've been informed that nine star ships with twenty two thousand troops will be arriving in the next thirty six hours. Mr Chapman, you as chancellor of New Earth will be in charge of the methodology.

If in two weeks there are any Palchek still on New Earth you will owe me an explanation."

Then Cpt. McCain said to Jerry, "It is possible that I've over-estimated your abilities, if you don't feel up to the task please say so now." You could have heard a pin drop and Jerry knew his title as chancellor depended upon his success. Kim squeezed my hand and said to me telepathically, "You better hope he's up to it. If he says no you will be appointed chancellor." I just about fell off my chair.

Jerry stood and said, "As chancellor of New Earth I will no longer tolerate the presence of the Palchek. I assure one and all that within a fortnight there will be no living Palchek on New Earth." That was the commitment that Cpt. McCain wanted to hear and she replied, "You may have any and all people and equipment you deem useful, from both the Freedom and the Horizon."

Jerry nodded and it was settled. That's as close as I ever want to come to power and fame.

Cpt. McCain stood and said, "We are at a crossroad in our history. Our earth, although not forgotten, is probably little more than a snowball now and will most likely remain that way for the next ten to one hundred thousand years.

We've had the good fortune to find this planet and although it is regrettably at the cost of an entire race we will make our future here. The high counsel of the federation has battled the Palchek for hundreds of years and what has taken place here was inevitable.

We will not be intimidated by any force or people. We have come too far and sacrificed too much. When my ship is finished I will turn over the power of decision to Jerry Chapman and he will lead us to a new and happier life.

To defy him is to defy me, which I must say is at best a fatal error. I will remain Captain and in control of our forces in space. This change of power will take place when I take command of the Adventure II."

I asked for the floor, "As we grow and our fleet in space grows, I find it confusing trying to separate the big captains from the little ones and would therefore like to suggest that Cpt. McCain receive the title of Admiral and Commander in Chief."

Jerry spoke, "I believe I am the only one capable of determining or assigning such a title. Hence, when Cpt. McCain takes command of the Adventure II she will also take the title of Admiral / Commander in Chief over all forces on land and in the air." Therewith he made it clear he would share the power. We all applauded and congratulated Cpt. McCain.

While all this was going on Kim had arranged for a glass of champagne to be served and we toasted our new leaders.

After the toast, Cpt. McCain announced that Victor Kofi and his family would be moving to New Earth and she added, "Should any of you have the wish to settle on New Earth rather than dashing around exploring outer space please make that wish known.

A chosen few of you are almost impossible to do without, but I want a crew that wants to explore and is not at the edge of their seat waiting to return home. The Adventure II will be my home and I would like to make it yours as well."

I stood and said, "You can count on me." Victor Vogel followed then Lars, then Kim, then Lin Chi, and last Simlayar.

Jimmy said, "What is supposed to become of us?" "Cpts. Cheedle, Zarka and Preston will have the job of guarding New Earth in four month intervals. The remaining eight months will be utilized as follows, one month R&R as you see fit and seven months exploration." Jimmy asked, "Is Emily Preston now a captain?" Cpt. McCain answered, "Someone has to fly the Freedom, you'll have the twin to the Horizon and I expect you to name it. By the way, it will be here tomorrow." We all applauded and Jimmy turned red. He said, "Thank you all and thank you Cpt. McCain for your faith in me."

She answered, "Faith, hogwash, you're the best pilot I've ever seen and you've won the hearts of everyone around you, you're family.

Send pilot Preston to me later today and do not tell her why she's been asked to the bridge. I like to see them sweat a little before they smile." "Yes mam, sir uh admiral." "Go back to sick-bay and stay there till you're fit." He got up, said good-by and left.

Cpt. Zarka said, "May I have the privilege of being the first to guard New Earth?" Cpt. McCain, "Chancellor Chapman will be the one to decide and please bear in mind, whoever goes first will have the obligation of finishing Cpt. Preston's training." He looked and Jerry said, "Yes, you may have the first guard."

Cpt. McCain adjourned the meeting and we returned to the bridge.

Bret Ambruse stopped me in the hall and said, "So who documents that meeting?" "We both do, I'll write it the way I saw it and you do the same." "What if we have discrepancies?" "There's no such thing, you'll never see things exactly the way I do. That's the neat part of being an individualist. Your version may even be better than mine." "Even if it were, I will always come in second to you." I said, "That's bull-shit! Do you really think I don't keep up-to-date with what you write? Do you think for one second that Cpt. McCain isn't up-to-date on your writing?" He said, "I've never heard a peep." "Congratulations. In this business no news is good news. No one is going to come around and pat you on the back and tell you what a great job you're doing but screw it up and they'll crucify you. That's the way it is." He said, "OK, then that means I've been doing alright. I still get pretty darnned nervous at high echelon meetings." "Get used to it. You're now the person documenting history and giving it form.

Our youth will learn it as you write it. Fuck it up and we'll be back in the stone-age." We both laughed. "Seriously Bret, you're doing a great job, just be you and write it as you see it. Let the critics in two hundred years figure out if we did it right.

When I got back to the bridge everyone was watching the big screen. The Adventure II was being towed away via tractor beam. As I looked on I couldn't help but say, "What a beautiful piece of art."

Its twelve hundred meters long, four hundred twenty wide and has seven levels. Although not necessary it is extremely aerodynamic and it's armed to the teeth.

I walked over to Lars and asked, "Where's it being taken to?" He looked at it for a moment then said, "I honestly don't know. It's part of the deal." "What deal?" "You'll have to get the rest of the information from Cpt. McCain. I don't have permission to discuss it."

I approached the captain with the same question and she said, "I of course want you to document this day but I do not want it made public for the next twenty years and then only after either I or my replacement OKs it.

I made a deal with Kotar that he could inspect my ship from top to bottom if he installed a cloaking system in it. He said he needed two days to install it and one for the inspection.

Not even the high counsel knows this is going on." "Is it really that big of an advantage to be cloaked?" "That's a silly question. Don't you read what you write?" "Yes, remember how nerve wracking it was to know that an unknown vessel was near us, we couldn't see it and our sensors couldn't detect it."

"From what Kotar has told me we will even have the ability to fire our weapons while cloaked. Of course that's only good for one shot but that's usually all it takes." "I understand, while in the ship we won't know if we're cloaked or not so the knowledge of us having this ability serves no rational purpose and could induce jealousy in others." "Very good Mr. Manning, so now you know and I'll cut your tongue out with a laser if you tell anyone." "That's fair." And therewith the conversation was over.

Lin Chi came over and asked if I would take him for a ride in a fighter. I said, "Are you sure you want me to fly it. We have over thirty qualified pilots now." "I'm sure, they're all young and overestimate their abilities. I developed most of the propulsion system and some other parts and would love to fly in it. You must not tell my wife, she worries far too much."

I'll ask Cpt. McCain if I may and if she says yes then I'd be happy to." "Thank you, I'll be waiting for your answer."

Cpt. McCain said yes and therewith I was actually allowed to take one of the fighters for a spin. I told Lin to meet me in bay 01 and we could go right away.

When I got there Emily Preston was there to help me get ready. While putting on the flight-suit I asked her, "Did you graduate and get your permit to teach?" "Yes I did and I actually did pretty well.

Maybe some day I'll be allowed to apply for a captain's patent." "From what I've heard you've certainly got the ability, I wish you the best of luck." She smiled and thanked me. In less than twenty four hours she would be Captain of the star ship Freedom. I felt very happy for her.

Lin Chi joined us and said, "So this is Emily Preston?" She looked up surprised and said, "How do you know me?" "I know all the pilots and study their abilities and methods. That's why you are so comfortable flying a machine that I design." She smiled and helped him into his flight suit.

Lin and I did an inspection of the vessel inside and out and then were seated and strapped in.

I started the engine and headed for the hatch. Lin said, "Who will open the door?" "I said, "It's magic" and accelerated. I herd him gasp and the door flashed open and we were in space.

I flew very close to the Enterprise dodging mirrors, dishes and the occasional green-house. Then out into open space. We circled New Earth's two moons and then flew over to the Horizon. After circling it we returned to bay 01.

I said as we got out, "How'd you like it?" "The flight was fantastic and to see things from that perspective is very special and I thank you."

We stopped for a tea on the way back to the bridge and chatted for a while. His wife is pregnant again and they are very happy about it. He wants to stay with Cpt. McCain on the Adventure II until his first born starts school. Then relocate to New Earth. I could only wish him the best.

Once back on the bridge Kim asked if I would talk to one of her classes. "Sure but what should I say?" She said, "Tell them an event that didn't happen. You know what I mean. I'm trying to see how good their perception is." "You mean you know every time someone says an untruth?" "She smiled and said, "Classroom 11 in fifteen minutes." "I'll be there."

While giving my speech several of the students hesitated but none stopped me and questioned what I was saying.

Later Kim told me all but two caught me by the second untruth and the other two on the third one. I asked, "Why didn't they question me?" "That's not their job or their right.

They are to pass their knowledge on to their superiors nothing more." Where do they work when they're done?" "They'll be assigned to star ships as councilors or will work with politicians who deal with unknown aliens or wherever they can be useful."

I asked, "Do any of them have your talents?" "One or two of them are very promising. Thank you for taking such an interest." "You're welcome, you are the most important thing in my life, the interest comes automatically but my timing isn't always what it could be." "It's just fine, for example right now. The answer to all that stuff in your head is yes. Yes I do have time this evening, yes I would love to go to the Out Look for dinner and yes I'd love to wake up next to you. Now get out of here. You're disrupting my students."

There were nine muffled laughs behind me so I said good-by and left the room before I embarrassed myself even more.

I went to sick bay to pay Jimmy Cheedle a visit. He was up and exercising and asked if I'd like to join him. I changed into a training suit and we worked out for almost an hour. I asked, "Did Dr Khan say when you can leave?" "Not exactly, he said if I was here in the morning he'd put me in the O R and remove something vital. I think he's trying to get rid of me."

"I'm happy you made it through whatever it was." "What was it that they fired at me?" "What did it feel like?" "It was as if it could vibrate everything in and around me until everything fell apart. It vibrated straight through my shield. Thank goodness the shuttles are riveted and the seams are welded.

I'll bet all the gauges had to be replaced." "It was worse than that, the ship has been scrapped and a new one is being built.

You are the only thing that made it through and I would say it's because we have a doctor who knows magic." Jimmy said, "I'm inclined to think you're right. It's very irritating, I didn't even film it." "What difference does that make? It would have been destroyed by the vibrations anyway." "Maybe they'll find another one when they sweep the planet."

Jimmy's expression suddenly changed. He almost shouted, "Underground, they have to look underground! I'll bet they have a network and there's a lot more of them down there than we think." I asked, "Do you feel like going to the bridge? I think you better share all this with Cpt. McCain and chancellor Chapman." "Sure if Dr khan will release me." A voice came from behind us, "He will. Give them the information they need to finish the job. Besides, everyone down there is in a lot more danger than they can possibly imagine."

We went to the bridge and jimmy explained his hypothesis to Cpt. McCain. This, of course, created a general alert. All the shuttles and fighters were fitted with sensors that detect tunnels, caves and cavities that could hold Palchek or weapons and other sensors that detected life forms. We couldn't rely on infrared because they could be cold blooded and we wouldn't see them.

The shuttle that was equipped with the pulse cannon was to destroy the areas as found. One would however not be enough so more were being installed in fighters. Penetrating weapons such as torpedoes and missiles are being installed on anything that flies.

Cpt. McCain approached me and said, "You will of course join the pilots in bay 01. Be safe, without pity and come back alive."

I looked at Kim and a single tear plummeted from her right eye. I turned and went to bay 01. Dakota Dryden, Eric's fiancé, was there to assist me with my flight suit. No one was speaking, this was an all-out war and we knew it.

Jimmy Cheedle approached me and asked if he could have a minute alone. After Dakota was gone he said, "Mr Manning you're good, you're real good but you're not one of us.

I'd like you to secure an observation point on the back side of moon two in order to document what is taking place." I said, "Thank you Jimmy I'm grateful but you and I know what has to be done and that it is often a matter of one single pilot being in the right place at the right time. Let's go do what we've got to do."

"It's an honor sir."

We boarded our fighters and Jimmy returned to the Freedom. He is once again going to enter the atmosphere with that gigantic space ship and this time Cpt. Zarka was joining him.

We exited the bay in single file and headed toward New Earth at maximum speed. If they could see us coming they knew that all hell was about to break loose.

After entering the atmosphere I switched on the sensors and immediately saw a network below the surface. I placed a missile in it every two hundred meters until my supply was spent and immediately returned to the Enterprise for more. The other pilots were doing the same.

They were of course ready for us when we got back and we didn't even have to get out of the fighter. It was armed in less than five minutes. This went on for over four hours and the Palchek were now firing back with everything they had. They knew it was the end.

I spotted another large cavity that probably held weapons or Palchek in hiding and headed for it. Suddenly I felt a tremendous blow to my left side and immediately lost control of the fighter. I was hit and going down at three thousand miles an hour. Needless to say, these things don't have ejection seats or parachutes.

New Earth was racing at me with an incredible speed and a million things were going through my mind as I pushed every button and pulled every lever in an attempt to regain control. I remember yelling SHIT!! As loud as I could in anticipation of the impact and then everything just stopped. I was about two hundred feet from the ground and steadily going backwards.

Jimmy's voice came over my headphone, "Cpt. McCain's going to be pissed that you got her ship all shot up." He had caught me with his tractor beam and was pulling me to safety. That was more than I could take and I passed out.

I woke up in sick bay with Kim at my side. She said, "You took a hell of a beating just to get some time off." "I smiled and said, "Jimmy saved me." "Well, he saved most of you and Dr Khan said he has put the rest back together."

Then I noticed I couldn't move my left side. I asked, "What's the deal?" Dr Khan came over and said, "The deal is your left arm was broken in three places, two ribs broken the collar bone broken in two places and the hip bone is fractured. You're a wreck!" I asked, "How much of it can you fix?"

"What a stupid question, all of it of course. Now talk for a few minutes and then I'm going to put you to sleep for a week in order to fix everything and get the heeling process mostly completed." He walked away and I said, "I'm surrounded by all the right people. She smiled and said relax and again I passed out.

It seemed like only minutes had passed and I heard Doctor Khan in his squeaky Indian dialect saying, "Wake up wake up I have other patients that need this bed. Get out of here I'm tired of looking at you." My eyes opened slowly. As I began focusing I could see everyone from the bridge gathered around to greet me.

Cpt. McCain smiled and said, "Welcome back Mr. Manning." Kim was holding my hand, Lars and Lin were on the other side of my bed and Simlayar was one step behind the captain.

Dr. Khan said, "I believe you will be able to get up and walk around this afternoon and you may leave sick bay tomorrow. Now please excuse me I have sick people to tend to." I asked Cpt. McCain "Is it over?" She said, "Yes, it's over, the Palchek are gone and New Earth has officially been claimed by humans. We have you and of course many others to thank and we're happy you're still with us."

Jimmy came through the door and said, "Sorry I'm late." Everyone turned to him and applauded. Lars said, "Many thanks to the greatest pilot there ever was." He smiled and came over to me. "How are you my friend?" I couldn't say anything and my eyes filled with tears. Then he saved the moment, "They're still trying to put that damned ship back together." Everyone laughed, we spoke for a while and then Kim shooed them away saying, "He's mine now we'll see you on the bridge tomorrow. They said good-by and left. I was very happy to be alive and to have such friends and an angel at my side.

The next morning at eight Kim met me at the entrance of the clinic. She asked, "Have you checked out?" "Yes mam I have, Dr Khan has been called to the Adventure II so I checked out with the nurse. I hope you're taking me to breakfast." "Sure there's a café right around the corner."

After breakfast we went to the bridge. Cpt. McCain met us there and asked if we'd like to join her on a walk-through of the Adventure II. We of course said yes. Lars, Lin Chi and Simlayar joined us.

When we got to the bay I saw a lot of faces I knew and was thankful that they had survived. Dakota Dryden, Eric's soon to be wife is our pilot. It's her last official duty aboard the Enterprise before moving to New Earth.

We boarded the shuttle and departed for Adventure II. It was very quiet as we circled the gigantic vessel we had called home for over six years. Then the Adventure came into view. It was a majestic masterpiece of all the science, technology and knowledge we had acquired wrapped in absolute perfection.

Cpt. McCain directed Dakota to circle it and land on deck four. She did so with perfection and Cpt. McCain said, "It's a shame we're loosing you. I wish you all the best." Dakota thanked her and we entered the Adventure II.

It was a marvel from the inside as well. There were no sharp corners everything was rounded and seamless which increased its structural integrity. The windows were nothing more than holes with force fields separating us from space. It was truly amazing.

We toured for over two hours viewing the energy source, fighter bays, living quarters and clinic and so on then

Lars said, "Admiral McCain, I would like to see the bridge." She smiled and said, "That (Admiral) is going to take some getting used to, follow me please."

The Bridge was spacious and very practical. The entire front was open to offer a 170 degree panorama. The main screen was now a hologram and only visible when activated.

Instead of a lone captain's chair in the middle there were three chairs: the chairs on either side of the center chair were facing slightly inward and were on swivels. This made eye contact possible. Lin and Lars found their stations immediately and were pressing all kinds of buttons and trying everything out.

Adm. McCain turned to me and said, "I suppose you realize that your job no longer exists?" I had no idea what to say or how to react. "Yes, uh I uh realize I,…. She stopped me from stuttering and said, "Mr. Manning, you have gone from a secret agent to an observer to the history writer of our species to pilot and trusted comrade in arms. I would be honored to have you as my first mate." I stood there staring at her and Lars yelled, "Say yes and thank you."

I said, "It would be an honor to be your first mate. I thank you." Everyone applauded. We took our seats on the bridge. Kim on the right, Adm. McCain in the middle and me on the left.

At 11:00hrs on March 17, 2126, Adm. McCain gave her first official command, "Number 1, take us out of here."

C2009JayJDrummond